HALF A HERO

A NOVEL

ANTHONY HOPE

Half a Hero

Anthony Hope

© 1st World Library, 2009
PO Box 2211
Fairfield, IA 52556
www.1stworldlibrary.com
First Edition

LCCN: 2009923334

Softcover ISBN: 978-1-4218-8809-5
Hardcover ISBN: 978-1-4218-8908-5
eBook ISBN: 978-1-4218-8710-4

Purchase *"Half a Hero"*
as a traditional bound book at:
www.1stWorldLibrary.com/purchase.asp?ISBN=978-1-4218-8809-5

1st World Library is a literary, educational organization
dedicated to:

- Creating a free internet library of downloadable ebooks

- Hosting writing competitions and offering book publishing
  scholarships.

Interested in more 1st World Library books? contact:
literacy@1stworldlibrary.com
Check us out at: www.1stworldlibrary.com

1st World Library Literary Society

Giving Back to the World

"If you want to work on the core problem, it's early school literacy."

- James Barksdale, former CEO of Netscape

"No skill is more crucial to the future of a child, or to a democratic and prosperous society, than literacy."

- Los Angeles Times

"Literacy... means far more than learning how to read and write... The aim is to transmit... knowledge and promote social participation."

- UNESCO

"Literacy is not a luxury, it is a right and a responsibility. If our world is to meet the challenges of the twenty-first century we must harness the energy and creativity of all our citizens."

- President Bill Clinton

"Parents should be encouraged to read to their children, and teachers should be equipped with all available techniques for teaching literacy, so the varying needs and capacities of individual kids can be taken into account."

- Hugh Mackay

CONTENTS

CHAPTER I

THE IMPOSSIBLE—INEVITABLE

In the garden the question was settled without serious difference of opinion. If Sir Robert Perry really could not go on—and Lady Eynesford was by no means prepared to concede even that—then Mr. Puttock, *bourgeois* as he was, or Mr. Coxon, conceited and priggish though he might be, must come in. At any rate, the one indisputable fact was the impossibility of Mr. Medland: this was, to Lady Eynesford's mind, axiomatic, and, in the safe privacy of her family circle (for Miss Scaife counted as one of the family, and Captain Heseltine and Mr. Flemyng did not count at all), she went so far as to declare that, let the Governor do as he would (in the inconceivable case of his being so foolish as to do anything of the kind), she at least would not receive Mr. Medland. Having launched this hypothetical thunderbolt, she asked Alicia Derosne to give her another cup of tea. Alicia poured out the tea, handed it to her sister-in-law, and asked,

"But, Mary, what is there so dreadful about Mr. Medland?"

"Everything," said Lady Eynesford.

"Still," suggested Miss Scaife, "if the creatures are bent on having him—"

"My dear Eleanor, what is a Governor for?" demanded Lady Eynesford.

"To do as he's told and subscribe to the Cup," interposed Dick Derosne. And he added, "They are having a palaver. Old Perry's been in an hour and a half."

Captain Heseltine and Mr. Flemyng looked at their watches and nodded gravely.

"Poor Willie!" murmured Lady Eynesford. "He'll miss his ride."

Poor Willie—that is to say, His Excellency William Delaporte, Baron Eynesford, Governor of New Lindsey—deserved all the sympathy his wife's exclamation implied, and even more. For, after a vast amount of fencing and an elaborate disquisition on the state of parties in the colony, Sir Robert Perry decisively refused the dissolution the Governor offered, and ended by saying, with eyebrows raised and the slightest shrug of his shoulders,

"In fact, sir, it's my duty to advise you to send for Mr. Medland."

The Governor pushed his chair back from the table.

"You won't try again?" he asked.

"Impossible, until he has failed."

"You think Puttock out of the question?"

"Quite. He has not following enough: people wouldn't stand Medland being passed over. Really, I don't think you'll find Medland hard to get on with. He's a very able man. For

Anthony Hope

myself, I like him."

The Governor sat silent for a few minutes. Sir Robert, conceiving that his interview was at an end, rose to take leave. Lord Eynesford expressed much regret at being obliged to lose his services: Sir Robert replied suitably, and was at the door before the Governor reverted to Mr. Medland.

"There are queer stories about him, aren't there?" he asked. "I mean about his private life."

"Well, there is some vague gossip of the kind."

"There now! That's very awkward. He must come here, you know, and what shall I say to my wife?"

"She's been dead three or four years now," said Sir Robert, not referring to the Governor's wife. "And it's only rumour after all. Nothing has ever come to light on the subject."

"But there's a girl."

"There's nothing against the girl—except of course—"

"Oh, just so," said the Governor; "but that makes it awkward. Besides, somebody told me he used to get drunk."

"I think you may disregard that," said Sir Robert. "It only means that he likes his glass of wine as most of us do."

Sir Robert retired, and presently Dick Derosne, who acted as his brother's private secretary, came in. The Governor was in an easy-chair, smoking a cigar.

"So you've settled it," said Dick.

"Yes. Perry won't hear of going on."

"Well, he hardly could after being beaten by seventeen on his biggest bill. What's going to happen?"

Now the Governor thought fit to assume that the course he had, after so much hesitation, determined upon was, to every sensible man, the only possible course. Perhaps he fancied that he would thus be in a stronger position for justifying it to a sensible woman.

"Of course," he said, in a tone expressive of some surprise at a question so unnecessary, "I am sending for Medland."

Dick Derosne whistled. The Governor relapsed into sincerity.

"No help for it," he pleaded. "You must back me up, old man, with Mary. Women can't understand constitutional obligations."

"She said she wouldn't have him to the house," remarked Dick.

"Oh, Eleanor Scaife must persuade her. I wish you'd go and tell them, Dick. I'm expecting Medland in half-an-hour. I wish I was out of it. I distrust these fellows, both them and their policy."

"And yet you'll have to be civil to them."

"Civil! I must be just as cordial as I was with Perry. That's why it's so important that Mary should be—"

"Reasonable?" suggested Dick.

"Well, yes," said Lord Eynesford.

"How does Perry take it?"

"Oh, I don't think he minds much. He thinks Medland's gang will soon fall to pieces and he'll come back. Besides, the K.C.M.G. softens the blow."

"Ah! It's the cheap defence of nations now—*vice* chivalry, out of fashion," laughed Dick.

Hitherto Lord Eynesford and his wife had enjoyed their reign. Everything had gone well. The Governor agreed heartily with the measures introduced by Sir Robert Perry's ministry, and his relations with the members of the government, and especially with its chief, had been based on reciprocal liking and respect: they were most of them gentlemen and all of them respectable men, and, what was hardly less important, their wives and families had afforded no excuse for the exercise of Lady Eynesford's somewhat fastidious nicety as to manners, or her distinctly rigid scrutiny into morals. Under such conditions, the duty and the inclinations of Government House went hand-in-hand. Suddenly, in the midst of an apparently peaceful session, came what the Governor considered an unhallowed combination between a discontented section of Perry's party, and the Opposition under Medland's leadership. The result was the defeat of the Government, the resignation of Sir Robert, and the inevitability of Mr. Medland.

Entering the Legislative Assembly as the representative of an outlying constituency, Medland had speedily made himself the spokesman of the growing Labour Party, and now, after fifteen years of public life, and a secret and subterranean struggle with the old middle-class element, was established as the leader of a united party, so powerful in numbers that the accession of some dozen deserters had placed it in a majority. Mr. Coxon had led the revolt against Sir Robert Perry, and the Governor disliked Coxon even more thoroughly than he distrusted Medland. Miss Scaife said that Medland was the more dangerous, inasmuch as he was sincere and impetuous, while Coxon was neither; but then, the Governor would reply, Coxon was a snob, and Medland, if not exactly a gentleman according to the ideas of Eton and Christchurch—and Lord Eynesford adhered to these ideas—scorned a bad imitation where he could not attain the reality, and by his simplicity and freedom from pretension extorted the admission of good breeding. But why compare the men? He would have to accept both, for Medland must offer Coxon a place, and beyond doubt the offer would be accepted. The Governor was alarmed for the fate of New Lindsey under such ruling, and awaited with apprehension his next interview with his wife.

Dick Derosne had fulfilled his mission, and his tidings had spread dismay on the lawn. Lady Eynesford reiterated her edict of exclusion against the new Premier; Eleanor Scaife smiled and told her she would be forced to receive him. Alicia in vain sought particulars of Mr. Medland's misdeeds, and the *aides-de-camp* speculated curiously on the composition of the Cabinet, Captain Heseltine betting Mr. Flemyng five to two that it would include Mr. Giles, the leading tailor of Kirton, to whose services the captain had once been driven to resort with immense trepidation and disastrous results. As a fact, the captain lost his bet; the Cabinet did not include Mr. Giles, because that gentleman, albeit an able speaker, and a man of much greater intellect than most of his customers, was suspected of paying low wages to his employés, though, according to the captain, it was impossible that he should pay them as little as their skill deserved.

"I don't think I ever saw Mr. Medland," said Alicia, who had come out from England only a few months before.

"I have seen him," said Eleanor Scaife. "In fact, I had a little talk with him at the Jubilee Banquet."

"Was he sober?" Lady Eynesford, in her bitterness of spirit, allowed herself to ask.

"Mary! Of course he was. He was also rather interesting. He was then in mourning for Mrs. Medland, and he told me he only came because his absence would have been put down to disloyalty."

The mention of Mrs. Medland increased the downward curve of Lady Eynesford's mouth, and she was about to speak, when Dick Derosne exclaimed,

"Well, you can see him now, Al. He's walking up the drive."

The party and their tea-table were screened by trees, and they were able, themselves unseen, to watch Mr. Medland, as, in obedience to the Governor's summons, he walked slowly up to Government House. A girl of about seventeen or eighteen accompanied him to the gate, and left him there with a merry wave of her hand, and he strode on alone, his hands in his trousers pockets and a soft felt hat on the back of his head.

James—or, as his followers called him, "Jimmy"—Medland was forty-one years of age, once an engineer, now a politician, by profession, a tall, loose-limbed, slouching man, with stiff black hair and a shaven face. His features were large and had been clear-cut, but by now they had grown coarser, and his deep-set eyes, under heavy lids and bushy eyebrows, alone survived unimpaired by time and life. Deep lines ran either side from nose to mouth, and the like across his forehead. He had cut himself while shaving that morning, and a large patch of black plaster showed in the centre of his long, prominent chin: as he walked, he now and then lifted a hand to pluck nervously at it; save in this unconscious gesture, he betrayed no sign of excitement or preoccupation, for, as he walked, he looked about him and once, for a minute, he whistled.

"Awful!" said Lady Eynesford in a whisper.

"He wants a new coat," said Captain Heseltine.

"He looks rather interesting, I think," said Alicia.

At this moment a rare and beautiful butterfly fluttered close over Mr. Medland's head. He paused and watched it for a moment. Then he looked carefully round him: no one was in sight: the butterfly settled for a moment on a flowerbed. Mr. Medland looked round again. Then he cautiously lifted his soft hat from his head, wistfully eyed the butterfly, looked round again, suddenly pounced down on his knees, and pressed the hat to the ground. He was very close to the hidden tea-party now, so close that Alicia's suppressed scream of laughter almost betrayed its presence. Mr. Medland put his head down and, raising one corner of the hat, peered under it. Alicia laughed outright, for the butterfly was fluttering in the air above him. Medland did not hear her; he looked up, saw the butterfly, rose to his feet, put on his hat, and exclaimed, in a voice audible by all the listeners—

"Missed it, by heaven!"

"You see the sort of man he is," observed Lady Eynesford.

"An entomologist, I suppose," suggested Miss Scaife.

"He chases butterflies in the Governor's garden, and swears when he doesn't catch them!"

"He fears not God, neither regards the Governor," remarked Dick, with a solemn shake of his head.

"Don't be flippant, Dick," said Lady Eynesford sharply.

"He might at least brush the knees of his trousers," moaned Captain Heseltine.

Meanwhile Mr. Medland walked up to the door and rang the bell. He was received by Jackson, the butler; and Jackson was flanked by two footmen. Jackson politely concealed his surprise at not seeing a carriage and pair, and stated that his Excellency would receive Mr. Medland at once.

"I hope I haven't kept him waiting," answered Medland. "The pony's lame, and I had to walk."

The footmen, who were young, raw, and English, almost smiled. A Premier dependent on one pony! Jackson redoubled his obsequious attention.

The Governor used to say that he wished his wife had imbibed the constitutional spirit as readily as Jackson.

CHAPTER II

A POPULAR DEMONSTRATION

Miss Eleanor Scaife was *gouvernante des enfants de* New Lindsey; but she found the duty of looking after two small children, shared as it was with a couple of nurses, not enough to occupy her energies. So she organised the hospitality of Government House, and interested herself in the political problems of a young community. In the course of the latter pursuit, a study of Mr. Medland appeared appropriate and needful, and Miss Scaife was minded to engage in it, in spite of the hostility of Lady Eynesford. She had studied Sir Robert Perry for three years, but Sir Robert was disappointing. That he was a charming old gentleman she freely admitted, but he was not in any special way characteristic of a young community. He was just like half-a-hundred members of Parliament whom she had known while she lived with the Eynesfords at home: in fact he was irredeemably European. Accordingly she was glad to see him, but she mentally transferred him to the recreative department, and talked to him about scenery, pictures, and light literature. Lady Eynesford admired Sir Robert because there was no smack of the young community about him; Miss Scaife conceded that point of view, but maintained that there was another: and from that other she ranked Mr. Medland above a thousand Sir Roberts. All this she explained to Alicia Derosne, after Lady Eynesford had retired in dudgeon, and while the Governor was closeted with the new Premier.

"But," objected Alicia, "Captain Heseltine says—"

"Unless," interrupted Eleanor, "it's something about a coat, I don't care what Captain Heseltine says. He's an authority on that subject, but on no other under the sun."

Alicia abandoned Captain Heseltine's authority and fell back on her sister-in-law's; Eleanor, in spite of the unusual relations of intimate friendship, dating from old school-days, between her employer and herself, could not treat Lady Eynesford's opinion with open disrespect. She drew certain distinctions, which resulted in demonstrating that a close acquaintance between Mr. Medland and Alicia was inadvisable, but that as regards herself the case was different.

"In short," said Alicia, summarising the distinctions, "you are thirty and I am twenty-two. But I don't want to know the man, only I liked him for hunting that butterfly. I wonder what Miss Medland is like. Captain Heseltine says she's very pretty."

"I don't know."

"Is she out? Oh, but does one come out in New Lindsey?"

"It will be much more convenient if she isn't out," said Miss Scaife, rising and beginning to walk towards the house.

Alicia accompanied her. Before they had gone far, Mr. Medland and Dick Derosne appeared in the drive. The interview was ended, and Dick was escorting Mr. Medland.

"I'm afraid we can't avoid them," said Miss Scaife.

"I'm afraid not," said Alicia. "I wonder what they're talking about."

Mr. Medland's voice, though not loud in ordinary speech, was distinct and penetrating. In a moment Alicia's wonder was satisfied.

"Only be sure you get the right gin," he said.

"Good gracious!" said Alicia. "Is that characteristic of a young community, Eleanor?"

Miss Scaife made no reply. The two parties met, and Mr. Medland was presented. At this instant, Alicia, glancing at the house, thought she saw a disapproving face at Lady Eynesford's window; but it seemed hardly likely that the Governor's wife would be watching the Premier out of the window. Alicia wondered whether they had met in the house; Miss Scaife felt no doubt that they had not. She knew that Lady Eynesford's surrender would be a matter of time.

"Well," she said, "are we to congratulate you, Mr. Medland?"

"I believe my tongue is supposed to be sealed for the time," he answered, smiling.

"Mine isn't," laughed Dick, "and I think you may offer him your felicitations."

"You think it, yourself, a subject for congratulation?" asked Eleanor, getting to work at once.

"Oh, Eleanor!" protested Alicia. "Poor Mr. Medland!"

Anthony Hope

Medland glanced from one to the other, smiling again.

"Whatever may be the sacrifice of personal inclination involved," he began solemnly, "when the Governor calls on me I have no—"

"You're making fun of us," said Alicia, seeing the twinkle in his eye.

"I am quoting Mr.—Sir Robert Perry's speech when he last came in."

"Sir Robert is a great friend of mine," declared Alicia.

"Seriously," said Medland, turning to Eleanor, "I am very pleased."

"Why?" she asked. "The responsibility must be frightful."

Alicia and Dick laughed irreverently.

"Eleanor's always talking about responsibility," said the former. "I hate the idea of it, don't you, Mr. Medland?"

"Call it power and try then," he answered.

"Power? Oh, but I have none!"

"No?" he asked, with a look that made Alicia think he might have been "nice" when he was a young man.

"Oh, of course, if it's mere ambition—" began Eleanor impatiently.

"Not altogether," he interposed.

"Then what else?"

"Listen!" he said, holding up his hand.

They were now within twenty or thirty yards of the road, and, listening, they heard the murmur of many voices. Government House stood on the shore of the bay, about half a mile outside the town, and a broad road ran by the gates which, on reaching Kirton, was merged in one of the main thoroughfares, Victoria Street.

Another turn brought the party in the garden in sight of the road. It was thronged with people for a considerable distance, people in a thick mass, surging up against the gate and hardly held back by a cordon of police.

"Whatever can be the matter?" exclaimed Eleanor.

"I am the matter," said Medland. "They have heard about it."

When the crowd saw him, cheer after cheer rang out, caps and handkerchiefs were waved, and even flags made a sudden appearance. Moving a pace in advance of his companions, he lifted his hat, and the enthusiastic cries burst forth with renewed vigour. He signed to them to be still, but they did not heed him. Alicia caught hold of Eleanor's hand, her breath coming and going in sudden gasps. Eleanor looked at Medland. He was moistening his lips, and she saw a little quiver run through his limbs.

"By Jove!" said Dick Derosne.

Medland turned to Eleanor, and pointed to the crowd.

"Yes, I see," she said.

Anthony Hope

He held out his hand to bid them farewell, and walked on towards the gate. They stood and watched his progress. Suddenly a different cry rose.

"Let her pass! Let her pass! Let her through to him!"

The crowd slowly parted, and down the middle of the road, amid the raising of hats and pretty rough compliments, a young girl came walking swiftly and proudly, with a smile on her lips.

"It's his daughter," whispered Alicia. "Oh!"

Medland opened the gate and went out. The girl, her fair hair blowing out behind her and her cheeks glowing red, ran to meet him, and, as he stooped and kissed her, the crowd, having, as a crowd, but one way to tell its feelings, roared and cheered again. Medland, with one hand on his daughter's shoulder and the other holding his hat, walked down the lane between human walls, and was lost to sight as the walls found motion and closed in behind him.

After some moments' silence Dick Derosne recovered himself, and remarked with a cynical air,

"Neat bit of acting—kissing the girl and all that."

But Alicia would not have it. With a tremulous laugh, she said,

"I should like to have kissed him too. Oh, Eleanor, I didn't know it was like that!"

Perhaps Eleanor did not either, but she would not admit it. What was it but a lot of ignorant people cheering they knew not what? If anything, it was degrading. Yet, in spite of these most reasonable reflections, she knew that her cheeks had flushed and her heart beat at the sight and the sound.

They were still standing and watching the crowd as it retreated towards Kirton, when the Governor, who had come out to get some fresh air after his arduous labour, joined them.

"Extraordinary the popularity of the man in Kirton," he observed, in answer to Alicia's eager description of Mr. Medland's triumph.

"What has he done for them?" asked Eleanor.

"Done? Oh, I don't know. He's done something, I suppose; but it's what he's going to do that they're so keen about."

"Is he a Socialist?" inquired Alicia.

"I can't tell you," replied Lord Eynesford. "I don't know what he is—and I'm not sure I know what a Socialist is. Ask Eleanor."

"A Socialist," began Eleanor, in an authoritative tone, "is—"

But this much-desired definition was unhappily lost, for a footman came up and told Lord Eynesford that his wife would like to see him if he were disengaged.

The Governor smiled grimly, winked imperceptibly, and departed.

"It's been quite an entertaining day," said Miss Scaife. "But I'm very sorry for Sir Robert."

"What was Mr. Medland talking to you about, Dick?" asked Alicia.

"Oh, a new sort of drink. You take a long glass, and some pounded ice and some gin—only you must be careful to get—"

"I don't want to hear about it."

"Well, you asked, you know," retorted Dick, with the air of a man who suffers under the perpetual illogicality of woman.

CHAPTER III

HOSPITALITY *EX OFFICIO*

"I confess to being very much alarmed," said Mr. Kilshaw, "and I think Capital generally shares the feeling."

"If I thought he could last, I should share it myself," said Sir Robert Perry.

"He may easily last long enough to half ruin my business. Large concerns are delicate concerns."

"Come, Kilshaw, Puttock's a capitalist; he'll see Capital isn't wronged."

"Puttock is all very well in his way; but what do you say to Jewell and Norburn?"

"Jewell's an old-style Radical: he won't do you much harm. You hit the nail on the head when you mention Norburn. Norburn would be very pleased to run your factory as a State work-shop for two pound a week."

"And pickings," added Mr. Kilshaw, with scornful emphasis.

A third gentleman, who was sitting near in the large

bow-window of the Central Club, an elderly man, with short-clipped white hair and a pleasant face, joined in the talk.

"Norburn? Why, is that the fellow I tried? Is he in Medland's government?"

"That's the man, Sir John," answered Kilshaw; and Sir Robert added,

"You gave him three months for inciting to riot in the strike at the Collieries two years ago. He's made Minister of Public Works; I hear the Governor held out for a long while, but Medland insisted."

"And my works are to be Public Works, I suppose," grumbled Kilshaw, finding some comfort in this epigrammatic statement of the unwelcome prospect before him.

"Red-hot, isn't he?" asked Sir John Oakapple, who, as Chief Justice of the colony, had sent the new Minister to gaol.

Kilshaw nodded.

"Will he and Puttock pull together?" continued the Chief Justice.

"The hopeful part of the situation is," said Sir Robert, "that Puttock is almost bound to fall out with somebody, either with Norburn, for the reason you name, or with Coxon, because Coxon will try to rule the roast, or with Medland himself."

"Why should he quarrel with Medland?"

"Why does the heir quarrel with the king? Besides, there's the Prohibition Question. I doubt if Medland will satisfy

Puttock and his people over that."

"Oh, I expect he will," said the Chief Justice. "I asked him once—this is in confidence, you know—if he didn't think it a monstrous proposal, and he only shrugged those slouched shoulders of his, and said, 'We've got Sunday Closing, and we go in the back way: if we have Prohibition the drink'll go in the back way—same principle, my dear Chief Justice'": and that High Officer finished his anecdote with a laugh.

"The odd thing about Medland is," remarked Sir Robert, "that he's utterly indifferent about everything except what he's utterly mad about. He has no moderate sympathies or antipathies."

"Therefore he's a most dangerous man," said Kilshaw.

"Oh, I think he sympathises, in moderation, with morality," laughed Sir John.

"Ay," rejoined Perry quickly, "and that's all. What if Puttock raised the Righteous on him?"

"Oh, then I should stand by Medland," said the Chief Justice decisively. "And young Coxon's to be Attorney-General. He's safe enough."

"A man who thinks only about himself is generally safe," remarked Sir Robert dryly; and he added, with a smile, "That's why lawyers are such a valuable class."

The Chief Justice laughed, and took his revenge by asking,

"How many windows did they break, Perry?"

"Only three," rejoined the Ex-Premier. "Considering the

Anthony Hope

popular enthusiasm I got off cheap."

"You can't stir a people's heart for nothing. All the same, the reception they gave him was a fine sight."

"Extraordinary, wasn't it?"

"I call it most ominous," said Mr. Kilshaw, and he rose and went out gloomily.

"I haven't had my invitation to meet them at Government House yet," said the Chief Justice.

He referred to the banquet which the Governor was accustomed to give to a new Ministry, when the leading officials of the colony were always included in the party.

Sir Robert looked round for possible eavesdroppers.

"There's a hitch," he said in a low voice. "Lady Eynesford makes difficulties about having Medland."

"Oh, that's nonsense!"

"Utter nonsense; but it seems she does. However, I suppose you'll get your card in a day or two."

"And renew my acquaintance with Mr. Norburn under happier circumstances."

"Norburn will feel as one used to when one breakfasted with the school-master—as a peacemaking after another sort of interview."

Sir Robert Perry proved right in supposing that Lady Eynesford's resistance could not last for ever. It was long enough and fierce enough to make the Governor very unhappy and the rest of the family very uncomfortable, but it was foredoomed to failure. Even the Bishop of Kirton, whom she consulted, told her that high place had its peculiar duties, and that however deplorable the elevation of such a man might be, if the Queen's representative invited him to join his counsels, the Queen's representative's wife must invite him to join her dinner-party: and the Bishop proved the sincerity of his constitutional doctrine by accepting an invitation to meet the new Ministry. Lady Eynesford, abandoned by Church and State alike, surrendered, thanking heaven that Daisy Medland's youth postponed another distasteful necessity.

"You'll have to face it in a few months' time," said Eleanor Scaife, who was not always as comforting a companion as a lady in her position is supposed to be.

"Oh, they'll be out in a month," answered Lady Eynesford confidently. "The Bishop says they can't last. Do you know, Eleanor, Mr. Coxon is the only Churchman among them?"

"Shocking!" said Eleanor, with no more suspicion of irony than her reputation as an *esprit fort* demanded. It really startled her a little: the social significance seemed considerable.

Mr. Medland's invitation to dinner caused him perhaps more perturbation than had his invitation to power. A natural sensitiveness of mind supplied in him the place of an experience of refined society or an impulse of inherited pride. He cared nothing that his advent to office alarmed and displeased many; but it gave him pain to be compelled to dine at the table of a lady who, by notorious report, did not desire his company.

Anthony Hope

"I don't want to go, and she doesn't want to have me," he protested to his daughter; "yet she must have me and I must go. The great god Sham again, Daisy."

"You'll meet him everywhere now," said Daisy, with a melancholy shake of her young head.

"And rout him somewhere?"

"Oh yes, everywhere—except at Government House."

"I hate going."

"I believe mother would have liked it. Don't you think so, dear?"

"Perhaps. Should you?"

"I should be terribly afraid of Lady Eynesford."

"Just my feeling," said Medland, stroking his chin.

When he entered the drawing-room at Government House, and was presented to his hostess by the Governor, on whose brow rested a little pucker of anxiety, Lady Eynesford was talking to the Bishop and to Mr. Puttock. Puttock had accepted the office of Minister of Trade and Customs, but not without grumbling, for he had aspired to control the finances of the colony as Treasurer, and considered that Medland underrated his influence as a political leader. He was a short man, rather stout, with large whiskers; he wore a blue ribbon in the button-hole of his dress-coat. Lady Eynesford considered him remarkably like a grocer, and the very quintessence of nonconformity; but he at least was indisputably respectable, a devoted husband, and the father of a large family, behind whose ranks he was in the habit of walking to chapel twice every Sunday. Sometimes he preached when he got there. Just to his right, talking briskly to Alicia Derosne, stood Mr. Coxon, the Attorney-General, very smart in English-made clothes, and discussing the doings of people at home whom he had known or seen in the days when he was at Cambridge, and had the run of a rich uncle's house in Park Lane. In the distance the Roman Catholic Archbishop was talking to Eleanor Scaife, and suffering Sir John Oakapple's jests with a polite faint smile. This mixture of the sects ranked high among the trials of Lady Eynesford's position, and contained precious opportunities for Miss Scaife's inquiring mind.

It seems true beyond question that moral estimation counts for more in the likings of women than in those of men. Medland, in spite of the utter insignificance, as he conceived, of the lady's judgment considered as an intellectual process, was too much of a politician, and perhaps a little too much of a man also, not to wish to conciliate the Governor's wife; but his courteous deference, his clever talk, and his search for points of sympathy broke ineffectually on the barriers of Lady Eynesford's official politeness and personal reserve. She was cruel in her clear indication of the footing upon which they met, and the Governor's uneasy glance of appeal would produce nothing better than a cold interest in the scenery of the Premier's constituency. Medland was glad when Lady Eynesford turned to the Chief Justice and released him; his relief was so great that it was hardly marred by finding Mrs. Puttock on his other side. Yet Mrs. Puttock and he were not congenial spirits.

"We are sending a deputation to you," said Mrs. Puttock, directly Medland's change of position gave her an opportunity.

He emptied his glass of champagne, and asked,

"Which of your many 'We's,' Mrs. Puttock?"

"Why, the W.T.A.A."

"I won't affect ignorance—Women's—Total—Abstinence—Association."

"The enthusiasm this afternoon was enormous. Of course Mr. Puttock could not be there; but I told them I felt sure that with the new Ministry an era of real hope had dawned," and Mrs. Puttock looked inquiringly at the Premier, who was in his turn looking at the foaming wine that fell into his glass from Jackson's practised hand.

"A new era?" he answered. "Oh, well, you didn't get much out of Perry. What do you want of me?"

"We want to strengthen your hands in dealing drastically with the problem. Of course, it will be one of your first measures."

"We have at least six first measures already on the list," remarked the Premier, smiling.

"I saw your daughter to-day," Mrs. Puttock continued. "I went to ask her to join us."

"Isn't she rather young to join things?" pleaded Mr. Medland. "Poor child! She would hardly understand what she's giving—I mean, what she's going in for. What did she say?"

"Well, really, Mr. Medland, I think you might speak a word to her. She told me she loved champagne and tipsy-cake. The tipsy-cake doesn't matter, because it can be made without alcohol.—I beg your pardon?"

"I didn't speak," said the Premier.

"But champagne! At her age!"

"She's only tasted it half-a-dozen times."

"Well, I hope every one will have to give it up soon. My husband says that the Cabinet—"

"Here's treason! Has he been telling you our secrets?"

"Secrets! Why, two-thirds of the party are pledged—"

But here Lady Eynesford again claimed the Premier's attention, and he was really glad of it.

Dick Derosne walked home with Mr. Medland. He had intended to go only to the gate, but Medland pressed him to go further, and, engrossed in conversation, they reached Medland's house without separating.

"Come in and see Daisy," said Medland. "She's been alone all the evening, poor girl, and will be glad of better company than mine."

"Oh, come, I expect she likes your society better than any one else's."

"Well, that won't last long, will it?"

They went in and found Daisy supping on the wing of a chicken, and some wine-and-water. Medland led the way, and, as soon as his daughter saw him, she exclaimed,

"Was it very awful, father?"

"Well, was it, Mr. Derosne?" he asked of Dick. "Daisy, this is the Governor's brother, Mr. Derosne."

"It was awful!" said Dick, executing his bow. "Those great feeds always are."

"Why, Daisy," exclaimed Mr. Medland, "you're drinking wine. How about Mrs. Puttock?"

"Oh, she told you? She said it was very wicked."

"And you?"

"Oh, I said it wasn't, because you did it."

"Luckily, a conclusion may be right, though the reason for it is utterly wrong," said the Premier.

"I," said Dick, "always admit things are wicked, you know, and say I do 'em all the same. It saves a lot of argument."

The door opened and Mr. Norburn walked in.

"Is it too late for me to come?" he asked.

"Of course not," said Daisy, greeting him with evident pleasure, and ensconcing him in an armchair. "We expect you to come at all the odd times. That's the part of an intimate friend, isn't it, Mr. Derosne?"

Medland was speaking to Norburn, and Dick took the opportunity of remarking,

"Mayn't I come at an odd time now and then?"

"Oh do. We shall be so pleased."

"Mr. Norburn doesn't come at all of them, does he?"

"At most. Do you mind that?"

"Of course I do. Who wouldn't?"

"I don't."

"No, if you did I shouldn't."

Dick was, it must be admitted, getting along very well, considering that he had only been presented to the young lady ten minutes before. That was Dick's way; and when the young lady is attractive, it is a way that has many recommendations, only sometimes it leads to a pitfall—a cold answer, or a snub.

"But why," asked Daisy, in apparent surprise, "should you mind about what I thought? I'm afraid I should never think about whether you liked it or not, you know."

"Good-night," said Dick. And when he got outside and was lighting his cigar, he exclaimed, "Confound the girl!" And after a pause he added, "Hang the fellow!" and shook his head and went home.

CHAPTER IV

WEEDING OUT THE WEAK-KNEED

In a short time it happened that Lady Eynesford conceived a high opinion of Mr. Coxon. He was, she declared, the one bright spot in the new Ministry; he possessed ability, principle, sound Churchmanship, and gentlemanly demeanour. A young man thus equipped could hardly fail of success, and Lady Eynesford, in spite of the Governor's decidedly lukewarm approbation, was pleased to take the Attorney-General under her special protection. More than once in the next week or two did Mr. Coxon, tall-hatted, frock-coated, and new-gloved, in obedience to cordial invitations, take tea in the verandah of Government House. He was naturally gratified by these attentions, and, being not devoid of ambition, soon began to look upon his position as the starting-point for a greater prize. Lady Eynesford was, here again, with him—up to a point. She thought (and thoughts are apt to put themselves with a bluntness which would be inexcusable in speech) that it was high time that Eleanor Scaife was married, and, from an abstract point of view, this could hardly be denied. Lady Eynesford took the next step. Eleanor and Coxon would suit one another to perfection. Hence the invitations to tea, and Lady Eynesford's considerate withdrawals into the house, or out of sight in the garden. Of course it was impossible to gauge

Eleanor's views at this early stage, but Lady Eynesford was assured of Mr. Coxon's gratitude—his bearing left no doubt of it—and she congratulated herself warmly on the promising and benevolent scheme which she had set afoot.

Now the danger of encouraging ambitious young men—and this remark is general in its scope, and not confined at all to one subject-matter—is that their vaulting imaginations constantly overleap the benevolence of their patrons. Mr. Coxon would not have been very grateful for permission to make love to Miss Scaife; he was extremely grateful for the opportunity of recommending himself to Alicia Derosne. The Governor's sister—none less—became by degrees his aim and object, and when Lady Eynesford left him with Miss Scaife, hoping that Alicia would have the sense not to get in the way, Mr. Coxon's soaring mind regarded himself as left with Alicia, and he hoped that the necessary exercise of discretion would be forthcoming from Miss Scaife. Presently this little comedy revealed itself to Eleanor, and, after an amused glance at the retreating figure of her misguided friend, she would bury herself in *Tomes on the British Colonies*, and abandon Alicia to the visitor's wiles. A little indignant at the idea of being "married off" in this fashion, she did not feel it incumbent on her to open Lady Eynesford's eyes. As for Alicia—Alicia laughed, and thought that young men were much the same all the world over.

"Tomes," said Eleanor on one occasion, looking up from the first volume of that author—and perhaps she chose her passage with malice—"clearly intimates his opinion that the Empire can't hold together unless the social bonds between England and the colonies are strengthened."

"Does he, dear?" said Alicia, playing with the pug. "Do look at his tongue, Mr. Coxon. Isn't it charming?"

"Yes. Listen to this: 'It is on every ground to be regretted that the divorce between society at home and in the colonies is so complete. The ties of common interest and personal friendship which, impalpable though they be, bind nations together more closely than constitutions and laws, are to a great extent wanting. Even the interchange of visits is rare; closer connection by intermarriage, in a broad view, non-existent.'"

"There's a great deal of sense in that," said Coxon.

"Well, Mr. Coxon," laughed Alicia, "you should have thought of it when you were in England."

Eleanor's eyes had dropped again to Tomes, and Mr. Coxon answered, in a tone not calculated to disturb the reader,

"I hope it's not altogether too late."

"The choice is so small out here, isn't it? Now, according to Tomes, Mr. Medland ought to marry a duchess—well, a dowager-duchess—but there isn't one."

"I should hardly have thought the Premier quite the man for a duchess," said Coxon, rather superciliously.

"Well, I like him much better than most dukes I've seen. Why do you shake your head?"

"I've the greatest respect for Mr. Medland as my leader, but—come, Miss Derosne, he's hardly—now is he?"

"I like him very much indeed," declared Alicia. "I think he's the most interesting man I've ever met."

"But thinking a man interesting and thinking him a man one would like to marry are quite different, surely?" suggested fastidious Mr. Coxon.

"Thinking him interesting and thinking him a man one would be *likely* to marry are quite different," corrected Eleanor, emerging from Tomes.

"By the way, who was Mrs. Medland?" asked Alicia.

Coxon hesitated for a moment: Eleanor raised her eyes.

"I believe her name was Benyon," he answered. "I—I know nothing about her."

"Didn't you know her?"

"No, I was in England, and she died a year after I came back—before I went into politics at all."

"I wonder if she was nice."

"My dear Alicia, what can it matter?" asked Eleanor.

"If you come to that, Eleanor, most of the things we talk about don't matter," protested Alicia. "We are not Attorney-Generals, like Mr. Coxon, whose words are worth—how much?"

"Now, Miss Derosne, you're chaffing me."

"Come and feed the swans," said Alicia, rising.

"What will Mary think?" said Eleanor, settling herself down again to Tomes. "And why is Alicia so curious about the Medlands?"

It was perhaps natural that Eleanor should be puzzled to

answer the question she put to herself, but in reality the interest Alicia felt admitted of easy explanation. She had first encountered Medland under conditions which invested him with all the attraction that a visibly dominant character exercises over a young mind, and the impression then created had been of late much deepened by what she heard from her brother. Dick felt that the Governor would be a cold, and Lady Eynesford a thoroughly unfavourable, auditor of his views on the Medlands, but, in spite of Daisy's cruel indifference, he had taken advantage of her permission to pay her more than one visit, and he poured out his soul to his sister. His outpourings consisted of enthusiastic praises of both father and daughter.

"By Jove!" he said, "it's simply—you know, Al—simply fetching to see them together. He's a splendid chap—not an ounce of side or nonsense about him. And she's awfully pretty. Don't you think she's awfully pretty, Al?"

"I only saw her for a moment, dear."

"It's too bad of Mary to go on as she does. She simply ignores Miss Medland."

"Miss Medland's still very young, Dick. Is he—how does he treat her?"

"I don't know. It's almost funny—they're always jumping up to get one another things, don't you know!" answered Dick, whose feelings outran his powers of elegant description.

"Do you go there much, Dick?"

"Now, Al, don't try to do Mary to me."

Alicia laughed.

"I think Mary will 'do' as much 'Mary' to you as you want, if you don't take care, you foolish boy. But, Dick, tell me. How do Willie and Mr. Medland get on?"

"Oh, pretty well, but—You won't tell?"

Alicia promised secrecy, and Dick, conscious of criminality, lowered his voice and continued,

"I believe there's a row on in the Cabinet already. Willie said Puttock and Jewell were at loggerheads with Norburn, and Medland was inclined to back Norburn."

"And Mr. Coxon?"

"He's supposed to be lying low. And then I was down at the club and met old Oakapple there, and he told me that Kilshaw had boasted of having done a deal with Puttock."

"What did he mean?"

"Why, that he and his gang—the rich capitalists, you know—were to back up old Puttock's temperance measures, provided Puttock (and Jewell, if Puttock could nobble him) prevented Medland from bringing in—what the deuce was it?—some Socialistic labour legislation or other—I forget what. Anyhow the Chief Justice thought Perry would be back soon."

"What? That Mr. Medland would be turned out? What a shame! He hasn't had a fair chance, has he?"

The gossip which Dick had picked up was not very wide of the mark. It was perhaps too early to talk of absolute dissensions, but it was tolerably well known that a struggle was likely to occur in the Cabinet, nominally on the question of the relative priority to be given to different measures, more truly perhaps on the issue whether the advanced labour party, represented by Norburn, or the Radicals of the older type, headed by Puttock and Jewell, were to control the policy of the Premier and the Government. The latter section was inextricably connected, and, in its *personnel*, almost identical with the party who set the Prohibition question above and before all other matters. The concrete form taken by this conflict of abstract principles seemed likely to be— should the Government begin with a Temperance measure, or should it, in the first place, proceed to give to Labour that drastic Factory and Workshop Act which Norburn had advocated and Medland accepted, and which would, Mr. Kilshaw declared, reduce every manufacturer to the position of a slave of Government and a pauper to boot, would drive capital from the colony, and shut up every mill in New Lindsey? Now Mr. Kilshaw would, if he were reduced to choose, rather close the public-houses than the mills. So he told Sir Robert Perry, who was very quiet, but very watchful just now; and the story was that Sir Robert said, "Puttock has got shares in the Southern Sea Mill—and Puttock's a Prohibition man," and refused to say any more; but that was enough—so the talk ran—to send Mr. Kilshaw straight to Puttock's hall-door.

These public matters gave Mr. Coxon much food for thought. His own attitude was, at present, considered to be one of neutrality towards the rival factions in the Government. He was in the habit of defining his aim in political life as being a steady and gradual removal of obstacles to the progress of the colony; to attain complete truth, it was only necessary to alter the definition by substituting "Mr. Coxon" for "the colony"; and the question which now occupied him was how he might best secure the best possible position for himself, without, as he hastened to protest, abandoning his principles. He disliked Puttock, and he was envious of

Norburn, who threatened to supplant him as the "rising man" of his party. Should he help Puttock to remove Norburn, or lend Norburn a hand in ousting Puttock?

Down to the very week before the Legislative Assembly met, Mr. Medland kept his own counsel, disclosing his mind not even to his colleagues. Then he called a Cabinet, and listened to the conflicting views set forth by Puttock and Norburn.

"And what do you say, Mr. Coxon?" he asked, when Puttock's vehement harangue came to an end.

"I shall follow your judgment implicitly," replied Mr. Coxon, with touching fidelity.

"I feel bound to state," said Mr. Puttock, "and I believe I speak for my friend Jewell also" (Mr. Jewell nodded), "that with us priority for Temperance legislation and a cautious policy in imposing hampering restrictions on commercial undertakings are of vital moment. We cannot agree to give way on either point."

"And you, Norburn?" asked Medland, turning to his devoted follower, and smiling a kindly smile.

Norburn was about to speak, when Puttock broke in,

"It is best that the Premier should understand our position; what we have stated is absolutely essential to our continuance in the Government."

Mr. Medland thought that the function of a follower was to follow, and of a leader to lead. He always found it difficult to put up with opposition, and patience was not among whatever qualities of statesmanship he possessed.

Drumming gently on the table, he said,

"Oh, no Temperance this session. We'll give 'em a Labour session." He paused, and added, "And give it 'em hot and strong."

So that evening Puttock and Jewell resigned, and the Cabinet, meeting the House shorn and maimed, was established in power by the magnificent majority of ten.

"If so soon as this I'm done for,
I wonder what I was begun for!"

quoted Sir John Oakapple. "If they never agreed at all, what did they take office together for?"

"The screw," suggested Captain Heseltine.

"Then why haven't they stuck to it?"

Silence met this question, and the Chief Justice turned a look of bland inquiry on Mr. Kilshaw.

Mr. Kilshaw coughed and turned the pages of the *Kirton World*.

The Chief Justice winked at Dick Derosne, and said that it was refreshing to see there were still men who would sacrifice office to conviction.

"Oh, uncommon, Sir John," said Dick Derosne, and these cynics, having done entire injustice to two deeply sincere men, went off and joined in a game of pool. The Chief Justice took the pool.

CHAPTER V

A TALK AT A DANCE

Immediately after the Assembly had so narrowly confirmed Mr. Medland's position, it adjourned for a fortnight in order to allow time for the reorganisation of the Government, and the preparation of its legislative projects. The Governor seized the opportunity and started on a shooting expedition, accompanied by his wife. His absence somewhat diminished the *éclat* of Sir John Oakapple's dance, but nevertheless it was agreed to be a very brilliant affair. Everybody came, for Sir John's position invited hospitality to all parties alike, and the host, as became a well-to-do bachelor, provided a sumptuous entertainment. Even Mr. Medland was there, for it was his daughter's first public appearance, and he and Sir Robert Perry had interchanged some friendly remarks on the existing crisis.

"I suppose I mustn't ask who you're going to give us instead of your deserters," said Sir Robert jokingly.

"Oh," answered Medland, "I'm going to fill up with Labour men. I haven't quite fixed on the men yet."

"Then you'll be all one colour—all red? But I must congratulate you on your daughter's *début*. She and Miss

Anthony Hope

Derosne are the *belles* of the evening."

Then Sir Robert, in his pretty way, must needs be led up to Daisy Medland and dance a quadrille with her, apologising politely to Dick Derosne, who had arranged to sit out the said quadrille with the same lady, and became a violent anti-Perryite on the spot.

Alicia passed on Mr. Coxon's arm, and stopped for a moment to condole.

"I didn't know Premiers danced," she said, and perhaps her glance conveyed a shy invitation to Medland.

"If I ask you now, I shall have another secession," he replied, smiling at Coxon. "Besides, I can't dance."

"You must sit out with me then," she said, growing bolder. "You don't mind, do you, Mr. Coxon?"

Coxon and Dick were left to console one another, and Alicia sat down with Medland. At first he was silent, watching his daughter. When the quadrille ended, he rose and said,

"Come into the garden."

"But my partner for the next won't be able to find me."

"Well, supposing he can't?" said the Premier.

"It makes one very conceited to be a Premier," thought Alicia, but she went into the garden.

Then began what she declared to herself was the most interesting conversation to which she had ever listened. From silence, the Premier passed to a remark here and there, thence to a conversation, thence, as the evening went on and they strolled further and further away from the house, into a monologue on his life and aims and hopes. Young man after young man sought her in vain, or, finding the pair, feared to intrude and retired in discontent, while Medland strove to draw the picture of that far-off society whose bringing-near was his goal in public life. She wondered if he talked to other women like that: and she found herself hoping that he did not. His gaunt form seemed to fill and his sunk eyes to spring out to meet the light, as he painted for her the time when his dreams should have clothed themselves with the reality which his persuasive imagination almost gave them now.

Then he suddenly turned on himself.

"And I might have done something," he said; "but I've wasted most of my life."

"Wasted it?" she echoed in a wondering question.

"I don't know why I talk about it to-night, still less why I talk about it to you. I talked about it last to—to my wife."

"Ah! But your daughter?"

"Daisy!" he laughed tenderly. "Poor little Daisy! I don't bother her with it all." Then he added, "Really I've no business to bother you either, Miss Derosne. I break out sometimes. I'm afraid I'm not 'a silent, strong man.' Does it bore you?"

"You know—you know—" Alicia stammered.

"And now," he said, rising in his excitement, "even now, what have I? The place—the form—the name of power; and these creatures hold me back and hang on my flank and—I can do nothing." He sank back on the bench where she sat.

Alicia put her hand out and drew it back. Then she stretched it out again, and laid it on his arm.

"I am so sorry," she said, and her voice faltered. "Oh, if I could—but how absurd!"

Medland turned suddenly and looked her in the face.

"You will help some one," he answered, "some better man. And I—I beg your pardon. Come."

Alicia asked herself afterwards if she ought to be ashamed of what she did then. She caught the Premier by the arm, and said,

"But I want to stay with you." And then she sat trembling to hear his answer.

For a moment he did not answer. He passed his hand over his brow; then he smiled sadly.

"Nearly twenty years ago a woman said that to me," he said. "But she—well, it wasn't to talk politics."

"Oh, to call it *talking politics*!" she answered, with a little gasping laugh.

With another swift turn of his head, he bent his eyes on hers. She turned her head away, and neither spoke. Alicia played nervously with one glove which she had stripped off, while Medland gravely watched her face, beautiful in its pure outline and quivering with unwonted emotions. With a start he roused himself.

"Come," he said imperiously, offering his arm. She took it, and, without more words, they turned towards the house.

They had not gone far, when Eleanor Scaife met them. She was walking quickly, looking round as she went, as though in search. When she saw them she started, and cried,

"Oh, I want you, Alicia."

Medland immediately drew aside, and with a bow took his way. Alicia, calming herself with an effort, asked what was the matter.

"Why, it's that wretched brother of yours. I really do not know what Mary will say. I shall be afraid—"

"But what has Dick done?"

"Done? Why he's danced six dances out of eight with that Medland child. The whole room's talking about them."

"Eight dances? There can't have been eight dances?"

"Don't be silly," said Eleanor sharply. "I suppose you danced? No! I remember I didn't see you. Where have *you* been?"

"I—I've been sitting out."

"Not—not—Alicia, with one man? Worse and—"

"Yes."

"Mr. Coxon, then, I hope? At least he's safe."

"No."

"Who then?"

"I don't know why you should ask—"

"Alicia! Was it—?" exclaimed Eleanor, with a gesture towards where she had found her friend.

"Mr. Medland? Yes," answered Alicia. And, in her effort to exclude timidity, she infused into her voice a note of defiance.

Eleanor sat down on the nearest seat. Surprise dominated her faculties. Dick's behaviour was reprehensible, but, given such creatures as young men, natural. But Alicia? The thing was too surprising to cause uneasiness.

"Well, you are a queer child! Here's all the room looking for you to dance with you, and you go and sit in the garden with a politician of five-and-forty! What in the world were you doing?"

"Talking politics," said Alicia, now quite calmly.

"And you've been here since—?"

"The first quadrille."

"Six mortal dances!" said Eleanor, in an envious tone. Alicia had had a grand opportunity. "Did you remember to ask him about that description of the Cabinet meetings in Tomes? You remember we agreed to?"

"I'm afraid I forgot, dear."

"Oh, how stupid of you! If I'd been—but good gracious! I forgot Dick. Do come, Alicia, and get him away from her.

We seem to have nothing but Medlands to-night!"

The first person they met inside the ball-room was Mr. Coxon. He was enveloped in gloom. Alicia's conscience smote her.

"Oh!" she cried, "I forgot Mr. Coxon! I must go and scold him for not coming for me. Nonsense, Eleanor! I can't help about Dick," and, shaking off Miss Scaife's detaining hand, she went to play the usual imposture.

Eleanor looked round in bewilderment. Seeing Lady Perry, she was struck with an idea, crossed the room, and joined the ex-Premier's smiling, pleasant wife. Lady Perry had noticed enough to be *au fait* with the situation at a word. She rose and went to where Medland was now leaning listlessly against the wall. She spoke a word to him; he started, smiled, and shrugged his shoulders.

"I know you'll forgive me. One can't be too careful," she urged. "No one can be father and mother both."

Mr. Medland beckoned to his daughter; she came to him, Dick standing a few feet off.

"Whenever, Daisy," said Medland, "a thing is pleasant, one must not, in this world, have much of it. Is that the gospel, Lady Perry?"

"You'll make young Mr. Derosne too conceited, my dear," whispered Lady Perry, very kindly; but she favoured Dick, who knew well that he was a sinner, with a severe glance.

Thus Eleanor Scaife, having rid her party of the Medlands— for the moment, as she impatiently added—was at liberty to listen to the conversation of Mrs. Puttock. Mrs. Puttock was always most civil to any of the Government House party, and she entertained Eleanor, who resolutely refused all invitations to dance, with plenty of gossip. Amidst their talk and the occasional interruptions of men who joined and left them, the evening wore away, and Eleanor had just signed to Alicia to make ready to go, when Mrs. Puttock touched on the Premier, who was visible across the room, chatting merrily with his host, and laughing heartily at the Chief Justice's stories.

"The Premier seems in good spirits," said Mrs. Puttock, a little acidly.

"Oh, I expect he's only bearing up in public," laughed Eleanor. "But there certainly is a great change in him since I first recollect him."

"Indeed, Miss Scaife."

"Yes," said Eleanor, rising, for she saw Alicia approaching under Captain Heseltine's escort. "It was about the Jubilee time. He seemed then quite overcome with grief at the loss of his wife. Ah, here's Alicia!"

"Wife!" exclaimed Mrs. Puttock, bestowing on Eleanor a look of deep significance. "It's my belief he never had a wife."

Eleanor started.

"What do you mean?" she began, but she checked herself when she found that Alicia was close beside her. She hastily bade Mrs. Puttock good-night.

"I mean what I say," observed that lady, with an emphatic nod. Eleanor escaped in bewilderment.

"Who never had a wife?" asked Alicia, with a laugh, as they were putting on their cloaks.

After a moment's pause, Eleanor answered,

"Sir John Oakapple," and she excused this deviation from truth by the sage reflection that girls like Alicia must not be told everything.

"We all know that," commented Alicia, contemptuously. "I hoped it was something interesting."

Eleanor enjoyed a smile in the sheltering gloom of the carriage. She felt very discreet.

Anthony Hope

CHAPTER VI

A CANDIDATE FOR OFFICE

The Premier sent his daughter home alone in a fly and walked with Coxon, whose road lay the same way. As they went, they talked of plans and prospects, and Medland unconsciously exasperated his companion by praising Norburn's character and capacity.

"Depend upon it, he's the coming man of New Lindsey," he said. "He thinks the world will get better sooner than it will, you may say. Well, perhaps I share that illusion. Anyhow he has enthusiasm and grit, and I love his utter disinterestedness."

Coxon acquiesced coldly in his rival's praises.

"That," continued Medland, "is where we have the pull. Who is there to follow Perry? Now Norburn is ready to step into my shoes the moment I'm gone, or—or come to grief."

They had reached Digby Square, a large open place, laid out with walks and trees, and named after Sir Jabez Digby, K.B., first Governor of New Lindsey. The Premier paused to light a cigar. Coxon watched him with a morose frown; he was angry and envious at Medland's disregard of the pretensions which he thought his own achievements justified. Though he was conscious that it would be wisest to say nothing, he could not help observing,

"Well, I hope it will be a long time before I am asked to change service under you for service under Norburn."

Medland's quick ear caught the note of anger.

"Well," he said, "it's ill prophesying. Time brings its own leaders. I know Norburn and you will work loyally together anyhow, whatever positions you hold to one another."

This polite concession did not appease Coxon.

"There is much that I distrust in his methods and aims," he remarked.

"I mustn't listen to this, my dear fellow."

"Of course I say it in strict—"

"Yes, but still—I should say the same to Norburn."

They walked on a few steps, and the Premier had just taken his cigar from his mouth in order to resume the conversation, when a man stepped up to him, appearing, as it seemed, from among the trees, and said,

"May I have a word with you, Mr. Medland?"

The speaker was dressed smartly, but not well, in a new suit of light clothes. He was tall and strongly built; a full grey beard made it a matter of difficulty to distinguish his features clearly in the dim light.

"I beg pardon, I don't think I've the pleasure of knowing you, but I shall be very happy. What is it, sir?"

"A word in private," said the stranger, "if this gentleman will excuse me."

In response to a glance from his chief, Coxon said goodnight and strolled on, hearing Medland say,

"I seem to know your voice, but I can't lay my hand on your name."

The stranger drew nearer to him.

"I pass by the name of Benham now," he said; "I haven't forgotten you. I've too good cause to remember you."

Medland looked at him closely.

"It's only the beard that puzzles you," said the stranger, with a grim smile.

"Benyon!" exclaimed the Premier. "I thought you had left the country. What do you want with me, sir?"

"I have not left the country, and I want a good deal with you, Mr. Premier Medland."

"I lost touch of you four years ago."

"Yes; it ceased to matter what became of me about then, didn't it?"

"Have you been in the same place?"

"No; I broke. I have been up country."

Half a Hero   57

"What brings you here? If you wanted money you could have written."

"I've never asked you for money. I wouldn't come to you if I wasn't hard put to it."

"What do you want then?"

"Is that all you have to say to me? Have you no regret to express to me?"

"Not an atom," said the Premier, puffing at his cigar. "If I'd felt any regret I should have expressed it long ago."

"Time doesn't seem to bring repentance to you."

"Don't talk nonsense. What do you want with me?"

"Well, yes, business is business. Look here! I am a respected man where I live. My name is known at Shepherdstown. Benham is, I say, a respected name."

"Well?"

"Now, here in Kirton I'm not known. I was never here in my life before. No one would recognise me as the man whose—"

"As Benyon? I suppose not. Well?"

"Taking all that into account, I see no reason why I shouldn't get the vacant Inspectorship of Railways. It's a nice place, and it's in your gift."

Mr. Medland raised his eyebrows and smiled.

"It involves travelling most of the time," pursued Benham,

"and I needn't live in Kirton, if you preferred that arrangement."

"You are very considerate."

"You see you owe me something."

"Which I might pay out of the public purse? Is that your suggestion?"

"Oh, come, we're men of business. You're not on a platform."

"No," said Mr. Medland meditatively. "I am not on a platform. Consequently I feel at liberty to tell you—" he paused and smiled again.

"Well?"

"To go to the devil!" said the Premier.

"Take care! I know a good deal about you. There are many men would be glad to know, definitely, what I know."

"Then ask them for an Inspectorship."

Benham drew a step nearer.

"Ay, and I can hit you nearer home."

"You might have, once. What can you do now? She's safe from you," answered Medland, with a frown.

"Yes, she's safe, but there's the daughter."

"Daisy!"

"Yes, Daisy." And he added, in slow, emphatic tones—"Yes, my daughter Daisy."

Medland was about to answer violently, but he curbed his temper and said quietly,

"Your daughter? Come, don't talk nonsense."

"A daughter born to my wife in wedlock is my daughter. If I claim her, what answer is there?"

"I can prove that she's not your daughter."

"Perhaps; and what an edifying sight! The Premier proving—" Mr. Benham broke off with a laugh that sounded loud and harsh in the silent night air.

Medland ground his heel into the gravel.

"How it will please your Methodist friends, and the swells at Government House! You can tell 'em all about that trip to Meadow Beach under the name of—what was it?—Christie, wasn't it? And about your night-flitting, and—"

"Hold your tongue."

"Oh, there's no one to hear now. You won't like proving all that, will you? No, no, the girl will come to her loving father! Take a minute to think it over, Medland—take just a minute. An Inspectorship's no great matter to a politician, you know. You're not so mighty pure as all that! Take a minute. I can wait," and he flung himself on to a bench and lit a cheroot.

Then, in Digby Square, at two o'clock in the morning, the devil tempted "Jimmy" Medland. The man had indeed hit him close—very close. He had hit him in the love he bore his daughter, and in the love he bore her mother and her mother's fame. He had hit him in his love of place and power, and his nobler joy in using them for what seemed to him good purposes. Love and tenderness—pride and ambition—the man shot his arrow at all. And as Medland stood motionless in thought, across these abiding reflections came now and again a new one—the image of a face that had been that night upturned to his almost in worship, and would, if this thing were done, be turned away in sorrow, shame, and scorn.

What, after all, was an Inspectorship? It was only doing what the world said all politicians did. What, compared with losing love and power and fair fame, was it to—job an Inspectorship? Besides, from one point of view, the man had a kind of claim upon him: he had done him wrong.

"I dare say," interrupted Benham, "that you're thinking there's nothing to prevent me 'asking for more' next month. Well, of course there isn't. But I shan't. I only want a decent position and a decent income, and then I'll let you alone. Come, Medland, rancour apart, you know I'm not a common blackmailer."

This remark tickled Medland, and he smiled. Still, it was true in its way. He had known the man very well, and, harsh though he was to all about him, the man had been fairly honest and had borne a decent name. Probably what he was doing now did not seem to him much worse than any other backstairs method of getting on in the world. Medland thought that in all likelihood, if he gained his request, he would keep his word. That thought made the temptation stronger, but it forced itself on him when he remembered the number of years during which he had been even more vulnerable in one respect than he was now, and yet the man had left him alone. He could say neither yes nor no.

"You must give me a few days for consideration," he said.

Benham shrugged his shoulders in amazement.

"Have you promised the berth?" he asked.

"No, I haven't promised it."

"Got another candidate?"

"Only the man who ought to have it," answered the Premier, and Benham's air so infected him that he felt the answer to be a very weak one.

"You see," objected Benham, "from what I can learn you're only in office from day to day, so to speak, and where shall I be if you get turned out?"

"We're safe anyhow till the Assembly meets, ten days hence."

"All right. I'll give you till then. And really, Jimmy Medland, little reason as I have to love you, I should advise you not to be a fool. Here's my address. You can write."

"I shan't write. I may send or come."

Benham laughed.

"He's got some wits about him, after all! Good-night. Mind giving me a fair start? You used to be a hot-tempered fellow and—however, I suppose Premiers can't afford the luxury of assaults."

"I'm sorry to say they can't," said Mr. Medland. "I'll wait five minutes where I am."

"All right. Good-night," and Mr. Benham disappeared among the trees.

At the end of five minutes the Premier resumed his interrupted walk and soon reached his home. His study showed signs of his daughter's presence. Her fan was on the table, her gloves beside it; on the mantelpiece lay a red rose, its stalk bound round with wire. Medland recognised it as like the bud Dick Derosne had worn in his button-hole.

"The young rascal!" he said, as he mixed himself some brandy-and-water, and sat down to his desk. The table was covered with drafts of his new bill, and he pulled the papers into shape, arranged his blotting-pad, and dipped his pen in the ink. Then he lit his pipe and rested his head on the back of his chair, staring up at the ceiling. And there he stayed till the servant, coming in at six o'clock, found him hastily snatching up the pen and seeming to make a memorandum. Being Premier, she said, was killing him, and, "for my part," she added, "I don't care how soon we're out."

CHAPTER VII

A COMMON SPECTACLE

After some anxious consideration, Eleanor Scaife decided to keep silence for the present about Mrs. Puttock's strange remark. That lady had deluged her with such a flood of gossip, that Eleanor felt that a thing was not likely to be true merely because Mrs. Puttock asserted it, while, if the suggested scandal had a basis in fact, it was probable that some of the men of the Governor's household, or indeed the Governor himself, would be well informed on the matter. If so, Lord Eynesford would use his discretion in telling his wife. Eleanor was afraid that, if she interfered, she might run the risk of appearing officious, and of receiving the polite snub which Lady Eynesford was somewhat of an adept in administering. After all, the woman, whoever she was, was dead and gone, and Eleanor, in the absence of fuller knowledge, declined to be shocked. A woman, she reflected, who studies the problems of society, must be prepared for everything. Still, she felt that intimacy with the Medlands was not to be encouraged, and began to range herself by Lady Eynesford's side so far as the Premier was concerned.

"We had a delightful trip," said Lady Eynesford, on the afternoon of the day following the dance. "I hope everything has been going on well here, Eleanor. What was it like at

Sir John's?"

"They missed you and the Governor very much."

"Oh, I don't matter, and I hope Dick represented Willie, and danced with everybody's wife in turn. That's poor Willie's duty."

This programme was so very different from that which Dick had planned and carried out on his own account, that Eleanor shrank from the deceit involved in acquiescence.

"I'm afraid not," she said. "You see, Dick's young and hasn't got a wife of his own."

"*Tant mieux*, he'd feel the contrast less," replied Lady Eynesford, with airy assurance. "Who did he dance with?"

Eleanor racked her memory and produced the names of four ladies with each of whom Dick had danced one hasty waltz.

"That's only four dances," objected Lady Eynesford.

"Oh, I didn't notice. I was talking to Sir John and to Mrs. Puttock."

"Eleanor!"

"Well then, he danced once or twice with little Daisy Medland. It was her first ball, you know."

"He needn't have done it twice; I suppose he was bound to once. Dear me! We shall have to consider what we're to do about her now."

"She's a pretty girl, Mary."

"Did Dick think so?" asked Lady Eynesford quickly.

Eleanor distinguished between Mrs. Puttock's remark and Dick's conduct. "Well, it looked like it," she answered.

"What do you mean?"

"To tell the truth, Mary, he danced with her half the evening, and, I think, would have gone on all night if Lady Perry hadn't stopped it."

"The wretched boy!"

At this moment the wretched boy happened to enter Lady Eynesford's boudoir. Dick was dressed for riding, was humming a tune, and appeared generally well pleased with himself and the world.

"You wretched boy!" said his sister-in-law.

Dick gave her one glance. Then, assuming an air of trepidation, he murmured reproachfully,

"*Nous sommes trahis.*"

"What have you to say for yourself? No, I'm not joking. I particularly wanted to avoid being mixed up with these Medlands one bit more than we could help, and, directly my back is turned, you go and—"

"Have you seen Alicia yet?" asked Dick.

"Seen Alicia? No, not to talk to."

"Well then, keep some of it. Don't spend it all on me. You'll want it, Mary."

"Dick, you're very impertinent. What do you mean?"

Dick was about to answer, when he saw Eleanor frowning at him. He raised his brows. Eleanor rapidly returned the signal.

"She flirted disgracefully with Sir John," he said.

"How dare you make fun of me like that? It was most foolish and—and wrong of you. I shall speak to Willie about it."

"I thought it was the constitutional thing to do," pleaded Dick, but Lady Eynesford was already on her way to the door, and vanished through it with a scornful toss of her head.

"You gave me away," said Dick to Eleanor. "Never trust a woman! And, Eleanor, what were you nodding like an old mandarin for?"

"I thought it just as well we shouldn't vex Mary just now by telling her how—how friendly Alicia was with Mr. Medland."

"Oh, I see. I wish you'd thought it just as well not to vex Mary by telling her how—how friendly I was with Miss Medland."

"It's quite different," said Miss Scaife coldly. "In Alicia, it was merely strange. Mr. Medland might be her father. Now, Miss Medland—"

"I never let on about you and Coxon," said Dick, who wished to change the subject, and made his escape under shelter of Miss Scaife's indignant repudiation.

Still humming his tune, he mounted his horse and rode to the Public Park. At a particular turn of the avenue he pulled up and waited under a tree. Presently a pony-carriage appeared in the distance.

"Good!" said Dick, throwing away his cigarette and feeling if his neck-cloth were in its place. The pony-cart drew near. Dick saw with pleasure the figure of the driver, but he also perceived, to his great disgust, that a man was sitting by her side.

"That's the way they"—he meant women—"let you in!" he remarked. "Anybody would have supposed she meant she drove alone. Who the deuce has she got there?"

Miss Medland had Norburn with her, and Norburn was just explaining to her—for he did not imitate her father's forbearance—the methods by which he proposed to banish the evil monster, competition, from the world. There is, however, one sort of competition, at least, which Norburn's methods will hardly banish, and it was into the clutches of this particular form of the evil monster that Mr. Norburn was, little as he thought it, about to be pushed. A long period of intimacy and favour excluded from his mind the suspicion that he might have to fight for his position with Daisy Medland; and, if he could have brought himself to entertain the thought of a successful rival—of some one who, coming suddenly between, should break the strong bonds of affection well tried by time—he certainly would not have expected to find such a competitor in Dick Derosne. In fact, neither of the young men was capable of appreciating the attractions of the other: Dick considering Norburn very doubtfully a gentleman, and very certainly what in his University days he dubbed a "smug"; Norburn regarding him with the rather impatient contempt that such a man is apt to bestow on those for whom dressing themselves and amusing themselves are the chief labours of a day. Moreover, Norburn did not frequent dances, and young men who do not frequent dances often go wrong by forgetting how much may happen between the afternoon of a Tuesday and the morning of a Wednesday.

No doubt those of us who are men, having been more or less pretty fellows in our time, have had our triumphs, concerning which we are, as a rule, becomingly mute, but occasionally, in the confidences of the smoking-room, undesirably loquacious. For this fault there is no excuse, unless such a one as justifies the practice of inflicting reprisals in international quarrels; it being quite certain that our failures are no secret—indeed there must be covertly (but extensively) circulating somewhere a *Gazette* wherein such occurrences are registered—there is a kind of "wild justice" even in smoking-room disclosures. But whatever our bad or good fortune may have been, it is not to be supposed for a moment that any of us enjoy such an enchanting revelation as comes to a young girl who, by nature's kind freak, has been made beautiful. Daisy Medland was radiant as she turned from Norburn's pale thoughtful face and careless garb to Dick Derosne, the outward perfection of a well-born, well-made, well-dressed Englishman, bowing, smiling, and debonair. Daisy liked Norburn very much—how much she never quite knew—but there was no doubt that two young men were a pleasant change from one, and the contrast between them increased the charm—a novel charm to her—of the situation, for she was well aware that, different as they were from one another, strong as the contrast was, they were both at this moment thinking precisely the same thought, namely, "Who's this fellow, and what does he want?"—a coincidence which again shows that Norburn's theories had much to do before they conquered the world.

It is not a very uncommon sight to see a clever man sit mum, abashed by the chatter of a cheery shallow-pate, who is happily unconscious of the oppressive triviality of his own conversation. Norburn's eager flow of words froze at the contact of Dick's small-talk, and he was a discontented auditor of ball-room and club gossip. It amazed him that a man should know, or care, or talk about more than half the things on which Dick descanted so merrily; it astounded him that they should win interest as keen and looks as bright as had ever rewarded the deepest truth or the highest aspiration. All of which, however, was not really at all odd, if only Mr. Norburn would have considered the matter a little more closely. But then an old favourite threatened by a new rival is not in a mood for cool analysis.

"And they say," pursued Dick, "that Puttock's coming back to your father because Sir Robert trod on Mrs. P.'s new black silk and tore it half off her—tore it awfully, you know."

Daisy laughed gaily.

"You weren't there, were you, Mr. Norburn? Well, it was worth all the money only to see old Mrs. Grim eat ices—you remember, Miss Medland? She bolted three while Sir John was proposing the Queen's health, and two more in the first verse of 'God save—'" and so Dick ran on.

Mr. Norburn consulted his watch.

"I'm afraid I must go," he said. "I'm due at the office."

"Oh," exclaimed Daisy penitently, "I forgot. But can't I drive you back?"

"I couldn't trouble you to do that. You're not going back so soon?"

"But of course I can, Mr. Norburn; it's so far to walk."

"I don't mind the walk."

"Are you really quite sure? It is a beautiful morning to be out, isn't it?"

Norburn took his leave, thinking, no doubt, of his official duties and nothing else, and Daisy touched her pony.

"I must go on," she said.

"So must I," said Dick, "mustn't keep my horse standing any longer."

"Why not? He can't catch cold to-day."

"Oh, he'd take root and never go away—just as I do, when I stand near you, you know."

It is not proposed to set out the rest of their conversation. Daisy forgot Norburn's gloomy face, Dick forgot every face but Daisy's, and the usual things were said and done. An appeal to the memory of any reader will probably give a result accurate enough. Imagine yourself on a pretty morning, in a pretty place, by a pretty girl, and let her be kind and you not a numskull, and there's half-a-dozen pages saved.

It was, however, a little unfortunate that, at the last moment, when the third good-bye was being said, Lady Eynesford should come whirling by in her barouche.

"The deuce!" said Dick under his breath.

Lady Eynesford's features did not relax. She bowed to her

brother-in-law gravely and stiffly; her gaze appeared to travel far over the top of the low pony-carriage which contained Daisy Medland. Dick flushed with vexation. True, the Governor's wife did not yet know the Premier's daughter, but she need not have insisted on the fact so ostentatiously. Dick turned to his companion. She was laughing.

"Why are you laughing?" he asked, rather offended. A man seldom likes to be thought to value the opinion of the women of his family, valuable as it always is.

"You know very well," she answered. "Oh, I dare say I've got into trouble too."

"I don't care," said Dick valiantly.

"Neither do I—at least, not much."

"I don't see how you can have got into trouble."

"Ah, perhaps you don't see everything, Mr. Derosne."

"I say, you don't mean that Mr.—?"

"Good-bye," said Daisy, whipping up her pony.

Dick was left wondering what she had meant, and whether anything so preposterous and revolting as the idea of Norburn having any business to control her doings or her likings could possibly have any truth in it. And, as a natural result of this disturbing notion, he determined to see her again as soon as he could.

Anthony Hope

CHAPTER VIII

FOR THE HIGHEST BIDDER

Shepherdstown, the spot where Mr. Benham said that his was a respected name—and he said quite truly, for he had managed to pay his debts as they fell due, and nothing was known against his character—lay in Puttock's constituency, and Benham thought it well to call upon his representative. The only secret part of his enterprise had been transacted with the Premier in Digby Square: for the rest, a plausible overtness of action was plainly desirable. He obtained an interview with Puttock, and laid before him his hopes and his qualifications. Mr. Puttock was graciousness itself; he remembered, with gratitude and surprising alacrity, his visitor's local services to the party; had he been still in office, it would have been his delight no less than his duty to press Benham's incontestable claims; he would have felt that he was merely paying a small part of the debt he owed Shepherdstown and one of its leading men, and would, at the same time, have enjoyed the conviction that he was enlisting in the public service a man of tried integrity and ability.

"Unhappily, however," said Mr. Puttock, spreading out his plump hands in pathetic fashion, "as you might conjecture, Mr.—" he glanced at the visitor's card—"Benham, my influence at the present juncture is less than *nil*. I am powerless. I can only look on at what I conceive to be a course of conduct fraught with peril to the true interests of New Lindsey, and entirely inconsistent with the best traditions of our party."

"Your views are heartily shared at home," responded Benham. "Speaking in confidence, I can assure you of that, sir. Our confidence in the Ministry ended when you retired."

"As long as my constituents approve of my action, I am content. But I am grieved not to be able to help you."

"But, in spite of present differences, surely your good word would carry weight. My name is, I believe, already before the Premier, and if it was backed by your support—"

"Let me recommend you," said Puttock sourly, "to try to obtain Mr. Norburn's good word. That is, between ourselves, all-powerful."

Benham frowned.

"Norburn! Much Norburn would do for me."

"Why, does he know you?" asked Puttock. "Have you any quarrel with him?"

"There's no love lost between us. He organised my shearers when they struck two years ago."

"What are you?"

"Sheep, sir. The fellow came down and fought me, and—well, sir, he said things about me that you'd hardly credit."

"Oh, I hope," said Puttock earnestly, "that that would not influence his judgment. But, to be frank—well, it's common knowledge that Mr. Norburn and I found we could not work together."

"But surely, sir, the Premier will take his own line?"

"I don't know. As likely as not, Norburn will have some Labour man to press."

"Ah, if we could see you at the head of the Government!"

"I don't deny that I am deeply disappointed with the Premier's course of action—so deeply that I can give him no support."

Mr. Benham remained silent for a minute, meditating. He perceived that, in case Medland proved unreasonable, a second string lay ready to his hand. He wondered how much Puttock already knew—and what he would pay for more knowledge. The worst of it was that Puttock had the reputation of being an uncommonly good hand at a bargain.

"Yet Mr. Medland's a very clever man," he observed.

"Oh, clever, yes; but I fear unstable, Mr. Benham."

"I suppose so. After all a man's private life is some guide, isn't it?"

"Some guide!" exclaimed Puttock. "Surely you understate the case. If a man's private life is discreditable—"

"But would you go so far as that about the Premier?" inquired Benham, with a pained air.

"There's no smoke without fire, I'm afraid. It's a painful subject, and of course only a matter of rumour, but—"

"You see, I've been living in the country, and I'm not up in all that's said here."

"I wouldn't mention it to everybody, but to you I may venture. According to the report among those in a position to know, there was the gravest doubt as to the regularity of—his domestic relations."

"Dear, dear!"

"Nothing, as I say, is known or could, probably, be proved. It would damage him most seriously, of course, if that sort of thing were proved."

"I should think so indeed. He could hardly remain where he is."

"I don't know. Well, perhaps not. A little while ago I should have deeply regretted anything calculated to lessen his influence, but now—well, well, we shall see."

"Your secession has so weakened him that he couldn't stand up against it," said Benham, with conviction. "And then—why, we might have a real leader."

Mr. Benham's admiring gaze left no doubt as to the heaven-sent leader who was in his mind, and he had the satisfaction of detecting a gleam of eagerness in Mr. Puttock's eye.

"He may be of use to me, if Medland kicks," reflected Benham as he walked away. But he hoped that the Premier would not prove recalcitrant. He had counted on the sufficiency of threats, and it would be an annoyance if he were forced to resort to action; for he could not deny that his respected name would suffer some stain in the process of inflicting punishment, if the victim chose to declare the terms on which the chastisement might have been averted.

Now this aspect of the case had presented itself to Medland also, reinforcing the considerations which weighed against giving Benham the appointment he sought. The Premier hated yielding, and he hated jobs: Benham asked him to acknowledge himself beaten, and, as ransom, to perpetrate a peculiarly dirty job. At most times of his life he would not even have looked at such a proposal, but his new-won position, with its possibilities and its risks, made him timid: he was fearful as a child of anything that would jeopardise what he had so hardly and narrowly achieved; and this unwonted mood increased his dread of Benham's disclosures to an almost superstitious terror. Under the influence of this feeling, he was so far false to his standard of conduct as tentatively to mention Benham's name to Norburn as that of a possible candidate for the vacant post. He expected to hear in reply nothing more than a surprised inquiry as to the man's claims, but Norburn, despite his faithfulness to every wish of his leader's, besought him earnestly to make no such choice.

"You don't know about him," he said; "but in his own neighbourhood he's known far and wide as a hard employer and a determined enemy of the Unions. Such an appointment would do us immense harm."

"I didn't know that. You're sure?"

"I believe it might cost us a dozen votes. I couldn't defend the choice myself. I fought him once, and I know all about him. Who recommended him to you?"

"No one. He came himself."

Norburn laughed.

"It needs some assurance," he remarked, "for a man with his record to come to you. He must have known that I could tell you all about him."

The Premier smiled: to tell him all about Benham was exactly what his zealous young colleague could not do.

"Then it's quite out of the question?" he asked.

"If you take my opinion, quite."

The Premier gave a sigh of relief. He was glad to have the matter settled for him, and to be saved from the temptation that had been besetting him these ten days past.

"The fellow must be mad to expect such a thing," continued Norburn. "Why doesn't he go to the other side?"

"Perhaps he will now," answered Medland. It seemed not at all unlikely.

When his mind was finally made up, Medland found at first a reckless pleasure in, as he expressed it to himself, "chancing it." He had always been fond of a fight against odds. The odds were against him here, and the stakes perilously high. His spirits rose; his mouth was set firm, and his eyes gleamed as they had gleamed when the crowd led him in triumph to his house three weeks ago. The battle was to begin to-morrow; the House met then, and all his foes, public and private, would close round him and his band of friends. And, when the fresh attack had been delivered, how many would his friends be? Rousing himself, he got up.

"You stay with Daisy," he said to Norburn. "I must go out for an hour."

It was nine o'clock, and he made his way swiftly to the address which Benham had given him. He found that gentleman in a quiet and respectable lodging, and was received with civility.

"You are just to your time," said Benham.

"I'm not behind it. I had till to-morrow."

"And you have brought the appointment?"

"No."

"The promise of it, then?"

"No; I can't do it."

"Why not?"

"Well, I don't know why I should tell you, but for two good reasons—it's difficult and it's dirty. Difficult because you're not popular with my friends—dirty, because—but you know that."

"You really mean to refuse?"

"Yes."

"Then what are you going to do for me?"

"I can't do anything for you."

"That's final?" asked Benham, facing him squarely. "You utterly refuse to do me a small favour, though you were ready enough to ruin my life?"

Medland was doubtful if he had ruined the man's life, but he only answered—

"I can't job you into anything. That's what you want, and it's what I can't do for you."

"Very well. I've got a thing of value, haven't I? Well, I shall sell it to the highest bidder. Ay, and I tell you what, James Medland, I'll be level with you before I die, God help me I will! You shall be sorry for this, before I've done with you."

"I take the chance of that. If you're in want, I'll supply you with money, as far as my means allow."

"Your means? What are they? You won't have your salary long, if I can help it. I think I can find a better market, thank you."

Medland turned on his heel. He had come with a vague idea of trying in some way to smooth over matters between them. It was plainly impossible; he had no wish to bribe, and, if he had, clearly he could not bribe high enough. He was still in his confident mood, and Benham's rude threats roused him to defiance.

"Have it your own way," he said; "but people who attack me in Kirton run some risks," and he went out with a smile on his face.

As he strolled home again, his exultant temper left him. The springiness of his step relaxed into a slouching gait, and his head fell forward. He stopped and turned half round, as though to go back; then, with a sigh, he held on his way. Far off, he could see the twinkling lights of ships, and, in the still of evening, catch the roll of the sea as it broke on the beach, and an odd fancy came over him of sailing far away with his daughter over the sea—or, perhaps better still, of walking quietly into the water until it closed over his head. Now and then he grew tired of fighting, and to him life was all fighting now.

"Meditating new resolutions, Medland?" asked a cheery voice at his side.

Turning with a start, he saw the Chief Justice, who continued,

"You'll be in the thick of it to-morrow, I suppose?"

"I have left off thinking where I shall be to-morrow," he answered. "To-day is enough for a Minister."

"And to-morrow may be too much? Young Heseltine offered just now to lay me six to five you'd be out in a month."

"Confound him! Who is he?"

"One of the Governor's young fellows."

"Oh, yes, I remember."

"Talking of that, I had some very kind inquiries about you at Government House to-day."

"Ah!"

"From Miss Derosne. She's a warm admirer of yours, and really a most charming girl. Well, good-night. I shall try and get down to hear your statement to-morrow."

Sir John bustled off, leaving the Premier with a new bent of thought. In his mind he rehearsed his interview with Alicia

Derosne, wondering, as men wonder after they have been carried away by emotion into unrestrained disclosures of their hearts, whether she had really been impressed; whether, after all, he had not been, or seemed, insincere, theatrical, or absurd; wondering again in what light she would look on him, when she knew what it looked likely all Kirton would know soon; wondering last whether, if he had not met the woman who had been his partner in life for so long, and had, in youth, met such a girl as Alicia Derosne, his fate would have been different, and he need not now have trembled at his story being told. Immersed in thought he wandered on, out of the town and down to the shores of the bay, and checked himself, with a sudden laugh, only on the very brink of the sea. The absurdity struck him; he laughed again, as he lit a cigar and rebuked himself aloud.

"Here I am, a Premier and forty-one! and I'm going on for all the world like a cross between a love-sick boy and a runaway criminal!"

He paused and added—

"And the worst of it, I am rather like a criminal and—"

He paused abruptly. A thought struck him and made him frown angrily at his folly. It was stupid to think of himself as love-sick, even in jest. He had not come to that. And to think of himself as a lover was not a thought that carried pleasant memories to Mr. Medland.

Anthony Hope

CHAPTER IX

TWO HASTY UTTERANCES

"Thank God, there's the Legislative Council, anyhow!" exclaimed Mr. Kilshaw.

Sir Robert Perry pursed up his lips. He had fought with that safeguard of stability behind him once or twice before, and the end had been defeat. There were better things than the support of the Legislative Council.

"I'd rather," he remarked, "have a dissolution and a thumping campaign fund. If I'd known they were at sixes and sevens like this, I'd have taken the Governor's offer."

"Hum," said Mr. Kilshaw, who would be expected to subscribe largely to the suggested fund. "But how do you propose to get your dissolution now? Besides, I believe he'd beat us."

"That would depend on Puttock—and one or two more."

"What did you think of Puttock's explanation?"

"The whole performance reminded me of a highly religious rattlesnake: it was a magnificent struggle against natural venom."

"I thought it very creditable."

"Oh, I suppose so: it would be, if you think of it, in the snake. But Medland will be replying soon. Come along."

They hurried into the House, and found the Premier already on his legs. The floor and the galleries were crowded, and the space allotted to ladies—there was no grating in New Lindsey, as Eleanor Scaife had already recorded in her notebook—was bright with gay colours. Sir Robert and Mr. Kilshaw slipped into their places just in time to see Medland stoop down to Norburn, who sat next him, and whisper to him. Norburn nodded with a defiant air, and Medland, with a slight frown, proceeded. The Premier had no easy task. Puttock had fallen on his flank with skill and effect, and Norburn, who followed, had increased his leader's difficulties by a brilliant but indiscreet series of tilts against every section except that to which he himself belonged; Jewell had answered powerfully, and Coxon had coughed and fidgeted. The Premier was now skilfully paring away what his lieutenant had said, and justifying every proposition he advanced by a reference to Mr. Puttock's previous speeches. Mr. Puttock, in his turn, fidgeted, and Coxon smiled sardonically. The Premier, encouraged by this success, pulled himself together and approached the last and most delicate part of his task, which was to defend or palliate a phrase of Norburn's that had been greeted with angry groans and protests. Mr. Norburn had in fact referred to the Capitalist class as a "parasitic growth," and Medland was left to get out of this indiscretion as best he could. He referred to the unhappy phrase. The storm which had greeted its first appearance broke out again. There were cries of "Withdraw!" Mr. Kilshaw called out, "Do you adopt that? Yes or no;" Norburn's followers cheered; redoubled groans answered them; Eleanor made notes, and Alicia's eyes were fixed on Medland, who stood silent and smiling.

Anthony Hope

Kilshaw cried again, "Do you adopt it?"

Medland turned towards him, and in slow and measured tones began to describe a visit he had paid to Kilshaw's mill. He named no name, but everybody knew to whose works he referred.

"There was a man there," he said, "working with a fever upon him; there was a woman working—and by her, her baby, five days old; there were old men who looked to no rest but the grave, and children who were always too tired to play; there were girls without innocence, boys without merriment, women without joy, men without hope. And, as I walked home in the evening, back to my house, I met a string of race-horses; they were in training, I was told, for the Kirton Cup; their owner spent, they said, ten thousand pounds a year on his stables. Their owner, Sir, owned the mill—and them that worked there."

He paused, and then, with a gesture unusual in that place, he laid his hand on Norburn's shoulder, and went on in a tone of gentle apology:

"What wonder if men with hot hearts and young heads use hard words? What wonder if they confound the bad with the good? Yes, what wonder if, once again, good and bad shall fall in a common doom?"

He sat down suddenly, still keeping his hand on his young colleague's shoulder, and Sir Robert rose and prayed leave to say a few words in reference to the—he seemed to pause for a word—the remarkable utterance which had fallen from the Premier. Sir Robert's rapier flashed to and fro, now in grave indignation, now in satirical jest, and, at the end, he rose almost to eloquence in bidding the Premier remember the responsibility such words, spoken by such a man, carried with them.

"You may say," said Sir Robert, "that to prophesy revolution is not to justify it—that to excuse violence is not to advocate it. Ignorant men reck little of wire-drawn distinctions, and I am glad, Sir—I say, I am glad that not on my head rests the weight of such wild words and open threats as we have heard to-day. For my head is grey, and I must soon give an account of what I have done."

The debate ended, leaving the general impression that the Government stood committed to a policy which some called thorough and some dangerous. Mr. Kilshaw, passing Puttock in the lobby, remarked,

"You'll have some fine opportunities for your 'independent and discriminating support,' Puttock, and I hope your banking account will be the fatter for it."

Puttock made a slight grimace, and Kilshaw smiled complacently. He had great hopes of Puttock, and was pleased when the latter remarked,

"By the way, Kilshaw, here's a friend of mine who's anxious to know you," and he introduced his influential constituent, Mr. Benham of Shepherdstown. The three men stood talking together and saw Medland pass by. Kilshaw, assuming Benham loved the Premier no more than Mr. Puttock, remarked,

"I'd give something handsome to see that fellow smashed."

"Would you?" asked Benham, with an eager smile; Kilshaw promised him a better opening than Puttock. He stepped across to Medland, raising his hat.

"A moment, Mr. Medland. You have not changed your mind on that little matter?"

"The appointment was made this morning," replied Medland, somewhat surprised to see him in the lobby.

"I am here with Mr. Puttock," said Benham, answering his look, "and Mr. Kilshaw."

Medland smiled.

"The appointment is made all the same," he remarked.

Benham bowed and returned to his friends. The Premier, seeing Eleanor and Alicia in front of him, overtook and joined them.

"Are you walking home?" he asked.

"Mr. Coxon is escorting us," answered Eleanor, indicating that gentleman, who was walking with them.

Perhaps Mr. Coxon in his day-dreams looked forward to the time when he should fight the Premier for his place and defeat him. He did not expect to have to fight with him for a position by a girl's side. Nevertheless he found, to his chagrin, that Medland did not pair off with Eleanor Scaife, but continued to walk by and talk to Alicia. Being a man of much assurance, he hazarded a protesting glance at Alicia: she met it with an impossible intensity of unconsciousness, and Eleanor maliciously opened fire upon him out of the batteries with which Tomes supplied her, at the same time quickening her pace and compelling him to leave the others behind.

Alicia glanced up at Medland.

"I thought of what you said the other night all the time," she began; "but you did not say it so well to-day."

"Ah, you remember the other night?"

"You were bold and straightforward then. I thought—I thought you fenced with it a little to-day."

"I'm not used to be charged with that."

"I suppose it was only by comparison."

"Yes. And nobody but you could make the comparison."

"I shall always like best to remember you by what you said then."

"Ah, I had to please so many people to-day. The other night I didn't think of pleasing any one—not even you! But I hope it's not coming to 'remembering' me yet. You're not going to leave us?"

"We're only birds of passage, you know. My brother's term will be up in fifteen months now."

"Well, Miss Derosne, I'm afraid fifteen months are likely enough to see an end of most of the dreams I talked about to you."

"No, no," she exclaimed eagerly. Then checking herself she added, "But what right have I to talk to you about it?"

"I talked to you."

"Oh, I happened to be there."

"Yes, and so I happened to talk. That's the way when people get on together."

Alicia looked up with a smile. Short as her acquaintance had been, she felt that the Premier was no longer a stranger. By opening his mind to her as he had done, he had claimed nothing less than friendship. He was, she told herself, like an old friend. And yet he was also unlike one; for, in intercourse with old friends, people are not subject alternately to impulses towards unrestrained intimacy and reactions to shy reserve. She liked him, but she was afraid of him; in fine, she was hardly happy with him, and not happy—The confession could not be finished even to herself.

"Shall you be glad to go home, or sorry?" he asked.

"Oh, I shall be very sorry."

"Then," he suggested, smiling, "why not stay?"

The question came pat in tune with those thoughts that would not be suppressed. Before she knew what she was doing—before she had time to reflect that probably his words were merely an idle civility or the playful suggestion of an impossibility, she exclaimed,

"What do you—?"

She stopped suddenly, in horror at herself; for she found him looking at her with surprise, and she felt her face flooded with colour.

"I beg your pardon?" said Medland.

Full of anger and shame, she could not answer him. Without a shadow of excuse—she could not find a shadow of excuse—she had read into his words a meaning he never thought of. She could not now conceive how she had done it. If told the like about another, she knew how scornfully severe her judgment would have been. He had surprised her, caught her unawares, and wrung from her an open expression of a wild idea that she had refused to recognise even in her own heart. She felt that her cheeks were red. Would the glow that burnt her never go?—and she bit her lips, for she was near tears. Oh, that he might not have seen! Or had she committed the sin unpardonable to a girl such as she was? Had she betrayed herself unasked?

"Nothing," she stammered at last. "Nothing." But she felt the heat still in her cheeks. She would have given the world to be able to tell him not to look at her; but she knew his puzzled eyes still sought hers, in hope of light.

He might at least say something! Silently he walked by her side along the road to Government House—that endless, endless road. She could not speak—and he—she only knew that he did not. She felt, by a subtle perception, his glance turned on her now and again, but he did not break the silence. The strain was too much; in spite of all her efforts, in spite of a hatred of her own weakness that would have made her, for the moment, sooner die, a hysterical sob burst from her lips.

Medland stopped.

"You must let me go," he said. "I am very busy. You can overtake the others. Good-bye."

He held out his hand, and she gave him hers. It was kind of him to go and make no words about the manner of his going, yet it showed that her desperate hope that he had not noticed was utterly vain.

Anthony Hope

"Good-bye," she managed to murmur, with averted head.

"I shall see you again soon," he said, pressing her hand, and was gone.

In the evening, Lady Eynesford trenchantly condemned the ventilation of the Houses of Parliament.

"The wretched place has given Alicia a headache. I found the poor child crying with pain. I wonder you let her stay, Eleanor."

"I didn't notice that it was close or hot."

"My dear Eleanor, you're as strong as a pony," remarked Lady Eynesford. "A very little thing upsets Alicia."

CHAPTER X

THE SMOKE OF HIDDEN FIRES

"No, I don't like turn-down collars," remarked Daisy Medland.

"I'm very sorry," said Norburn. "You never said so before, and they're so comfortable."

"And why don't you wear a high hat, and a frock-coat? It looks so much better. Mr.—well, Mr. Coxon always does when he goes anywhere in the afternoon."

"I didn't know Coxon was your standard of perfection, Daisy. He didn't use to be in the old days."

"Oh, it's not only Mr. Coxon."

"I know it isn't," replied Norburn significantly.

"I wonder the Governor lets you come in that hat," continued Daisy, scornfully eyeing Norburn's unconventional headgear.

"It's very like your father's."

"My father's not a young man. What would you think if the

Governor laid foundation-stones in a short jacket and a hat like yours?"

"I should think him a very sensible man."

"Well, I should think him a *guy*," said Miss Medland, with intense emphasis.

This method of treating an old friend galled Norburn excessively. When anger is in, the brains are out.

"I suppose Mr. Derosne is your ideal," he said.

Daisy accepted the opening of hostilities with alacrity.

"He dresses just perfectly," she remarked, "and he doesn't bore one with politics."

This latter remark was rather shameless, for Daisy was generally a keen partisan of her father's, and very ready to listen to anything connected with his public doings.

"You never used to say that sort of thing to me."

"Oh,'used!' I believe you've said 'used' six times in ten minutes! Am I always to go on talking as I *used* when I was in the nursery? I say it now anyhow, Mr. Norburn."

Norburn took up the despised hat. Looking at it now through Daisy's eyes he could not maintain that it was a handsome hat.

"It's your own fault. You began it," said Daisy, stifling a pang of compunction, for she really liked him very much, else why should she mind what he wore?

"I began it?"

"Yes. By—by dragging in Mr. Derosne."

"I only mentioned him as an example of fashionable youth."

"You know you wouldn't like it if I went about in dowdy old things."

"I don't mind a bit what you wear. It's all the same to me."

"How very peculiar you are!" exclaimed Daisy, with a look of compassionate amazement. "Most people notice what I wear. Oh, and I've got a charming dress for the flower-show at Government House."

"You're invited, are you?" asked Norburn, with an ill-judged exhibition of surprise.

"Of course I'm invited."

"I'm sorry to hear it."

"Why, pray, Mr. Norburn? Are you going?"

"Yes. I suppose I must."

"Not in that hat!" implored Daisy.

"Certainly," answered Norburn, though it is doubtful if he had in truth intended to do so, but for Daisy's taunts.

A tragic silence followed. At last, Miss Medland exclaimed,

"What will Lady Eynesford think of my friends?"

"I didn't know you cared so much for what Lady Eynesford thought. Besides, I need not present myself in that character."

"Oh, if you're going to be disagreeable!"

"For my part, I'm sorry you're going at all."

"Thank you. Is that because I shall enjoy it?"

"I don't care for that sort of society."

"I like it above everything."

Matters having thus reached a direct issue, Norburn clapped the *causa belli* on his head, and walked out of the room, dimly conscious that he had done himself as much harm as he possibly could in the space of a quarter of an hour. When he grew cool, he confessed that the momentary, if real, pleasure of being unpleasant was somewhat dearly bought at the cost of enmity with Daisy Medland. Indeed this unhappy young man, for all that his whole soul was by way of being absorbed in reconstructing society, would have thought most things a bad bargain at such a price. But his bitterness had been too strong. It seemed as though all his devotion, ay, and—he did not scruple to say to himself—all his real gifts were to weigh as nothing against the cut of a coat and the "sit" of a cravat—for to such elemental constituents his merciless and jealous analysis reduced poor Dick Derosne's attractions.

Little recked Dick of Norburn's feelings in the glow of his triumph. He was convinced that he alone had persuaded Lady Eynesford into including Daisy in her invitation to luncheon at the opening of the flower-show. It would have been a pity, in the mere interests of truth, to interfere with this conceit of Dick's, and Eleanor forbore to disclose her own share in the matter, or to hint at that long interview between the Governor and his wife.

"We shall live to regret it," said Lady Eynesford, "but it shall be as you wish, Willie."

So the Medlands came with the rest of the world to the flower-show, and were received with due ceremony and regaled with suitable fare. And afterwards the Governor took Daisy for a stroll through the tents, and, having thus done his duty handsomely, handed her over to Dick; but she and Dick found the tents stuffy and crowded, and sat down under the trees and enjoyed themselves very much, until Mr. Puttock espied them and came up to them, accompanied by a friend.

"I hope you're not very angry with me, Miss Daisy?" said Puttock, thinking she might resent his desertion of the Premier.

"Oh, but I am!" said Daisy, and truly enough, whatever the reason might be.

"Well, you mustn't visit it on my friend here, who is anxious to make your acquaintance. Miss Medland—Mr. Benham."

Benham sat down and began to make himself agreeable. He had a flow of conversation, and seemed in no hurry to move. Captain Heseltine appeared with a summons for Dick, who sulkily obeyed. Puttock caught sight of Jewell, and, with an apology, pursued him. Benham sat talking to Daisy Medland. Presently he proposed they should go where they would see the people better, and Daisy, who was bored, eagerly acquiesced. They took a seat by the side of the broad gravel walk.

"Will no one rescue me?" thought Daisy.

"He's bound to pass soon," thought Benham.

Benham's wish was the first to be fulfilled. Before long the Premier came in sight, accompanied by Coxon.

"Ah, there's your daughter," said the latter. "You were wondering where she was."

Medland looked, and saw Daisy and Benham sitting side by side. He quickened his pace and went up to them. Benham rose and took off his hat. Medland ignored him.

"I was looking for you, Daisy," he said. "I want you."

Daisy stood up, with relief.

"Good day, Mr. Medland," said Benham. "I have enjoyed making" (he paused, but barely perceptibly) "Miss Medland's acquaintance."

Medland bowed coldly.

"Mr. Puttock was good enough to introduce me."

"I am ready, father," said Daisy. "Good-bye, Mr. Benham."

Benham took her offered hand, and, with a smile, held it for a moment longer than sufficed for an ordinary farewell. Still holding it, he began—

"I hope we shall meet often in the future and—"

Medland, in a sudden fit of anger, seized his daughter's arm and drew it away.

"I do not desire your acquaintance, sir," he said, in loud, harsh tones, "for myself or my daughter."

Benham smiled viciously; Coxon, who stood by, watched the scene closely.

"Ah!" said Benham, "perhaps not; but you know me—and so will she," and he in his turn raised his voice in growing excitement.

Daisy, frightened at the angry interview, clung to Medland's arm, looking in wonder from him to Benham. Some half-dozen people, seeing the group, stopped for a moment in curiosity and, walking on, cast glances back over their shoulders. A lull in the babble of conversation warned Medland, and he looked round. Alicia Derosne was passing by in company with the Chief Justice. Near at hand stood Kilshaw, watching the encounter with a sneering smile. The Chief Justice stepped up to Medland.

"What's the matter?" he asked, in a low tone.

"Nothing," said Medland. "Only I do not wish my daughter to talk to this gentleman."

The contempt of his look and tone goaded Benham to fury.

"I don't care what you wish," he exclaimed. "I have as good a right as anybody to talk to the young lady, considering that she's—"

Before he could finish his sentence, Kilshaw darted up to him, and caught him by the arm.

"Not yet, you fool," he whispered, drawing the angry man away.

Benham yielded, and Kilshaw caught Medland's look of surprise.

"Come, Mr. Benham," he said aloud, "you and Mr. Medland must settle your differences, if you have any, elsewhere."

Medland glanced sharply at him, but accepted the cue.

"You are right," he said. "Come, Daisy," and he walked away with his daughter on his arm, while Kilshaw led Benham off in the opposite direction, talking to him urgently in a low voice. Benham shook his head again and again in angry protest, seeming to ask why he had not been allowed his own way.

The group of people passed on, amid inquiries who Benham was, and conjectures as to the cause of the Premier's anger.

"Now what in the world," asked Sir John, fitting his *pince-nez* more securely on his nose, "do you make of that, Miss Derosne?"

Sir John thought that he was addressing an indifferent spectator, and Alicia's manner did not undeceive him.

"How should I know, Sir John? It must have been politics."

"They wouldn't talk politics here—and, if they did, Medland would not quarrel about them."

"Did you hear what he said, Chief Justice?" asked Coxon.

"Yes, I heard."

"Curious, isn't it?"

"It's most tantalisingly curious," said Sir John.

"But, all the same, we mustn't forget the flowers," remarked Alicia, with affected gaiety.

They moved on, and the onlookers, still canvassing the incident, scattered their various ways.

It was Coxon who told Lady Eynesford about it afterwards, and her comment to the Governor that evening at dinner was,

"There, Willie! Didn't I tell you something horrid would come of having those people?"

No one answered her. The Governor knew better than to encourage a discussion. Dick swore softly under his breath at Coxon, and Alicia began to criticise Lady Perry's costume. Lady Eynesford followed up her triumph.

"I hope all you Medlandites are satisfied now," she said.

And Lady Eynesford was not the only person who found some satisfaction in this unfortunate incident, for when Daisy told Norburn about it, he remarked, with an extraordinary want of reason,

"I knew you'd be sorry you went."

"I'm not at all sorry," protested Daisy. "But why was father angry?"

"I'm sure I don't know. Didn't he tell you?"

"No."

"Oh, I recollect. This Benham has been worrying him about

Anthony Hope

some appointment."

"That doesn't account for his saying that he had as good a right as anybody to talk to me. I don't understand it."

"Well, neither do I. But you would go."

"Really, you're too absurd," said Daisy pettishly.

And poor Norburn knew that he was very absurd, and yet could not help being very absurd, although he despised himself for it.

The real truth was that Daisy had told him that, except for this one occurrence, she had had a most charming afternoon, and that Dick Derosne had been kindness itself.

This was enough to make even a rising statesman angry, and, when angry, absurd.

CHAPTER XI

A CONSCIENTIOUS MAN'S CONSCIENCE

A very few hours after its occurrence, the scene at the flower-show was regretted by all who took part in it. Medland realised the foolishness of his indiscretion and want of temper; Benham was afraid that he might have set inquiring minds on the track of game which he wished to hunt down for himself; Kilshaw was annoyed at having been forced into such an open display of his relations with and his influence over Benham. Even to himself, his dealings with the man were a delicate subject. Almost every one has one or two matters which he would rather not discuss with his own conscience; and his bargain with Benham was one of these tabooed topics to Kilshaw. For, in spite of what he had done in this instance, he belonged to a class which some righteous and superior people will have it does not exist. He was a conscientious politician—a man who, in the main, was honest and straightforward; prone indeed to think that what he had was necessarily identical with what he ought to have, and that any law not based on a recognition of this fact was an iniquitous law, but loyal to his friends, his class, his party, and his country; ready to spend and work for his own rights' sake, but no niggard of time or money in larger causes; sincere in his convictions, dauntless in affirming and upholding them, hardly conceiving that honest men could differ from them; strong in his self-confidence, believing that the best men always won, suspecting from the bottom of his heart every appeal to sentiment in the mouth of a politician. Such he was—a type of the man of success, with the hardness that success is apt to bring, but with the virtues that attain it; and his defects and merits had made him, for years past, Sir Robert Perry's most valued lieutenant, and a very pillar of the cautious conservative ideas on which that statesman's influence was based.

And now Mr. Kilshaw, impelled less by mere self-interest than by the rankling of a personal feud, had—dipped the end of his fingers in pitch. He had resented fiercely Medland's hardly disguised attack on him, and it had fanned into flame the wrath which the Premier's schemes, threatening the profits of himself and his fellow-capitalists, and the Premier's principles, redolent to his nostrils of the quackery and hypocrisy that he hated, had set alight in his heart. Against such a man and such a policy, was not everything fair? Was it not even fair to use a tool like Benham, if the tool put itself in his hand?

Yet he was ashamed; but, being in secret ashamed, he, as men often do, set his face and went on his way all the more obstinately.

He bought Mr. Benham, Mr. Benham and his secret; they were heartily at his disposal, for he could pay a better price than Puttock could; and he laid them by in his arsenal, for use, he carefully added to himself, only in the very last emergency.

"Not yet, you fool!" he had whispered to his tool in anger and alarm. The tool did not know how dirty it seemed to the hand that was to use it, and yet shrank from using it until the very last. But if it came to the very last—why, he would use it; and Mr. Kilshaw inspected the pitch on the end of his fingers, and almost convinced himself that it was not pitch at all.

Yet was this "very last" very far off? Since the flower-show, the Premier was displaying feverish activity. He was like a man who is stricken by mortal sickness, but has some work that he must finish before the time comes when he can do no more work, and know no more joy in the work he has done. Bill after bill was introduced embodying his schemes, and the popular praise of him and enthusiasm rose higher and higher at the sight of a minister doing, or at least attempting, all and more than he promised. The Ministry was worked to death; the Governor was apprehensive and uneasy; Capital was, as Kilshaw had said, alarmed; only Sir Robert Perry smiled, as he remarked to the Chief Justice at the Club,

"It can't last. His own men won't swallow all this. Medland must be mad to try it."

"Perhaps," suggested Sir John, "he doesn't mean business. He may only want a strong platform to dissolve on."

"Riding for a fall, eh?"

"I shouldn't wonder."

"My experience is," observed Captain Heseltine, looking up from the *Stud Book*, "that chaps who ride for a fall come more unholy crumplers than anybody else."

"I hope you're right," said Sir Robert, with a smile.

And they discussed the matter with much acumen, and would doubtless have arrived at a true conclusion, had they known anything about the matter. But, as it happened, they were all ignorant of the real reason which dictated Medland's conduct. He had gauged the character of his most uncompromising and powerful enemy to a nicety. He knew that Kilshaw would be loth to make use of Benham, and yet that he would make use of him. He saw that the danger which threatened him had become great and immediate. A stronger hand and a longer purse than Benham's were now against him. The chase had begun. He could not expect much law, and he was riding, not for a fall, but against time. He did not despair of escape, but the chances were against him. He must cover as much ground as he could before the pack was on his heels. So he brought in his bills, made his speeches, fluttered the dovecote of many a prejudice and many an interest, was the idol of the people, and never had a quiet hour.

Besides its more serious effects, the Premier's absorption in public affairs had the result of blinding him to the change that had gradually been coming over his own house. Norburn had always been in and out every hour; he was in and out still, but now he came straight from the street door to the Premier's room, and went straight back thence to the street door again. The visits to Daisy, which had been wont to precede and follow, perhaps even sometimes to occasion, business conferences, ceased almost entirely; and the young Minister's brow bore a weight of care that the precarious position of the Cabinet was not alone enough to account for. It would seem as if Daisy must have noticed Norburn's altered ways, although her father did not; but she made no reference to them, and appeared to be aware of nothing which called for explanation or remark. Perhaps she missed Norburn's visits less because his place was so often filled by Dick Derosne, who, unable to find, or perhaps scorning, any pretext of business, came with the undisguised object of seeing the Premier's daughter, and not the Premier.

Whatever differences Eleanor Scaife and other studious inquirers may discover between young communities and old, it is safe to say that there are many points of resemblance: one of them is that, in both, folk talk a good deal about their neighbours' affairs. The stream of gossip, which Dick's indiscreet behaviour at Sir John Oakapple's dance had set a-flowing, was not diminished in current by his subsequent conduct. Some people believed that he was merely amusing himself, and were very much or very little shocked according to their temperaments and their views on such matters; others, with great surprise and regret, were forced to believe him serious, and wondered what he could be thinking of; a third class took the line sanctioned by the eminent authority of Mr. Tomes, and hailed the possibility of a union of more than private importance. Such a diversity of opinion power-fully promoted the interchange of views, and very soon there were but few people in Kirton society, outside the two households most concerned, who were not watching the progress of the affair.

The circulating eddies of report at last reached Mr. Kilshaw, soon after he had, by his bargain with Benham, been put in possession of the facts that gentleman had to dispose of. Kilshaw knew Dick Derosne very well, and for a time he remained quiet, expecting to see Dick's zeal slacken and his infatuation cease of their own accord. When the opposite happened, Kilshaw's anger was stirred within him; he was ready to find, and in consequence at once found, a new sin and a fresh cause of offence in the Premier. Without considering that Medland had many things to do besides watching the course of flirtations or the development of passions, he hastily concluded that he had come upon another scheme and detected another manœuvre intended to strengthen the Premier's exposed position. He appreciated the advantage that such an alliance would be to a man threatened with the kind of revelation which menaced

Medland; it was clear to his mind that Medland had appreciated it too, and had laid a cunning trap for Dick's innocent feet. It did not suit him to produce yet the public explosion which he destined for his enemy; but he lost no time in determining to checkmate this last ingenious move by some private communication which would put Dick—or perhaps better still, Dick's friends—on guard.

Mr. Dick Derosne perhaps was not unaware that many people in Kirton frowned on him as an unprincipled deceiver, or, at best, a fickle light-o'-love; he would have been much more surprised, and also more displeased, to know that there was even one who thought of him as a deluded innocent, and had determined to rescue him from the snares which were set for his destruction. He did not feel like a deluded innocent. He was not sure how he did feel. Perhaps he also, as well as the man who was preparing to rescue him, had a subject which did not bear too much or too candid inward discussion; and he found it easier to stifle any attempt at importunity on the part of his conscience than Kilshaw did. Kilshaw could only appeal to the paramount interests of the public welfare as an excuse for his own doubtful dealing: Dick could and did look into Daisy Medland's eyes and forget that there was any need or occasion for excuse at all. Supposing she were fond of him—and he could not suppose anything else—what did he mean to do? Many people asked that question, but Dick Derosne himself was not among them. He knew that he would be very sorry to lose her, that she was the chief reason now why he found Kirton a pleasant place of residence, and that he resented very highly any other man venturing to engross her conversation. Beyond that he did not go; but the state of mind which these feelings indicated was no doubt quite enough to justify Kilshaw in deciding to have recourse to the Governor, and allow his message to Dick to filter through one who had more right than he had to offer counsel.

In a matter like this, to determine was to do. He got on his horse and rode through the Park towards Government House. In the Park he met Captain Heseltine, also mounted and looking very hot. The Captain mopped his face, and waved an accusing arm towards an inhospitable eucalyptus.

"Call that a tree!" he said. "The beastly thing doesn't give a ha'porth of shade."

"It's the best we've got," replied Kilshaw, in ironical apology for his country.

"As a rule, you know," the Captain continued, "coming out for a ride here, except at midnight, means standing up under a willow and wondering how the deuce you'll get home."

"Well, you're not under a willow now."

"No; I was, but I had to quit. Derosne and Miss Medland turned me out."

"Ah!"

"Yes."

"You felt you ought to go?"

"My tact told me so. I say, Kilshaw, what do you make of that?"

"Nothing in it," answered Kilshaw confidently.

Captain Heseltine had but one test of sincerity, and it was a test to which he knew Kilshaw was, as a rule, quite ready to submit. He took out a small note-book from one pocket and a pencil from the other.

Anthony Hope

"What'll you lay that it doesn't come off?" he asked.

"I won't bet."

"Oh," said the Captain, scornfully implying that he ceased to attach value to Mr. Kilshaw's judgment.

"I won't bet, because I know."

"The deuce you do!" exclaimed Heseltine, promptly re-pocketing his apparatus.

"And, if you want another reason why I won't bet," continued Kilshaw, who did not like the Captain's air of incredulity, "I'll tell you. I'm going to stop it myself."

"Oh, of course, if *you* object!" said the Captain, with undisguised irony. "I hope, though, that you'll let me have a shot, after Dick."

"You won't want it, if you're a wise man. You wait a bit, my friend," and with a grim nod of his head, Kilshaw rode on.

The Captain looked after him with a meditative stare. Then he glanced at his watch.

"That beggar knows something," said he. "I think I'll go and interrupt friend Richard." And he continued, apostrophising the absent Dick—"To stay out, my boy, may not be easy; but to get out when you're once in, is the deuce!"

CHAPTER XII

AN ABSURD AMBITION

Suave mari magno—Like so many of us who quote these words, Mr. Coxon could not finish the line, but the tag as it stood was enough to express his feelings. If the Cabinet were going to the bottom, he was not to sink with it. If he had one foot in that leaky boat, the other was on firm ground. He had received unmistakable intimations that, if he would tread the path of penitence as Puttock had, the way should be strewn with roses, and the fatted calf duly forthcoming at the end of the journey. He had a right to plume himself on the dexterity which had landed him in such a desirable position, and he was fully awake to the price which that position made him worth. Now a man who commands a great price, thought Mr. Coxon, is a great man. So his meditations—which, in this commercial age, seem hardly open to adverse criticism—ran, as he walked towards Government House, just about the same time as Mr. Kilshaw was also thinking of betaking himself thither. A great man (Mr. Coxon's reflections continued) can aspire to the hand of any lady—more especially when he depends not merely on intellectual ability (which is by no means everything), but is also a man of culture, of breeding, of a University education, and of a very decent income. He forbore to throw his personal attractions into the scale, but he felt that if he were in other respects a

Anthony Hope

suitable aspirant, no failure could await him on that score. Vanity apart, he could not be blind to the fact that he was in many ways different from most of his compatriots, still more from most of his colleagues.

"In all essentials I am an Englishman, pure and simple," thought he, as he entered the gates of Government House; but, the phrase failing quite to satisfy him, he substituted, as he rang the bell, "An English gentleman."

"Shall we go into the garden?" said Lady Eynesford, after she had bidden him welcome. "I dare say we shall find Miss Scaife there," and, as she spoke, she smiled most graciously.

Coxon followed her, his brow clouded for the first time that day. He was not anxious to find Miss Scaife, and he had begun to notice that Lady Eynesford always suggested Miss Scaife as a resource; her manner almost implied that he must come to see Miss Scaife.

"I can't think where she has got to," exclaimed Lady Eynesford, after a perfunctory search; "but it's too hot to hunt. Sit down here in the verandah. Eleanor has probably concealed herself somewhere to read the last debate. She takes such an interest in all your affairs—the Ministry's, I mean."

"I noticed she was very attentive the other day."

"Oh, at that wretched House! Why don't you ventilate it? It gave poor Alicia quite a headache."

"I hope Miss Derosne is not still suffering?"

"Oh, it's nothing much. I suppose she feels this close weather. It's frightful, isn't it? I wonder you had the courage to walk up. It's very friendly of you, Mr. Coxon."

"With such an inducement, Lady Eynesford—" Coxon began, in his laboriously polite style.

"I know," laughed his hostess, and her air was so kind and confidential that Coxon was emboldened. He did not understand why people called the Governor's wife cold and "stand-offish"; he always insisted that no one could be more cordial than she had shown herself towards him.

"What do you know?" he asked, with a smile, and an obviously assumed look of surprise.

"You don't suppose I think I'm the inducement—or even the Governor? And we can't find her! Too bad!" and Lady Eynesford shook her head in playful despair.

"But," said Coxon, feeling now quite happy, "isn't the—the inducement—at home?"

"Oh yes, she's somewhere," replied Lady Eynesford, good-naturedly ignoring her visitor's too ready acquiescence in her modest disclaimer.

"I'm afraid I'm a poor politician. I can conceal nothing."

"Your secret is quite safe with me, and no one else has guessed it."

"Not even Miss Scaife?" asked Coxon, with a smile. Eleanor had so often managed a *tête-à-tête* for him, he remembered.

"Oh, I can't tell that—but, you know, we women never guess these things till we're told. It's not correct, Mr. Coxon."

Anthony Hope

"But you say you guessed it."

"That's quite different. I might guess it—or—or anybody else (though nobody has)—but not Eleanor."

A slight shade of perplexity crossed Coxon's brow. The lady, if kind and reassuring, was also somewhat enigmatical.

"I believe," he said, "Miss Scaife has guessed it."

"Indeed! And is she—pleased?"

"I hope so."

"So do I—for your sake."

"Her approbation would be a factor, would it?"

"Really, Mr. Coxon, I suppose it would!" exclaimed Lady Eynesford in surprise.

"I mean it would be likely to weigh with—with your sister-in-law?"

"With Alicia? Why, what has Alicia got to do with it?"

"You mustn't chaff me, Lady Eynesford. It's too serious," pleaded Coxon, in self-complacent tones.

"What does the man mean?" thought Lady Eynesford. Then a glance at his face somehow brought sudden illumination, and the illumination brought such a shock that Lady Eynesford was startled into vulgar directness of speech.

"Good gracious! Surely it *is* Eleanor you come after?" she exclaimed.

"Miss Scaife! What made you think that? Surely you've seen that it's Miss Derosne who—"

"Mr. Coxon!"

At the tone in which Lady Eynesford seemed to hurl his own name in his teeth, Coxon's rosy illusion vanished. He sat in gloomy silence, twisting his hat in his hand and waiting for Lady Eynesford to speak again.

"You astonish me!" she said at last. "I made sure it was Eleanor."

"Why is it astonishing?" he asked. "Surely Miss Derosne's attractions are sufficient to—?"

"Oh, I'm so sorry, I am indeed. You must believe me, Mr. Coxon. If I had foreseen this I—I would have guarded against it. But now—indeed, I'm so sorry."

Lady Eynesford's sorrowful sympathy failed to touch Coxon's softer feelings.

"What is there to be sorry about?" he demanded, almost roughly.

"Why this—this unfortunate misunderstanding. Of course I thought it was Eleanor; you seemed so suited to one another."

Coxon, ignoring the natural affinity suggested, remarked,

"There's no harm done that I can see, except that I hoped I had you on my side. Perhaps I shall have still."

Sympathy had failed. Lady Eynesford, recognising that, felt

she had a duty to perform.

"I dare say I am to blame," she said, "but I never thought of such a thing. Really, Mr. Coxon, you must see that I wasn't likely to think of it," and her tone conveyed an appeal to his calmer reason. She was quite unconscious of giving any reasonable cause of offence.

"Why not?" he asked, the silky smoothness of his manner disappearing in his surprise and wounded dignity.

"The—the—oh, if you don't see, I can't tell you."

"You appear to assume that attentions from me to your sister-in-law were not to be expected."

"You do see that, don't you?"

"While attentions to your governess—"

"Miss Scaife is my friend and worthy of anybody's attentions," interposed Lady Eynesford quickly.

"But all the same, very different from Miss Derosne," sneered Coxon sullenly, putting her thoughts into her mouth with a discrimination that completed her discomfiture.

"I don't think there is any advantage in discussing it further," remarked Lady Eynesford, rising.

"I claim to see Miss Derosne herself. I am not to be put off."

"I will acquaint the Governor and my sister-in-law with your wishes. No doubt my husband will communicate with you. Good-morning, Mr. Coxon," and Lady Eynesford performed her stiffest bow.

"Good-morning, Lady Eynesford," he answered, in no less hostile tones, and very different was the man who slammed the gate of Government House behind him from the bland and confident suitor who had entered it half-an-hour before.

The moment he was gone, Lady Eynesford ran to her husband.

"The next time you take a Governorship," she exclaimed, as she sank into a chair, "you must leave me at home."

"What's the matter now?"

Lady Eynesford, with much indignant comment, related the tale of Coxon's audacity.

"Of course I meant him for Eleanor," she concluded. "Did you ever hear of such a thing?"

"But, my dear, he must see Alicia if he wants to. We can't turn him out as if he was a footman! After all, he's got a considerable position here."

"Here!" And the word expressed an opinion as comprehensive as, though far more condensed than, any to be found in Tomes.

"I suppose, Mary, there's no danger of—of Alicia being—?"

"Willie! I couldn't imagine it."

"Well, I'll just tell her, and then I'll write to Coxon and see what to do."

"Do make her understand it's impossible," urged Lady Eynesford.

"We've no reason to suppose she's ever thought of it," the Governor reminded his wife.

"No, of course not," she said. "I shall leave you alone with her, Willie."

Alicia came down at the Governor's summons.

"Well, here's another," said the Governor playfully.

Alicia's conquests had been somewhat numerous—such things were so hard to avoid, she pleaded—and it was not the first time her brother had had to confront her with the slain.

"Another what?"

"Another victim. Mary has been here in a rage because a gentleman is ready to be at your feet. Now who do you think it is?"

"I shan't guess. When I guess, I always guess wrong," said Alicia, "and that—"

"Tells tales, doesn't it? Well! it's a great man this time."

A sudden impossible idea ran through her head. Surely it couldn't be—? But nothing we think of very much seems always impossible. It might be! Her air of raillery dropped from her. She sat down, blushing and breathing quickly.

"Who is it, Willie?" she gasped.

"No, you must guess," said the Governor, over his shoulder; he was engaged in lighting a cigar.

"No, no; tell me, tell me," she could not help crying.

At the sound of her voice, he turned quickly and looked curiously at her.

"Why, Al, what's the matter?" he asked uneasily.

Surely she could not care for that fellow? But girls were queer creatures. Lord Eynesford always doubted if they really knew a gentleman from one who was—well, very nearly a gentleman.

Alicia saw his puzzled look and forced a smile.

"Don't tease me. Who is it?"

"No less a man than a Minister."

"A—Willie, who is it?" she asked, and she stretched out a hand in entreaty.

"My dear girl, whatever—? Well, then, it's Coxon."

"Mr. Coxon! Oh!" and a sigh followed, the hand fell to her side, the flush vanished.

She felt a great relief; the strain was over; there was nothing to be faced now, and, as happens at first, peace seemed almost so sweet as to drown the taste of disappointment. Yet she could not have denied that the taste of disappointment was there.

"Oh! how absurd!"

"It's rather amusing," said his Excellency, much relieved in his turn. "You won't chaff Mary—promise."

"What about? No, I promise."

Anthony Hope

"She thought he was sweet on Eleanor, and rather backed him up—asked him here and all that, you know—and it was you all the time."

Alicia laughed.

"I thought Mary used to leave him a lot to Eleanor."

"That's it."

"But Eleanor always passed him on to me."

"The deuce she did!" laughed Lord Eynesford.

"Don't tell Mary that!"

"Not I! Well, what shall I say? He wants to see you."

"How tiresome!"

"Look here, Al, Mary seems to have given him a bit of her mind; but I must be civil. We can't tell the chap that he's— well, you know. It wouldn't do out here. You don't mind seeing him, do you?"

Alicia said that she would do her duty.

"And shall I be safe in writing and telling him I can say nothing till he has discovered your inclinations?"

"You'll be perfectly safe," said Alicia with decision.

The Governor wrote his letter; it was a very civil letter indeed, and Lord Eynesford felt that it ought in some degree to assuage the wrath which his wife's unseemly surprise had probably raised in Coxon's breast.

"It's all very well," he pondered, "for a man to be civil all round as I am; but his womankind can always give him away."

He closed his note, pushed the writing-pad from him, and, leaning back in his chair, puffed at his cigar. In the moment of reflection, the impression of Alicia's unexplained agitation revived in his memory.

"I don't believe," he mused, "that she expected me to say Coxon. I wonder if there's some one else; it looked like it. But who the deuce could it be here? It can't be Heseltine or Flemyng—they're not her sort—and there's no one else. Ah! the mail came in this morning, perhaps it's some one at home. That must be it. I like that fellow's impudence. Wonder who the other chap is. Perhaps I was wrong—you can't tell with women, they always manage to get excited about something. I swear there was nothing before I came out, and there's no one here, and—"

"Mr. Kilshaw," announced Jackson.

CHAPTER XIII

OUT OF HARM'S WAY

"I don't see what business it is of his," said Dick to his brother the next afternoon. "I call it infernal impertinence."

Lord Eynesford differed.

"Well, I don't," he said. "He did it with great tact, and I'm very much obliged to him."

"I wish people would leave my affairs alone," Dick grumbled.

"Has it gone very far?" asked his brother, ignoring the grumble.

"Depends upon what you call far. There's nothing settled, if that's what you mean."

"I don't know that I've any exact right to interfere, but isn't it about time you made up your mind whether you want it to go any farther?"

"What's the hurry?"

"Because," pursued the Governor, "it seems to me that going on as you're doing means either that you want to marry her, or that you're making a fool of her."

This pointed statement of the case awoke Dick's dormant conscience.

"And a cad of myself, you mean?" he asked.

"Same thing, isn't it?" replied his brother curtly.

"I suppose so," Dick admitted ruefully. "Hang it, I am a fool!"

"I don't imagine you want to do anything a gentleman wouldn't do. Only, if you do, you won't do it from my house—that's all."

"All right, old chap. Don't be so precious down on me. I didn't mean any harm. A fellow gets led on, you know—no, I don't mean by her—by circumstances, you know."

"I grant you she's pretty and pleasant, but she won't have a *sou*, and—well, Medland's a very clever fellow and very distinguished. But—"

"No, I know. They're not our sort."

"Then of course it's no use blinking the fact that there's something wrong. I don't know what, but something."

"Did Kilshaw tell you that?"

"Yes, between ourselves, he did. He wouldn't tell me what, but said he knew what he was talking about, and that I'd better tell you that you and all of us would be very sorry before long if we had anything to do with the Medlands."

"What the deuce does he mean?" asked Dick fretfully.

"Well, you know the sort of gossip that's about. Compare that with what Kilshaw said."

"What gossip?"

"Nonsense! You know well enough. It's impossible to live here without noticing that everybody thinks there's something wrong. I believe Kilshaw knows what it is, and, what's more, that he means to have it out some day. However that may be, rumours of the sort there are about are by themselves enough to stop any wise man."

"Old wives' scandal, I expect."

"Perhaps: perhaps not. Anyhow, I'd rather have no scandal, old wives' or any other, about my wife's family."

"I'm awfully fond of her," said Dick.

"Well, as I said, it's your look-out. I don't know what Mary'll say, and—you've only got six hundred a year of your own, Dick."

"It seems to me we're in the deuce of a hurry—" began Dick feebly, but his brother interrupted him.

"Come, Dick, do you suppose Kilshaw would have come to me, if he hadn't thought the matter serious? It wasn't a very pleasant interview for him. I expect you've been making the pace pretty warm."

Dick did not venture on a denial. He shifted about uneasily

in his seat, and lit a cigarette with elaborate care.

"I don't want to be disagreeable," pursued the Governor, "but both for your sake and mine—not to speak of the girl's—I won't have anything that looks like trifling with her. You must make up your mind; you must go on, or you must drop it."

"How the devil can I drop it? I'm bound to meet her two or three times a week, and I can't cut her."

"You needn't flirt with her."

"Oh, needn't I? That's all you know about it."

The Governor was not offended by this rudeness.

"Then," he said, "if you don't mean to go on—"

"Who said I didn't?"

"Do you?"

Dick was driven into a corner. He asked why life was so ill-arranged, why he was poor, why a man might not look at a girl without proposing to her, why everybody was always so down on him, why people chattered so maliciously, why he was such a miserable devil, and many other questions. His brother relentlessly repeated his "Do you?" and at last Dick, red in the face, and with every sign of wholesome shame, blurted out,

"How can I marry her? You know I can't—especially after this story of Kilshaw's."

"Very well. Then if you can't marry her, and yet can't help making love to her—"

"I didn't say I made love to her."

"But you do—making love to her, I say, as often as you see her, why, you mustn't see her."

"I'm bound to see her."

"As long as you stay here, yes. But you needn't stay here. We can govern New Lindsey without you, Dick, for a time, anyhow."

This suggestion fell as a new light on Dick Derosne. He waited a moment before answering it with a long-drawn "O-oh!"

"Yes," said the Governor, nodding emphatically. "You might just as well run home and give a look to things: most likely they're going to the deuce."

"But what am I to say to people?"

"Why, that you're going to look after some affairs of mine."

"Will she believe that?"

"She? You said 'people!'"

"Hang it, Willie! I don't like bolting. Besides, it's not half bad out here. Do you think I've—I've behaved like a beast, Willie?"

"It looks like it."

"It's no more than what lots of fellows do."

"Not a bit: less than a great many, thank God, Dick. Come,

old chap, do the square thing—the squarest thing you can do now."

"Give me till to-morrow," said Dick, and escaped in a jumble of conflicting feelings—smothered pride in his fascinations, honest reprobation of his recklessness, momentary romantic impulses, recurrent prudential recollections, longings to stay, impatience to get rid of the affair, regrets that he had ever met Daisy Medland, pangs at the notion of not meeting her in the future—a very hotch-pot of crossed and jarring inclinations.

So the Governor did the right, the prudent thing, the only thing, the thing which he could not doubt was wise, and which all reasonable men must have seen to be inevitable. Nevertheless when he met Daisy Medland that afternoon in the Park, he felt much more like a pick-pocket than it is comfortable to feel when one is her Majesty's representative: for Dick was with him, and Daisy's eyes, which had lightened in joy at seeing them, clouded with disappointment as they rode past without stopping. Thus, when Dick turned very red and muttered, "I *am* a beast," the Governor moaned inwardly, "So am I."

It is perhaps creditable to Man—and Man, as opposed to Woman, in these days needs a word slipped in for him when it is reasonably possible—that these touches of tenderness fought against the stern resolve that had been taken. But of course they were only proper fruits of penitence, in Dick for himself, in Lord Eynesford for his kind, and it could not be expected that they would reproduce themselves in persons so entirely innocent of actual or vicarious offence as Lady Eynesford and Eleanor Scaife.

"I think," said Lady Eynesford, "that we may congratulate ourselves on a very happy way of getting out of the results of

Anthony Hope

Dick's folly."

"I can't think that Dick said anything really serious," remarked Eleanor.

"So much depends on how people understand things," observed Lady Eynesford.

It was on the tip of Eleanor's tongue to add, "Or wish to understand them," but she recollected that she had really no basis for this malicious insinuation, and made expiation for entertaining it by saying to Alicia,

"You think she's a nice girl, don't you?"

"Very," said Alicia briefly.

"The question is not what she is, so much as who she is," said Lady Eynesford.

"I expect it was all Dick's fault," said Alicia hastily.

"Or that man's," suggested the Governor's wife.

A month ago Alicia would have protested strongly. Now she held her peace: she could not trust herself to defend the Premier. Yet she was full of sympathy for his daughter, and of indignation at the tone in which her sister-in-law referred to him. Also she was indignant with Dick: this conduct of Dick's struck her as an impertinence, and, on behalf of the Medlands, she resented it. They talked, too, as if it were a flirtation with a milliner—dangerous enough to be trouble-some, yet too absurd to be really dangerous—discreditable no doubt to Dick, but—she detected the underlying thought —still more discreditable to Daisy Medland. The injustice angered her: it would have angered her at any time; but her anger was forced to lie deeply hidden and secret, and the suppression made it more intense. Dick's flighty fancy caricatured the feeling with which she was struggling: the family attitude towards it faintly foreshadowed the consternation that the lightest hint of her unbanishable dream would raise. And, worst of all—so it seemed to her—what must Medland think? He must surely scorn them all—this petty pride, their microscopic distinctions of rank, their little devices—all so small, yet all enough to justify the wounding of his daughter's heart. It gave her a sharp, almost unendurable pang to think that he might confound her in his sweeping judgment. Could he after—after what he had seen? He might think she also trifled—that it was in the family— that they all thought it good fun to lead people on and then— draw back in scorn lest the suppliant should so much as touch them.

In the haste of an unreasoning impulse, she went to Medland's house, full of the idea of dissociating herself from what had been done, only dimly conscious of difficulties which, if they existed, she was yet resolute to sweep away. Convention should not stand between, nor cost her a single unkind thought from him.

She asked for Daisy Medland, and was shown into Daisy's little room. She had not long to wait before Daisy came in. Alicia ran to meet her, but dared not open the subject near her heart, for the young girl's bearing was calm and distant. Yet her eyes were red, for it was but two hours since Dick Derosne had flung himself out of that room, and she had been left alone, able at last to cast off the armour of wounded pride and girlish reticence. She had assumed it again to meet her new visitor, and Alicia's impetuous sympathy was frozen by the fear of seeming impertinence.

At last, in despair of finding words, yet set not to go with her errand undone, she stretched out her arms, crying—

"Daisy! Not with me, dear!"

Daisy was not proof against an assault like that. Her wounded pride—for Dick had not been enough of a diplomatist to hide the meaning of his sudden flight—had borne her through her interview with him, and he had gone away doubting if she had really cared for him; it broke down now. She sprang to Alicia's arms, and her comforter seemed to hear her own confession in the young girl's broken and half-stifled words.

"Do come again," said Daisy, and Alicia, who after a long talk had risen to go, promised with a kiss.

The door opened and Medland came in. Alicia started, almost in fright.

"I came—I came—" she began in her agitation, for she assumed that his daughter had told him her story.

"It's very kind of you," he answered, and she, still misunderstanding, went on eagerly—

"It's such a shame! Oh, you don't think I had anything to do with it?"

He looked curiously from one to the other, but said nothing.

Alicia kissed Daisy again and passed by him towards the door: he followed her, and, closing the door, said abruptly,

"What's a shame, Miss Derosne? What's the matter with Daisy?"

"You don't know? Oh, I've no right—"

"No; but tell me, please. Come in here," and he beckoned her into his own study.

"Is she in any trouble?" he asked again. "She won't tell me, you know, for fear of worrying me, so you must."

Somehow Alicia, unable to resist his request, stammered out the gist of the story; she blamed Dick as severely as he deserved, and shielded Daisy from all suspicion of haste in giving her affection; but the story stood out plain.

"And—and I was so afraid," she ended as she had begun, "that you would think that I had anything to do with it."

"Poor little Daisy!" he said softly. "No; I'm sure you hadn't. Ah, well, I dare say they're right."

He was so calm that she was almost indignant with him.

"Can't you feel for her—you, her father?" she exclaimed. But a moment later she added, "I didn't mean that. Forgive me! I can't bear to think of the way she has been treated!"

He looked up suddenly and asked,

"Was it only—general objections—or—or anything in particular?"

"What do you mean? I don't know of anything in particular."

"I'm glad. I shouldn't have liked—but you won't understand. Well, you've been very kind."

She would not leave her doubt unsettled. His manner

puzzled her.

"Do you know of anything?" she found courage to add.

"'The fathers eat sour grapes,'" he answered, with a bitter smile. "Poor little Daisy!"

"I believe you're hinting at something against yourself."

"Perhaps."

He held out his hand to bid her good-bye, adding,

"You'd better let us alone, Miss Derosne."

"Why should I let you alone? Why mayn't I be her friend?"

He made no direct answer, but said,

"Your news of what has happened—I mean of your friends' attitude—hardly surprises me. You won't suppose I feel it less, because it's my fault—and my poor girl has to suffer for it."

"Your fault?"

"Yes."

"I don't understand," she murmured.

"I hope you never need," he answered earnestly, holding out his hand again.

This time she took it, but, as she did, she looked full in his face and said,

"I will believe nothing against you, not even your own

words. Good-bye."

Her voice faltered in the last syllable, and she ran hastily down the stairs.

Medland stood still for some minutes. Then he went in to his daughter and kissed her.

But even that night, in spite of his remorse and sorrow for her grief, his daughter was not alone in his thoughts.

Anthony Hope

CHAPTER XIV

A FATAL SECESSION

The sudden departure of Dick Derosne was, according to Kilshaw's view of it, a notable triumph for him over his adversary; but he was not a man to rest content with one victory. He had hardly achieved this success when a chance word from Captain Heseltine started him in a new enterprise, and a hint from Sir John Oakapple confirmed him in his course. He made up his mind not to wait for the slow growth of disaffection in Coxon's mind, but to accelerate the separation of that gentleman from his colleagues. The Captain had been pleased to be much amused at the cessation of Coxon's visits to Government House: Eleanor Scaife's contempt for her supposed admirer was so strong that, when playfully taxed with hardness of heart, she repelled the charge with a vigour that pointed the Captain straight to the real fact. Having apprehended it, he thought himself in no way bound to observe an over-strict reticence as to Coxon's "cheek" and his deserved rebuff.

"In fact," he concluded, "love's at a discount. With Coxon and Dick before one's eyes, it really isn't good enough. All a fellow gets is a dashed good snubbing or his marching orders." And he added, as if addressing an imaginary waiter, "Thank you, I'm not taking it to-day."

His words fell on attentive ears, and the next time Kilshaw had a chance of conversing with Coxon at the Club, he did not forget what he had learnt from Captain Heseltine.

"How d'you do, Coxon?" said he. "Haven't seen you for a long time. Come and sit here. You weren't at the Governor's party the other night?"

Coxon, gratified at this cordial greeting, joined Mr. Kilshaw. They were alone in the Club luncheon-room, and Coxon was always anxious to hear anything that Sir Robert or his friends had to say. There was always a possibility that it might be very well worth his while to listen.

"I wasn't there," he said. "I don't go when I can help it."

"You used to be so regular," remarked Kilshaw in surprise, or seeming surprise.

Coxon gave a laugh of embarrassed vexation.

"I think I go as often as I'm wanted," he said. "To tell you the truth, Kilshaw, I find my lady a little high and mighty."

"Women can never separate politics and persons," observed Kilshaw, with a tolerant smile. "It's no secret, I suppose, that she's not devoted to your chief."

Coxon looked up quickly. His wounded vanity had long sought for an explanation of the cruel rebuff he had endured.

"Well, I never put it down to that," he said.

"It can't be anything in yourself, can it?" asked Kilshaw, in bland innocence. "No, no; Lady Eynesford's one of us, and there's an end of it—though of course I wouldn't say it openly. Look at the different way she treats the Puttocks since they left you!"

"It's highly improper," observed Coxon.

"I grant it; but she's fond of Perry, and sees through his glasses. And then you must allow for her natural prejudices. Is Medland the sort of man who would suit her? Candidly now?"

"She needn't identify us all with Medland?"

"Come and have a cigar. Ah, there's Sir John! How are you, Chief Justice? Looks a bit shaky, doesn't he? Come along, Coxon."

So saying, Kilshaw led the way to the smoking-room, and, when the pair were comfortably settled, he recurred to his topic.

"I remember her asking me—in confidence of course, and, all the same, perhaps not very discreetly—what in the world made you go over, and what made you stay over."

"And you said—?"

"I didn't know what to say. I never did understand, and I understand less than ever now."

"Haven't I explained in the House?"

"Oh, in the House! I tell you what it is, Coxon,—and you must stop me if you don't like to hear it—I shall always consider Medland got your support on false pretences."

Coxon did not stop him. He sat and bit his finger-nail while

Kilshaw pointed out the discrepancies between what Medland had foreshadowed and what he was doing. He did not consciously exaggerate, but he made as good a case as he could; and he talked to an ear inclined to listen.

"He caught you and Puttock on false pretences—utterly false pretences," Kilshaw ended. "Puttock saw it pretty soon."

"I was too stupid, I suppose?"

"Well, if you like," said Kilshaw, with a laugh. "I suppose when one doesn't appreciate a man's game, one calls him stupid."

"I have no game," said Coxon stiffly.

"My dear fellow, I didn't mean it offensively. I'm sure you haven't, for if ever a man was sacrificing his position and his future on the altar of his convictions, you are."

Mr. Coxon looked noble, and felt uncomfortable.

"In a month or two," continued Kilshaw, laying his hand on his neighbour's arm and speaking impressively, "Medland will be not only out of office, but a discredited man."

"Why?" asked the other uneasily, for Kilshaw's words implied some hidden knowledge: without that he could not have ventured on such a prophecy to a colleague of the Premier's.

"Never mind why. You know you can't last, and time will show the rest. He'll go—and all who stick to him. Well, I've said too much. Have you heard the news? But of course you have, Ministers hear everything."

Anthony Hope

"What news?"

"The Chief Justice thinks of resigning: he told me himself that he had spoken to Medland about it, and Medland had asked him to wait a little."

"What for?"

"Oh, Medland wants to get hold of a good man from England, I understood. He thinks nobody here equal to it."

"Complimentary to my profession out here."

"I know. I wonder at Medland: he's generally so strong on 'Lindsey for the Lindseians,' as he once said. In this matter he and Perry seem to have changed places."

"Really? Then Sir Robert—?"

"Yes, he's quite anxious to have one of ourselves. I must say I heartily agree, and of course it could easily be managed, if Medland liked. Perry would do it in a minute. I really don't see why the best berth in the colony is to be handed over to some hungry failure from London. But no doubt you'll agree with Medland."

"Oh, I don't know," said Coxon. "It seems to me rather a point where the Bar here ought to assert itself."

"I know, if we were in and had a fit man, we should hear nothing more of an importation. The best man in the colony would be glad to have it: of course there's not the power a Minister has, or the interest of active political life, but it's well paid, very dignified, and, above all, permanent."

Now neither Kilshaw nor Coxon were dull men, and by this

time they very well understood one another. They knew what they meant just as well as though they had been indecent enough to say it. "Help us to turn out Medland, and you shall be Chief Justice," said Kilshaw, in the name of Sir Robert Perry,—"Chief Justice, and once more a *persona grata* at Government House." Chief Justice! Soon, perhaps, Sir Alfred! Would not that soften the Eynesford heart? Mr. Coxon honestly thought it would. The subtleties of English rank are not to be apprehended by a mere four years' visit to our shores.

"We expect Sir John to go on for a couple of months or so," Kilshaw continued. "I don't think he'll stay longer."

"Perhaps we shall be out by then."

"Not as things stand, I'm afraid," and Kilshaw shook his head. "Now if we could get you, Medland would be out in three weeks."

"I must do what I think right."

"My dear Coxon! Of course!"

Mr. Kilshaw returned to his office well pleased. A careful computation showed that Medland was supported now by a steady majority of not more than eight: Coxon's defection could not fail to leave him in a minority; for, although Coxon was a young man, and, as yet, of no great independent weight in politics, he had acquired a factitious importance, partly from the prestige of a successful University career in England, still more from the fact that he was the only remaining member of the Ministry to whom moderate men and vested interests could look with any confidence. Shorn of him, as it had been shorn of Puttock, the Government would stand revealed as the organ and expression of the

Anthony Hope

Labour Party and nothing else, and Perry and Kilshaw doubted not that six or eight members of the House would be found to enter the "cave," if Coxon showed them the way. Then,—"Why then," said Mr. Kilshaw to his conscience, "we need not use that brute Benham at all! There's a nice sop! Lie down like a good dog, and stop barking!"

Indeed, had it been quite certain that Benham's aid would not still prove needful, Kilshaw would have been very glad to be rid of him. Complete leisure and full pockets appeared not to be, in his case, a favourable soil for the growth of virtue. No doubt Mr. Benham's position was in some respects a hard one. All men who have money in plenty and nothing to do claim from the wise a lenient judgment, and, besides these disadvantages, Benham laboured under the possession of a secret—a secret of mighty power. What wonder if he spent much of his day in eating-houses and drinking-houses, obscurely hinting to admiring boon companions of the thing he could do an he would? Then, having drunk his fill, he would swagger, sometimes not over-steadily, out to the Park, and amuse himself by scowling at the Premier, or smiling a smile of hidden meaning at Daisy Medland, as they drove by. Also, he occasionally got into trouble: one zealous partisan of the Premier's rewarded an insinuation with a black eye, and Mr. Kilshaw's own servant, finding his master's pensioner besieging the house in a state of drink-begotten noisiness, kicked him down the street—an excess of zeal that cost Mr. Kilshaw a cheque next day. The danger was, however, of a worse thing than these. Kilshaw, suffering only what he doubtless deserved to suffer, went on thorns of fear lest some day Benham should not only explode his bomb prematurely, but publish to the world at whose charges and under whose auspices the engineer was carrying out his task. And when Mr. Kilshaw contemplated this possibility, he found it hopeless to deny that there was pitch on his fingers. Publicity makes such a difference in men's judgments of themselves.

In this way things hung on for a week or so, and then, one afternoon, the Chief Justice rushed into the Club in a state of some excitement. Spying Perry and Kilshaw, he hastened to them.

"You have heard?" he cried.

"What?" asked Sir Robert, wiping his glasses and smiling quietly.

"No? I believe I'm the first. Coxon told me himself: he came into my room when I rose to-day. He's asked Medland to accept his resignation."

Kilshaw sprang to his feet.

"What on?" asked Sir Robert.

"The Accident-Liability Clause in the Factory Act."

"A very good ground," commented the ex-Premier. "Very cleverly chosen."

"What does Medland say?" asked Kilshaw eagerly. "Will he give way, or will he let him go?"

"I think the man's mad," said the Chief Justice. "He won't budge an inch. So Coxon goes—and he says a dozen will go with him."

Then Mr. Kilshaw's feelings overcame him.

"Hurrah!" he cried. "By heaven, we've got him now! We shall beat him on the Clause! Perry, you'll be back in a week!"

Anthony Hope

"It looks like it," said Sir Robert, "but one never knows."

"Puttock's solid, and now Coxon! Perry, we shall beat him by anything from six to ten! I shan't die a pauper yet!"

Sir John bustled on, anxious to anticipate in other quarters the coming newsvendor, and Sir Robert turned to his lieutenant.

"I suppose he must have his price," he remarked, with deep regret evident in his tone.

"I can't look him in the face if he doesn't," answered Kilshaw. "By Jove, Perry, he's earned it."

"Oh yes, so did Iscariot," said Sir Robert. "But it wasn't a Judgeship."

"You won't go back on it, Perry?"

Sir Robert spread out his thin white hands before him, and shook his head sorrowfully.

"A bargain's a bargain, I suppose," said he, "even if it happens to be rather an iniquitous one," and having enunciated this principle, on which he had often insisted in public, he took up a volume of poetry.

Not so Mr. Kilshaw. He flitted from friend to friend, telling the good news and exchanging congratulations. The evening papers announced the resignation and its impending acceptance, and further stated that the rumour was that the Premier had convened a meeting of his remaining followers to consider their position.

"They may consider all night," said Mr. Kilshaw, "but they

can't change a minority into a majority," and he hailed a cab to take him home.

Suddenly he was touched on the shoulder. Turning, he found Benham beside him.

"Good news, eh?" said that worthy. "Shake hands on it, Mr. Kilshaw."

Kilshaw swallowed his first-formed words, and, after a moment's hesitation, put out his hand. Benham shook it warmly, saying,

"I guess we'll blow him up between us. There's my fist on it. See you soon," and, with a lurching step and a leer over his shoulder, he walked on.

Kilshaw looked at his hand.

"Thank God I had my glove on," he said, and got into his cab.

Certainly there is no rose without a thorn.

When the Governor announced to his household that he had accepted Coxon's resignation, and that it was understood that the retiring Minister would henceforward act with Sir Robert Perry, the news was variously received. Captain Heseltine's observation was brief, but comprehensive.

"Rats!" said he.

Alicia nodded to him with a smile. Eleanor Scaife began to argue the pros and cons of the Accident-Liability Clause, as to which, she considered, there might fairly be a difference of opinion. Lady Eynesford cut across the inchoate disquisition by remarking,

"I have never disliked Mr. Coxon, but he doesn't quite know his place," and nothing that anybody could say made her see any absurdity in this remark.

CHAPTER XV

AN ATTEMPT AT TERRORISM

All the world was driving, riding, or walking in the great avenue of the Park. The Governor had just gone by on horseback, accompanied by his sister and his A.D.C.'s, and Lady Eynesford's carriage was drawn up by the pathway. The air was full of gossip and rumours, for although it was an "off-day" at the House, and nothing important was expected to happen there before the following Monday, there had been that morning a meeting of the Premier's principal adherents, and every one knew or professed to know the decision arrived at. One said resignation, another dissolution, a third coalition, a fourth submission, and the variety of report only increased the confidence with which each man backed his opinion. Sir Robert Perry alone knew nothing, had heard nothing, and would guess nothing—by which adroit attitude he doubled his reputation for omniscience. And Mr. Kilshaw alone cared nothing: the Ministry was "cornered," he said, and that was enough for him. Eleanor Scaife was insatiable for information, or, failing that, conjecture, and she eagerly questioned the throng of men who came and went, paying their respects to the Governor's wife, and lingering to say a few words on the situation. Sir John Oakapple fixed himself permanently by the steps of the carriage, and played the part of a good-humoured though

Anthony Hope

cynical chorus to the shifting drama.

Presently, a little way off, Mr. Coxon made his appearance, showing in his manner a pleased consciousness of his importance. They all wanted a word with him, and laid traps to catch a hint of his future action; he had explained his motives and refused to explain his intentions half-a-dozen times at least. If this flattering prominence could last, he must think twice before he accepted even the most dignified of shelves; but his cool head told him it would not, and he was glad to remember the provision he had made for a rainy day. Meanwhile he basked in the sun of notoriety, and played his *rôle* of the man of principle.

"Ah," exclaimed Eleanor, "here comes the hero of the hour, the maker and unmaker of Ministries."

"As the weather-cock makes and unmakes the wind," said Sir John, with a smile.

"What? Mr. Coxon?" said Lady Eynesford, and, pleased to have an opportunity of renewing her politeness without revoking her edict, she made the late Minister a very gracious bow.

Coxon's face lit up as he returned the salutation. Had his reward come already? He had been right then; it was not towards him as himself, but towards the Medlandite that Lady Eynesford had displayed her arrogance and scorn. Smothering his recurrent misgivings, and ignoring the weakness of his theory, he laid the balm to his sore and obliterated all traces of wounded dignity from his response to Lady Eynesford's advance.

"My husband tells me," she said, "that I must leave my opinion of your exploits unspoken, Mr. Coxon. Why do you laugh, Sir John?"

"At a wife's obedience, Lady Eynesford."

"Then," said Coxon, "I shall indulge myself by imagining that I have your approbation."

"And what is going to happen?" asked Eleanor, for about the twentieth time that day.

Coxon smiled and shook his head.

"They all do that," observed Sir John. "Come, Coxon, admit you don't know."

"We'd better suppose that it's as the Chief Justice says," answered Coxon, whose smile still hinted wilful reticence.

"But think how uninteresting it makes you!" protested Eleanor.

"Oh, I don't agree," said Lady Eynesford. "I am studying every line of Mr. Coxon's face, and trying to find out for myself."

"I told you," he said in a lower voice, and under cover of a joke Sir John was retailing to Eleanor, "that I was a bad hand at concealment."

"I hope you have not remembered all I said then as well as all you said? I was so surprised and—and upset. Was I very rude?"

The implied apology disarmed Coxon of his last resentment.

"I was afraid," he said, "it meant an end to our acquain—"

"Our friendship," interposed the lady with swift graciousness. "Oh, then, I was much more disagreeable than I meant to be."

"It didn't mean that?"

"You don't ask seriously? Now do tell me—what about the Ministry?"

He sank his voice as he answered,

"They can't possibly last a week."

"You are sure?"

"Certain, Lady Eynesford. They'll be beaten on Monday."

Lady Eynesford, with a significant smile, beat one gloved hand softly against the other.

"That can't be seen outside the carriage, can it? You mustn't tell of me! And we owe it all to you, Mr. Coxon!" And for the moment Lady Eynesford's heart really warmed to the man who had relieved her of the Medlands. "When are you coming to see us?" she went on. "Or is it wrong for you to come now? Politically wrong, I mean."

"I was afraid it might be wrong otherwise," Coxon suggested.

"Not unless you feel it so, I'm sure."

"Perhaps Miss Derosne—" he began, but Lady Eynesford was on the alert.

"Her friendly feelings towards you have undergone no

change, and if you can forget—Ah, here are Alicia and my husband!" and Lady Eynesford, feeling the arrival excellently well timed, broke off the *tête-à-tête* before the protests she feared could form themselves on Coxon's lips.

It might be that Alicia's feelings had undergone no change, but, if so, Coxon was forced to recognise that he could never have enjoyed a large share of her favour, for she acknowledged his presence with the minimum of civility, and, when he addressed her directly, replied with the coldness of pronounced displeasure.

Lady Eynesford, perceiving that graciousness on her part was perfectly safe, redoubled her efforts to soothe the despised admirer. She had liked him well enough, he had served her against her enemies, and she was ready and eager to do all she could to soften the blow, provided always that she could rely on the blow being struck. Now, from Alicia's manner it was plain that the blow had fallen from an unfaltering hand.

Suddenly the Chief Justice said,

"Ah, it's settled one way or the other. Here come Medland and Miss Daisy."

In the distance the Premier appeared, walking by the pony his daughter rode. Lady Eynesford turned to her husband and whispered appealingly,

"Need they come here, Willie?"

He shook his head in indulgent disapproval, and said to Alicia,

"Come, Al, we'll go and speak to them," and before Lady

Anthony Hope

Eynesford could declare Alicia's company unnecessary, the pair had turned their horses' heads and were on the way to join the Medlands.

Lady Eynesford's eyes followed them. She saw the meeting, and presently she noticed the Governor ride on with Daisy Medland, while Alicia walked her horse and kept pace with the Premier. They passed by her on the other side of the broad avenue, Medland acknowledging her salutation but not crossing to speak to her. She saw Alicia's heightened colour and the eager interest with which she bent down to catch Medland's words. Medland spoke quickly and earnestly. Once he laughed, and Alicia's gay peal struck on her sister-in-law's ear. Lady Eynesford, as she looked after them, heard Sir John say to Eleanor,

"He's a wonderful man, with a very extraordinary attraction about him. Everybody feels it who comes into personal relations with him. I know I do. And Perry has remarked the same thing to me. Lady Perry, you know, like all women, openly admires him. It's very amusing to see Sir Robert's face when she praises him."

Lady Eynesford did not notice Eleanor's reply. A frown gathered on her brow as she still gazed after the two figures. What did they mean by talking about the man's attractiveness? He had never attracted her: and Alicia—It suddenly struck her that Alicia's former championship of the Premier had changed to a complete silence, and she was vaguely disturbed by the idea of this unnatural reticence. Alicia, she knew, was friendly, too friendly, with the girl; that did not so much matter now that Dick was safe on board ship. But if the friendship were not only for the daughter!

She roused herself from her reverie and turned again to Coxon. She found him looking at her closely, with a bitter smile on his lips. She had not noticed that Eleanor had got out and accepted Sir John's escort for a stroll. She and Coxon were alone.

"Miss Derosne's displeasure with me," he said, "is fully explained, isn't it?"

"What do you mean?" she asked sharply.

For reply he pointed with his cane.

"She favours the Ministry," he said. "Your views are not hers, Lady Eynesford."

"Oh, she knows nothing about politics."

"Perhaps it isn't all politics," he answered, with a boldly undisguised significance.

Lady Eynesford turned quickly on him, a haughty rebuke on her lips, but he did not quail. He smiled his bitter smile again, and she turned away with her words unspoken.

A silence followed. Coxon was wondering if his hint had gone too far. Lady Eynesford wondered how far he had meant it to carry. The idea of danger there was new and strange, and perhaps absurd, but infinitely disagreeable and disquieting.

"Well, good-bye, Lady Eynesford," he began.

"No, don't go," she answered. But before she could say more, there was a sudden stir in the footpath, voices broke out in eager talk, groups formed, and men ran from one to the other. Women's high voices asked for the news, and men's deep tones declared it in answer. Coxon turned eagerly to look, and as he did so, Kilshaw's carriage dashed up. Kilshaw sat inside, with the evening paper in his hand. He hurriedly greeted Lady Eynesford, and went on—

"Pray excuse me, but have you seen Sir Robert Perry? I am most anxious to find him."

"He's there on the path," answered Coxon, and Kilshaw leapt to the ground.

"Run and listen, and come and tell me," cried Lady Eynesford, and Coxon, hastening off, overtook Kilshaw just as the latter came upon Sir Robert Perry.

The news soon spread. The Premier, conscious of his danger, had determined on a demonstration of his power. On the Sunday before that eventful, much-discussed Monday, when the critical clause was to come before the Legislative Assembly, he and his followers had decided to convene mass-meetings throughout the country, in every constituency whose member was a waverer, or suspected of being one of "Coxon's rats," as somebody—possibly Captain Heseltine— had nicknamed them. This was bad, Kilshaw declared. But far worse remained: in the capital itself, in that very Park in which they were, there was to be an immense meeting: the Premier himself would speak, and the thousands who listened were to threaten the recreant Legislature with vengeance if it threw out the people's Minister.

"It's nothing more or less than an attempt to terrorise us," declared Sir Robert, in calm and deliberate tones. "It's a most unconstitutional and dangerous thing."

And Kilshaw endorsed his chief's views in less measured tones.

"If there's bloodshed, on his head be it! If he appeals to force, by Jove, he shall have it!"

Amid all this ferment the Premier walked by, half hidden by Alicia Derosne's horse.

"What is the excitement?" she exclaimed.

"My last shot," he answered, smiling. "Good-bye. Go and hear me abused."

Lady Eynesford would have been none the happier for knowing that Alicia thought, and Medland found, a smile answer enough.

CHAPTER XVI

A LEAKY VESSEL

It was the afternoon of the next day—the Friday—and Kirton was in some stir of bustle and excitement. Groups of working-men gathered and discussed the coming meeting; carts had already passed by on their way to the Park carrying materials for platforms, and had been cheered by some of the more eager spirits. The tradesmen were divided in feeling, some foreseeing a brisk demand for things to eat and drink in the next few days, the more timid not denying this but doubting whether payment might not be dispensed with, and nervously enlarging on the cost of plate glass. Organisers ran busily to and fro, displaying already, some of them, rosettes of office, and all of them as much hurry as though the great event were fixed for a short hour ahead. Norburn was about the streets, looking more cheerful than he had done for a long while—the scent of battle was in his nostrils—and enjoying the luxury of prevailing on his friends not to hiss Mr. Puttock when that worthy stepped across from his warehouse to the Club about five o'clock.

Inside the Club, also, excitement was not lacking. The Houses of Parliament were deserted for this more central spot, and many members anxiously discussed their principles and their prospects, and the relation between the two.

Medland's followers were not there in much force, being for the most part employed elsewhere, and indeed at no time much given to club-life, or suited for it, but there were many of Perry's, and still more of those who had followed Puttock, or were reported to be about to follow Coxon, and among them the members for several divisions in and near Kirton. These last, feeling that all the stir was largely for their benefit and on their account, were in a fluster of self-consciousness and apprehension, and very loud in their condemnation of the Premier's unscrupulous tactics.

"Surely the Governor can't approve of this sort of thing," said one.

"Is it *legal*, Sir John?" asked another of the Chief Justice, who had come in from court and was taking a cup of tea.

"It's mere bullying," exclaimed a third, catching Kilshaw's sympathetic eye.

"We'll not be bullied," answered that gentleman. "Every right-feeling and respectable man is with us, from the Governor—"

"The Governor? How do you know?" burst from half-a-dozen mouths.

"I do know. He's furious with Medland, partly for doing the thing at all, partly for not telling him sooner. He thinks Medland took advantage of his civility yesterday and paraded him in the Park as on his side, while all the time he never said a word about this move of his."

"Ah!" said everybody, and Coxon, who knew nothing about the matter, endorsed Kilshaw's account with a significant nod.

Anthony Hope

"It's a gambler's last throw," declared Puttock. "Honestly, I'm ashamed to have been so long in finding out his real character."

Some one here weakly defended the Premier.

"After all," he said, "there's nothing wrong in a public meeting, and perhaps that's all—"

Puttock overbore him with a solemnly emphasised reiteration—

"A discredited gambler's last throw."

"It's Jimmy Medland's last throw, anyhow," added Kilshaw. "I'll see to that."

"Look! There he is!" called a man in the bow-window, and the company crowded round to look.

Medland was walking down the street side by side with a short, thick-set man, whose close-cut, stiff, black hair, bright black eyes, and bristly chin-tip gave him a foreign look. The man seemed to be giving explanations or detailing arrangements, and Medland from time to time nodded assent.

"Who's that with him?" asked Puttock.

The desired information came from a young fellow in the Government service.

"I know him," he said, "because he applied to me for a certificate of naturalisation a month or two ago. François Gaspard he calls himself—heaven knows if it's his real name. He's a Frenchman, anyhow, and, I rather fancy, not a voluntary exile."

"Ah!" exclaimed Kilshaw, "what makes you think that?"

"Oh, I had a little talk with him, and he said he'd been kept too long out of his country to care about going back now, although the door had been opened at last."

"An amnesty, you suppose?"

"I thought so. And I happen to know he's very active among the political clubs here."

"Oh, that explains Medland being with him," said Kilshaw. "Some Communist or Socialist probably."

Attention being thus directed to the stranger, one or two of the Kirton politicians present recollected having encountered him in the course of their canvassings, and bore witness to the influence which he wielded among the extreme section of the labouring men. His presence with Medland was considered to increase appreciably the threatening aspect of affairs.

"One criminal in his Cabinet," said Mr. Kilshaw, with scornful reference to Norburn, "and arm-in-arm down the street with another. We're getting on, aren't we, Chief Justice?"

"I have seen too many criminals," answered Sir John, "to think badly of a man merely because he commits an offence against the law." The Chief Justice did not intend to be drawn into any exhibition of partisanship.

The occupants of the Club window continued to watch the Premier until he parted from his companion with a shake of the hand, and, as it seemed, a last emphatic word, and turned to Norburn, who was claiming his attention.

Now the last emphatic word whose unknown purport stirred much curiosity in the Club, carried a pang of disappointment to François Gaspard, for it was "Mind, no sticks," and it swept away François' rapturous imaginings of the thousands of Kirton armed with a forest of sturdy cudgels, wherewith to terrify the *bourgeoisie*. Still, François had made up his mind to trust Jimmy Medland, in spite of sundry shortcomings of faith and practice, and having sworn by his *foi*—which, to tell the truth, was an unsubstantial sanction—to obey his leader, he loyally, though regretfully, promised that there should be no sticks; for, "If sticks appear," the Premier had said, "I shall not appear, that's all, Mr. Gaspard."

The English illogicality which hung obstinately round even such gifted men as Medland and *le jeune* Norburn, so oppressed François—who could not see why, if you might hint at cudgels in the background, you should not use them—that, on his way to his next committee, he turned into a tavern to refresh his spirit. The room was fairly full, and he found, the centre of an interested group, an acquaintance of his, Mr. Benham. François imported no personal rancour into his politics; he hated whole classes with a deadly enmity, but he was ready to talk to or drink or gossip with any of the individuals composing them, without prejudice of course to his right, or rather duty, of obliterating them in their corporate capacity at the earliest opportunity, or even removing them one by one, did his insatiable principles demand the sacrifice. He had met Benham several times, since the latter had taken to frequenting music-halls and drinking-shops, and had enjoyed some argument with him, in which the loss of temper had been entirely on Benham's side. François gave his order, sat down, lit his cigarette, and listened to his friend's denunciation of the Government and its works.

Presently the company, having drunk as much as it wanted or

could pay for, or being weary of Benham's philippic, went its various ways, and François was left alone with his opponent. Benham had been consuming more small glasses of cognac than were good for him, and had reached the boastful and confidential stage of intoxication. He ranged up beside François, besought that unbending though polite man to eschew his evil ways, and hinted openly at the folly of those who pinned their faith on the Premier.

"He does not go all my way," responded François, with a smile and a shrug, "but he goes part. Well, we will go that part together."

Benham leant over him and whispered huskily, bringing his fist down on the counter—

"I can crush him, and I will."

"My dear friend!" murmured François. "See! Do not drink any more. It destroys the generally excellent balance of your mind."

"Ah, you may laugh, but I can do it."

François used the permission; he laughed gaily and freely.

"All your party tries," said he, "and it does not do it. And you will do it alone! Ah, *par exemple*!"

His cool scepticism unloosed Benham's tongue, when an eager curiosity might have revived his prudence and set a seal on his lips. He had chafed at being thought a nobody so long: Kilshaw's injunctions against gossip had been so hard to follow: he could not resist trying what startling effect a hint would have.

"I know enough to ruin him," he whispered, and something in his look or tone convinced François that he believed what he said. "Yes, and I'm going to do it. Others have got the money and'll back me—I've got the information. We shall ruin him, Mr. G-Gaspard, we shall drive him from the country, and where'll your precious party, and your precious schemes, and your precious meetings be then? Tell me that!"

"He would be a great loss," remarked François calmly. "But, come, what is this great thing that is to ruin him?"

"Wouldn't you like to know?"

"Eh, my friend, immensely!" smiled François, who spoke the mere truth, for all he took care to speak it very carelessly.

"I'll tell you this much, it's not a political matter—it's a private matter, and a public man's private character is everything."

"You think so? To me, it is not a great thing, so that he will do what I wish."

Benham smiled knowingly as he answered, with a wink,

"At any rate, most people think so. And I'll tell you what, Gaspard, I hate that fellow. He's wronged me—me, I tell you, and, by God, he shall smart for it!"

"Oh, if it is a personal quarrel," murmured François, with the air of not desiring to intrude in a matter which concerned two gentlemen alone.

"Every one'll know it in a few days," said Benham, "and then Mr. Medland's bust up, and all the lot of you with him. Put that in your pipe and smoke it, friend Gaspard."

"And at present no one knows it but you?"

If Benham had answered truly he would have been wise, but his vaunting mind persuaded him not to diminish his importance by confessing that he shared his secret with any one. After all, it was all his secret, though Kilshaw had bought it.

"Not a soul alive!" he answered, rising to go.

"Ah, then yours is a life valuable to your party. Wrap up, my friend, wrap up. It is chilly outside."

He buttoned Benham's coat for him with friendly solicitude, besought him not to get run over—a caution rather necessary—and started him on his way. Then he sat down again, ordered a cup of coffee, and smoked another cigarette.

"Decidedly," he said at last, "it would be a thousand pities if a creature like that were allowed to do any harm to the good Medland. Surely it would not be right to suffer that?"

And he sat thinking, and becoming more and more sure whither the finger of duty pointed, until some comrades came and carried him off to take the chair at an organising committee, where he made a very temperate speech, and announced that he should regard every one who carried a stick on Sunday as intentionally guilty of the grossest incivility to him, François Gaspard, and as an enemy to the cause to boot.

CHAPTER XVII

THE TRUTH ABOUT THE MAN

In arriving at the bold decision which had caused so much anger and alarm to his enemies, and some searchings of heart among many who still ranked themselves as his friends, the Premier had been moved by more than one motive. The sinister design of overawing the Legislature by the fear of physical force and armed attack did not form part of his intentions, but he did intend and desire what, to a man trained in the traditions of Sir Robert's school, was hardly less unconstitutional and wrong. Through the machinery of his great gatherings, it was to be plainly intimated to the members what course their constituents and masters willed them to follow. He proposed to take every precaution against riot—and the necessary measures fell within the sphere of his own official duties as Chief Secretary; but he was willing and eager that every form of suasion and threat, short of the cudgels for which François Gaspard pined, should be brought to bear on his renegade followers. And, in the second place, it was a vital object to him to probe as deep as he could into the secrets of the popular mind. In six months the life of the Legislative Assembly would expire by effluxion of time: at any moment before he had a right to demand a dissolution, provided that he could convince the Governor of the probability of his coming back with a majority; thus, if the meetings could not avert defeat, they would, he hoped, teach him what course to follow in face of it. Lastly, he anticipated a renewal of energy and confidence in his own followers as the result of an outward mani-festation of the support which he believed the masses of the electors accorded to his policy. His plans ignored the mine which was always beneath his feet. He had not forgotten it: it was constantly present to his mind with its menace of sudden explosion, but he was driven to disregard a chance that was entirely incalculable. He could not discern the mind of Benham, or of the man who pulled the strings to which Benham danced, accurately enough to forecast when the moment of attack would come. He felt sure that nothing short of the surrender and renunciation of all his policy could avert the blow—perhaps not even that would serve; if so, the blow must fall, when and where it would; for, whatever its effect on his position or his party, it would not leave him so powerless or so humbled in his own eyes as a voluntary submission to the terms his enemies chose to dictate.

The alternative of surrender would never have crossed his mind, had he been able to think only of the political side of the matter. But there was another, on which Benham's threats played with equal force. The episode of Dick Derosne's banishment had opened his eyes more fully to what the revelation might mean to his daughter; for, when he thought over the abrupt end that had been put to that romance, he could hardly fail to connect it with Benham or with Kilshaw. He shrank from the exposure to Daisy which he would have to undergo, and from the pain which he was doomed to inflict on her. Long years, no less than his own mode of thought, had veiled from him the character of what he would have to avow; the thing took on a new aspect when he forced himself to hear it as it would strike a daughter's ears. And, by this time, he was conscious—he could no longer affect to himself to be unconscious—that the blow which was to fall on Daisy would strike another with equal, perhaps greater, severity. He might remind himself, as he did over and over again, of the improbability, nay, the absurdity of what had happened; he might tell himself that he was no longer young, that time had robbed him of anything that could catch a girl's fancy, that the gulf of birth, associations, and surroundings yawned wide between. His own experience and insight into temperament rose up and contradicted him, and Alicia Derosne's face drove the truth into his mind. Seeking for a hero, she had strangely, almost comically, he thought, made one of him. Hero-worship, shutting out all criticism, had led her on till she made of him, a man whose life bore no close scrutiny, a battered politician, half visionary, half demagogue (for he did not spare himself in his thoughts)— till she had made of him an ideal statesman and a man worthy of all she had to give. A swift and gentle disenchantment was the best that could be wished for her: so he told himself, but he did not wish it. Time had not altogether changed him, and a woman's smile was to him still a force in his life, as much as it had been, or almost, when it led the boy of twenty-three to do all those rash and wrong things long ago. He could not bear to shut the door: dreaming of impossible transformations of obstinate facts, he drifted on, excusing himself for doing nothing by telling himself that there was nothing he could do.

Mr. Kilshaw's information as to the Governor's attitude had not been entirely incorrect, but, after an interview with the Premier, in which the latter explained his action, Lord Eynesford did not feel that more was required than a temperately expressed surprise and a hinted disapproval of the course adopted. He declined his wife's invitation to regard the matter in the most serious light, or to attribute any heinous offence to the Premier, contenting himself with remarking that Medland had a more powerful motive to maintain order than any one else; he also ventured to suggest that the best way of considering the question was not through a mist of prejudice against the Premier and all his belongings.

"Whatever you may do, Mary," he said, "I must keep the private and public sides separate."

"That's just what you don't do," retorted his wife—let it be added that they were alone. "The man has got round you as he gets round everybody."

"You, at least, seem safe so far," laughed the Governor. "Aren't you content with your triumph in the matter of Dick?"

"I heard from him to-day. He wants to come back."

Dick had obtained leave to visit Australia, instead of going home, and was therefore within comparatively easy distance of New Lindsey.

"Oh, I think we'll wait a bit."

"He seems to be having a splendid time, but he says he's lonely without us all."

"How touching!" remarked Lord Eynesford sceptically.

"Willie, be just to him. I was thinking how nice it would be if Alicia could join him for a little while. She's looking pale and wants a change."

"Does she want to go?"

"Well, I don't know."

Anthony Hope

"Haven't you asked her?"

"No, dear."

Lord Eynesford knew his wife's way. He rose and stood with his back to the fireplace.

"You'll be sending me away next, Mary," he remarked. "What's wrong with Alicia? She doesn't show signs of relenting about your friend Coxon, does she? If so, she shall go by the next boat, if I have to exert the prerogative."

"Mr. Coxon? Oh, dear, no! Poor man! There's no danger from him."

"What's in the wind then?"

"She's too intimate with these Medlands."

"My dear Mary! Forgive me, but you're in danger of becoming a monomaniac. The Medlands are not lepers."

Lady Eynesford shut her lips close and made no answer.

"What harm can they do her?" pursued the Governor. "Daisy's a nice girl, and Medland—well, the worst he can do is to make her a Radical, and it doesn't matter two straws what she is."

Lady Eynesford's foot tapped on the floor.

"I suppose you'll laugh at me," she said. "Indeed it's absurd enough to make any one laugh, but, Willie, I'm not quite sure that Alicia isn't too much—"

The sentence was cut short by the entrance of Alicia herself.

"Ah! Al!" cried the Governor. "Come here. Would you like to join Dick in Australia?"

Alicia started.

"He says he's lonely, and I thought it would be such a nice trip for you," added Lady Eynesford.

"Dick lonely! What nonsense! It only means he wants to come back, Mary."

Dick's pathos was evidently a broken reed. Lady Eynesford let it go, and said,

"Anyhow, you might take advantage of his being there to see Australia."

"I don't want to see Australia," answered Alicia. "I much prefer New Lindsey."

"You don't jump at Mary's proposal?"

"I utterly decline," laughed Alicia, and, taking the book she had come in search of, she went out.

"You see. She won't go," remarked Lady Eynesford.

"I never thought she would. What were you going to say when she came in?"

Lady Eynesford rose and stood by her husband.

"Willie," she said, "what is it about the Medlands? I'm tired of not knowing whether there is anything or whether there isn't."

"I don't know, my dear. There's some gossip, I believe," said Lord Eynesford discreetly.

"Do you know what Mrs. Puttock said to Eleanor? Eleanor ought to have told me at once, but she only did last night. Eleanor asked something about his wife, and Mrs. Puttock said, 'For my part, I don't believe he ever had a wife.'" Lady Eynesford repeated the all-important sentence with scrupulous accuracy.

"By Jove!" exclaimed the Governor. "That was what—" He checked himself before Kilshaw's name could leave his lips.

"Yes? Now, Willie, if that's true or—or anything like it, you know, is it right for Alicia to be constantly with Daisy Medland and—and in and out of the house, you know?"

The Governor looked grave. The thing was tangible enough now, and demanded to be dealt with more urgently than it ever had before.

"It's a pity Eleanor didn't speak sooner," he said.

"She thought less of it because Mrs. Puttock is a vulgar old gossip."

"Yes; but I'm afraid there may be something in it. Why did Eleanor tell you now?"

"Because I was speaking to her about the way Mr. Medland monopolised Alicia in the Park the other afternoon."

"Oh, that was my fault."

"It makes no difference how it came about. Willie, she had eyes and ears for no one else," and Lady Eynesford's voice became very earnest.

"But it's preposterous, Mary. You must be wrong. There couldn't possibly be anything of the kind."

"You know the sort of girl she is," his wife went on. "She's—well, she's easily caught by an idea, and rather romantic, and—really, dear, we ought to be careful."

"I can't believe it. If it's true, Medland has treated me very badly."

"What does he care?" asked Lady Eynesford. "How I wish she would go away! Nothing I say seems to make any impression on her."

"Perhaps Medland has noticed nothing, even if you're right about Alicia."

"He couldn't help noticing."

"What? Do you mean she makes it—?"

"I don't want to say anything unkind, but—well, yes, I'm afraid she does."

The Governor took a pace along the room.

"Upon my word," he exclaimed impatiently, "the way we get mixed up with these people is absurdly awkward. First there's Dick—"

"That's nothing to this. Dick was never really serious, and Alicia's always serious, if she thinks about a thing at all."

"Well, well, of course it must be stopped. What are you

going to do?"

"She must be told," said Lady Eynesford.

"I won't tell her."

"Then I must."

"I wonder if you're not wrong after all."

"Oh, watch them!" retorted Lady Eynesford, and, leaving her husband, she sought Alicia and invited her to come and have a talk in the verandah.

Alicia, when thus summoned, was sitting with Eleanor Scaife, and they were both watching Captain Heseltine's fox terrier jump over a walking-stick under his master's tuition. It was a suitable enough amusement for a hot day; and it was engrossing enough to prevent Eleanor raising her eyes at the sound of Lady Eynesford's voice. In fact, she was not over and above anxious to meet that lady's glance. Eleanor had, in the light of recent events, grown rather doubtful of the wisdom of her wonderful discretion, and Lady Eynesford had intimated, with her usual clearness of statement, a decided opinion that not Eleanor, but she herself was the proper person to judge what should and should not be told to Alicia. She had enforced her moral by hinting at very distressing consequences which might follow on Eleanor's unfortunate reticence.

"I sometimes think," Eleanor remarked to Heseltine, when Alicia had left them, "that perfect openness and candour are always best."

Captain Heseltine lowered the walking-stick and looked at her with an air of expectancy.

"It saves so much misunderstanding, if you tell everybody everything right out," continued Eleanor.

"For my part," returned Heseltine, with an earnestness which he rarely displayed, "I differ utterly. I've never in my life told anybody anything without being sorry I hadn't held my tongue."

"Oh, you mean your private affairs."

"Well, and you? Oh, I see. You only mean other people's. Agreed, agreed! Perfect openness and candour about them by all means!"

"I am quite serious. One never knows how much harm may be done by concealing them."

"Got a murder on your conscience?"

"Oh, not exactly," sighed Eleanor.

"You're like that chap Kilshaw. He's always talking as if he had something awful up his sleeve."

"Perhaps he has."

As Eleanor said this, she jumped up and ran to meet Alicia, whom she saw coming towards her. Lady Eynesford had wasted no time over her task.

The Captain, being left alone, did the appropriate thing. He soliloquised.

"She'd have told me in another half-minute," said he, with a chuckle. "It was choking her. Yet she's a sensible one as they go."

Whom or what class he meant by "they" it is merciful to his ignorant prejudices to leave unrevealed.

CHAPTER XVIII

BY AN OVERSIGHT OF SOCIETY'S

François Gaspard was a pleasant and cheerful man, good company, and genial to his neighbours and comrades, but it may be doubted whether Society had not made a grave mistake in not hanging him at the earliest opportunity. In his younger days he had lived in perpetual warfare against Society, its institutions and constitutions—a warfare that he carried on without scruple and without quarter: he would have had no cause for complaint had he been dealt with on this basis of his own choosing. Society, however, had chosen to fancy that it could reform François, or, failing that, could keep him alive and yet harmless. Thanks to this sanguine view, he found himself, at the age of forty-five, a free man in New Lindsey; and, thinking that he and his native country had had about enough of one another, he had enrolled himself as a subject of her Majesty, and had plunged into the affairs of his new home with his usual energy. François was not indeed quite the man he had been in his palmy time, his nerve was not so good, and his life was more comfortable, and therefore not so lightly to be risked; but he had made no renunciations, and often regretted that New Lindsey was a barren soil, wherein the seed he sowed bore little fruit. He could not be happy without a secret society, and that he had established in Kirton; but it was, he ruefully admitted, hardly

Anthony Hope

more than a toy, a mockery, the merest *simulacrum*. The members displayed no alacrity; they were but five all told, besides himself: a bookseller's assistant, a watchmaker (he was a German, but the larger cause harmonised all differences), two artisans, and—what is either natural or strange, according to one's estimation of parliamentary government—a doorkeeper in the Houses of Parliament. They used to meet at Gaspard's lodgings, regret, in tones as loud as prudence permitted, the abuses of the *status quo*, spend a social evening, and return to the outer world with a tickling sense of mystery and potential destructiveness. Gaspard held the very lowest opinion of them; he acknowledged that the "propaganda by action" took small root in New Lindsey, and when it came into his head that Mr. Benham was worse than superfluous, he admitted with a shrug the great difficulties that lay in the way of removing his acquaintance. A man could not do everything by himself, the matter was after all not very pressing, and he almost made up his mind to let Mr. Benham live. Such was the chain of his reflections, and if Society had clearly realised the way he looked at such things, it can hardly be supposed that Gaspard would have been left unhanged.

Nevertheless, almost academic as the question was, Gaspard indulged his humour by hinting to his associates that, in certain contingencies, there might be work for their hands. He would not be more explicit, for he was distrustful of them; but this vague hint was quite enough to cause some perturbation. The bookseller's assistant turned rather pale, and expressed a preference for waiting till one final, decisive, and overwhelming blow could be struck. He was understood to favour a wholesale massacre at Government House, but reminded his hearers of the dangers of hasty action. The watchmaker was strong on the division of functions: one man was valuable in counsel, another in the field; he belonged, he said, to the former category. The artisans smiled broadly over their drink, and openly declared that the President must "give 'em a lead." The doorkeeper reinforced this suggestion by reminding them that he was a husband and father, whereas Gaspard was a bachelor. All united in asking for further information, and were annoyed when Gaspard referred them to the rule governing such associations as theirs, namely, that the member to carry out the deed, if resolved upon, should be designated before the nature of the deed was discussed, or its desirability finally decided. If this were not so, he pointed out, a member's opinion on the merits of the scheme might be biased by the knowledge that he would, if fate so willed, have to carry it out. According to his rule, the designated member had no vote.

"Not know who it is?" exclaimed the doorkeeper. "Why, a man might be asked to take off his own brother!"

"Perfectly," smiled Gaspard. "It is to avoid any painful conflict of duties that the rule exists." He looked round the table with a broader smile, and added—"Shall it be the lot?"

The feeling of the meeting was against the lot. They preferred to choose their man.

"Let's vote by ballot," suggested the watchmaker.

"Agreed!" cried Gaspard, and they flung folded scraps of paper into a hat.

There was one vote for the doorkeeper: it came out first, and the doorkeeper wiped a bead of sweat from his brow. But soon he smiled again; the other four were all for Gaspard, who returned thanks for the honour in a few words.

"As soon as the information is complete, I will summon you

again," he said, dismissing them, and lighting his cigarette with a chuckle of mockery. Really, it seemed impossible to do anything with these creatures, and Gaspard did not feel quite so eager as he used to be to put his own neck in the noose. If he acted, he must, probably, fly from New Lindsey, and he was very comfortable and doing very well there. No; on second thoughts he doubted if the duty of removing Mr. Benham was absolutely imperative.

Meanwhile Benham would have been much surprised to hear that his latter end was a subject of dispassionate contemplation to the little Frenchman. No subject was more remote from his own thoughts. He was in high feather, the hour was fast approaching which was to witness his triumph and his revenge; the gag would soon be taken from his mouth, and his deadly disclosure would smite Medland like a sword. His sentiment was satisfied with the prospect, and Kilshaw took care that his pocket should have nothing to complain of. He refused indeed to provide for Benham in his own employ for obvious reasons; but he promised him a strong, though private, recommendation to an important house, in addition to the agreed price of his information, which was a thousand pounds, half to be paid in advance. The first five hundred pounds was paid on the day before the Premier's great meeting, for, if the Ministry weathered Monday's storm, the last weapon in the arsenal was to be brought into use. So said Mr. Kilshaw, still hoping to avoid the necessity, still resolute to face it if he must. Benham took his money and went his way, with one of those familiar, confidential looks and jocular speeches which filled Kilshaw's cup of disgust to the brim. Whenever the man did that sort of thing, Kilshaw was within an ace of kicking him down-stairs and throwing away the poisoned weapon; but he never did.

Mere chance willed that as Gaspard on Saturday evening was going home, having done a hard day's work at organising a trade procession for the next day, he should fall in with Benham. He stopped to speak, feeling an interest in all that concerned the man; and Benham, radiant and effusive from the process of "moistening his luck," would not be satisfied till Gaspard had agreed to sup with him and at his charges.

"Oh, if you like to do a good deed to an enemy," laughed the Frenchman, letting the other seize him by the arm and lead him off; and he thought to himself that he might as well spare so liberal a host. Might there not be other suppers in the future? Dead men, if they told no tales, paid for no suppers either.

After the meal they had another bottle of wine, and Benham called for a pack of cards. François won, and politely apologised.

"It is too bad of me," he said, "after your hospitality, *mon cher*."

"Oh, five pound won't hurt me, or ten either," cried Benham, draining his glass.

"No? Happy man!"

"I know where money comes from," continued Benham, with a wink.

"Ah, a man who knows what you do!" retorted Gaspard. "Have you forgotten telling me—you know—about our good Medland?"

"Did I tell you? Well, I had forgotten. Who cares! It's true—every word."

"Oh, I don't say it isn't," laughed Gaspard incredulously.

"But you don't believe it is?"

"We can't help our thoughts, but—" and another laugh ended his sentence.

Benham looked round. They were alone. Cautiously he drew a bag of money and a roll of notes from his pocket. For a moment he opened the bag and showed the gleam inside; wetting his forefinger, he parted the notes for a second.

"Some one believes it," he said, "up to five hundred pound."

"That's the sort of belief I'd like to inspire," laughed Gaspard, watching the money back into its pocket with a curious eye.

"Come, you're not drinking," urged the hospitable Benham.

"You don't show me the way," untruthfully answered the guest, as Benham complacently buttoned up his coat, little imagining that his neighbour was weighing a question, very momentous to him, in the light of fresh information.

Five hundred pounds! The duty of removing Benham began to look rather imperative again, but from a different point of view. François had of late worked for his living, a mode of existence which seemed to him anomalous, and ill suited to his genius. Five hundred pounds meant, to a man of his frugal habits and tact in eliciting hospitality three years' comfortable idleness. It was no doubt apparent now that Benham had already parted with his secret, and that, if anything happened to him, the secret would still remain to vex the good Medland. Gaspard regretted this; he would have liked to combine public and private advantage in the job. But a man must not ask everything, or he may end by having to take nothing. Here sat a drunken fool with five hundred pounds; opposite to him sat a sober sharp-wit with only five. The situation was full of suggestion. If the five hundred could be got from the fool without violence, well and good; but really, thought Mr. Gaspard, their transference to the sharp-wit must be effected somehow, or that sharp-wit had no title to the name.

"Care to play any more?" asked Benham.

"Not I, my friend, I have robbed you enough."

"And about time for the luck to turn, isn't it? Well, I don't care! What shall we do?"

"What you will," answered the Frenchman absently.

Benham pulled his beard, then leant forward and put a question with an intoxicated leer. A laugh of feigned reproof burst from Gaspard. Benham seemed to urge him, and at last he said,

"Oh, if you're bent on it, I can be your guide."

The two men left the house arm-in-arm, went down the street, and crossed Digby Square. It was late, and few people were about, but Gaspard saw one acquaintance. The door-keeper was strolling along on his way home, and Gaspard bade him good-night in a cheery voice as they passed him. The doorkeeper stood and watched the pair for a minute as they left the Square and turned down a narrow street which led to the poorer part of the town, and thence to the quays. He heard Gaspard's high-pitched voice and shrill laughter, and, in answer, Benham's thick tones and heavy shout of drunken mirth. Once or twice these sounds repeated themselves, then they ceased; the footsteps of the Frenchman and his companion died away in the distance. The door-keeper went on his way, thinking with relief that Mr.

Anthony Hope

Gaspard, for all his tall talk, was more at home with a bottle than with a knife or a bomb.

Notwithstanding his dissipation, Gaspard was afoot very early in the morning. It was hardly light, and the deep scratch of finger-nails on his face—it is so awkward when drunken fools wake at the wrong minute—attracted no attention from the few people he encountered. He did not give them long to look at him, for he hurried swiftly through the streets, towards the quays where the ships lay loading their cargoes. He seemed to have urgent business to transact down there, business that would brook no delay, and that was, if one might guess from his uneasy glances over his shoulder, of a private nature. With one hand he held tight hold of something in his trousers pocket, the other rested on his belt, hard by a little revolver. In his business it is necessary to be ready for everything.

Meanwhile Mr. Benham, having no affairs to trouble him, and no more business to transact, stayed where he was.

CHAPTER XIX

LAST CHANCES

At an early hour on Sunday all Kirton seemed astir. The streets were alive with thronging people, with banners, with inchoate and still amorphous processions, with vendors of meat, drink, and newspapers. According to the official arrangements, the proceedings were not to begin till one o'clock, and, in theory, the forenoon hours were left undisturbed; but, what with the people who were taking part in the demonstration, and those who were going to look on, and those who hoped to suck some profit to themselves out of the day's work, the ordinary duties and observances of a Sunday were largely neglected, and Mr. Puttock, passing on his way to chapel at the head of his family, did not lack material for reprobation in the temporary superseding of religious obligations.

The Governor and his family drove to the Cathedral, according to their custom, Eleanor Scaife having pleaded in vain for leave to walk about the streets instead. Lady Eynesford declined to recognise the occasion, and Eleanor had to content herself with stealthy glances to right and left till the church doors engulfed her. The only absentee was Alicia Derosne, and she was not walking about the streets, but sitting under the verandah, with a book unopened on her knees, and her eyes set in empty fixedness on the horizon. The luxuriant growth of a southern summer filled her nostrils with sweet scents, and the wind, blowing off the sea, tempered the heat to a fresh and balmy warmth; the waves sparkled in the sun, and the world was loud in boast of its own beauty; but poor Alicia, like many a maid before, was wondering how long this wretched life was to last, and how any one was ever happy. Faith bruised and trust misplaced blotted out for her the joy of living and the exultation of youth. If these things were true, why did the sun shine, and how could the world be merry? If these things were true, for her the sun shone no more, and the merriment was stilled for ever. So she thought, and, if she were not right, it needed a philosopher to tell her so; and then she would not have believed him, but caught her woe closer to her heart, and nursed it with fiercer tenderness against his shallow prating. Perhaps he might have told her too, that it is cruel kindness unasked to set people on a pinnacle, and, when they cannot keep foothold on that slippery height, to scorn their fall. Other things such an one might well have said, but more wisely left unsaid; for cool reason is a blister to heartache, and heartache is not best cured by blisters. Never yet did a child stop crying for being told its pain was nought and would soon be gone. Yet this prescription had been Lady Eynesford's—although she was no philosopher, to her knowledge—for Alicia, and it had left the patient protesting that she felt no pain at all, and yet feeling it all the more.

"What do you accuse me of? Why do you speak to me?" she had burst out. "What is it to me what he has done or not done? What do you mean, Mary?"

Before this torrent of questions Lady Eynesford tactfully retreated a little way. A warning against hasty love dwindled to an appeal whether so much friendliness, such constant meetings, either with daughter or with father, were desirable.

"I'm sure I'm sorry for the poor child," she said; "but in this world—"

"Suppose it's all a slander!"

"My dear Alicia, do they say such things about a man in his position unless there's something in them?"

"It's nothing to me," said Alicia again.

"Of course, you can do nothing abrupt; but you'll gradually withdraw from their acquaintance, won't you?"

Alicia had escaped without a promise, pleading for time to think in the same breath that she denied any concern in the matter. She was by way of thinking now, and all that Lady Eynesford had said repeated itself in her mind as she looked out on the garden and the glimpses of the town beyond. She understood now Dick's banishment, her sister-in-law's unresting hostility to the Medlands, and the reason why she had been pressed to go to Australia. She spared a minute to grief for Daisy, but her own sorrow would not be denied, and engrossed her again. In the solitude she had sought, she cried to herself, "Why didn't they tell me before? What's the use of telling me now?" Then she would fly back to the hope that the thing was not true, that her friends had clutched too hastily at anything which would save her from what they dreaded, and, she confessed to herself, rightly dreaded. No, she would not believe it yet; and, if it were not true, why should she not be happy? Why should she not, even though she did what Dick had not dared to do, and what, when Coxon asked her, she had laughed at for an absurdity?

There began to be more movement outside the gates. The first note of band-music was wafted to her ear, and the roll of wheels announced the return of the church-goers. She roused

Anthony Hope

herself and went to meet them. They were agog with excitement, partly about the meeting, partly about the murder. While Eleanor was trying to tell her of the state of popular feeling, the Governor seized her arm and began to detail the story of the discovery.

"You remember the man?" he asked. "He was at our flower-show—had a sort of row with Medland, you know. Well, he's been found murdered (so the police think) in a low part of the town! The woman who keeps the house found him. He didn't come down in the morning, and, as she couldn't make him hear, she forced the door, and found him with his throat cut."

"Awful!" shuddered Lady Eynesford. "He looked such a respectable man too."

"Ah, I fancy he'd gone a bit to the bad lately—taken to drinking and so on."

"He was a friend of Mr. Kilshaw's, wasn't he?" asked Alicia.

"A sort of hanger-on, I think. Anyhow, there he was dead, and with his pockets empty."

"Perhaps he killed himself," she suggested.

"They think not. They've arrested the woman, but she declares she knows nothing about it!"

"Poor man!" said Alicia; and, at another time, she might have thought a good deal about the horrible end of a man whom she had known as an acquaintance. But, as it was, she soon forgot him again, and, leaving the rest, returned to her solitary seat.

In the town, the news of the murder was but one ruffle more on the wave of excitement, and not a very marked one. Few people knew Benham's name, and when the first agitation following on the discovery of the body died away and the onlookers found there was no news to be had, they turned away to join the processions or to stare at them. The police were left to pursue their investigations in peace, and they soon reached a conclusion. The landlady of the house where Benham died lived alone, save for the occasional presence of her son: he was away at work in an outlying district, and she had been the only person in the house that night. She let beds to single men, she said, and the night before two men had arrived, one the worse for drink. They had asked for adjoining rooms. As they went up-stairs, she had heard the one who had been drinking say to the other, "What are you bringing me here for? This isn't the place for what I want." His companion, the shorter of the two, whom she thought she would know again, had answered—"All in good time; you go and lie down, and I'll fetch what you want." Soon after, the short one came down and asked if she had any brandy; she gave him a bottle half full and he went up-stairs again. She heard voices raised as if in dispute for a few minutes, and one of them—she could not say which—said something which sounded like "Well, finish the drink first, and then I'll go." Silence followed, at least she could not hear any more talking; and presently, it not being her business to spy on gentlemen, she went to bed, and knew nothing more till she woke at seven o'clock. Going up-stairs, she found one door open and the room empty, not the room the two men had been in together, but the other. The second door was locked, and she did not knock; gentlemen often slept late. At half-past ten she ventured to knock, got no answer, knocked again and again, and finally, with the help of the man from next door, broke the lock and found the taller of the two men dead on the bed. She had at once summoned the police; and that, she concluded, was all she knew about the matter, and she was a respectable, hard-working woman, a widow who could produce her marriage certificate in case any person present desired to inspect it.

The Superintendent listened to her protestations of virtue with an ironical smile, told her the police knew her house very well, frightened her wholesomely, took down her very vague description of the missing man, and kept her in custody; but he did not seriously doubt the truth of her story, and, if it were true, the man he wanted was evidently the sober man, the shorter man, who had introduced his friend to the house on a pretext, had called for drink, and vanished in the early morning, leaving a dead man behind him. Who was this man? Where did he come from? Had he been missing since last night? On these inquiries the Superintendent launched several intelligent men, and then was forced for the time to turn his attention to the business of the day.

To search a large town for a missing man takes time, and the searchers did not happen to fall in with Company B of Procession 3, which at one o'clock had mustered in Digby Square, prepared to march to the Public Park. Had they done so, it might or might not have seemed to them worth noticing that Company B of Procession 3, which was composed of carpenters and joiners, had missed some one, namely the officer whom they called their "Marshal," and who was to have ordered their ranks and marched at their head; and the name of their Marshal was none other than François Gaspard. The Superintendent himself was keeping watch over Company B, but, in a professionally Olympian scorn of processions, he was far from asking or caring to know who the Marshal was, and indeed, if he had known, he would scarcely have drawn such a lightning-quick inference as that the missing Marshal and the missing murderer were one and the same. So Mr. Gaspard's absence was passed over with a few curses on his laziness, or, from the more charitable, a surmise that there had been a misunderstanding, and Company B, having appointed a new Marshal, went on its way.

One demonstration of the public will is much like another in the shape it takes and the incidents it produces. This Sunday's was, however, as friends and foes agreed, remarkable not only for the numbers who took part, but still more for the spirit which animated it, and when the Premier and his colleagues made their appearance on the great platform there was no room to doubt that somehow, by his gifts or his faults, his policy or his demagogic arts, his love of humanity or his adroit wooing of popularity, Medland held a position in the eyes of the common people of the capital which had seldom or never been equalled in the history of the Colony. He had caused them to be called together in order to raise their enthusiasm, and to elicit from them a visible, unmistakable pledge of support. But, when he stood before them, bareheaded, in vain beckoning for silence, their cries and cheers told him that his task was rather to moderate than to stir up, and the first part of his speech was a somewhat laboured proof of the consistency of gatherings of that nature with the proper independence of representative assemblies. The people heard him through this argument in respectful silence, clapping their hands when, at the end of it, he paused before he passed to the second part of his speech. At the first sign of attack, at the first quietly drawn contrast between what the seceders had promised and what they were doing, his audience was a changed one. Fierce murmurs of assent and groans became audible now, and when Medland, caught by the contagion that spread to him from his listeners, gave rein to his feelings, and launched into a passionate declaration that, to his mind, the liberty claimed for members did not mean liberty to betray those who had trusted them, the murmurs and groans rose into one tumult of savage applause, and men raised both hands over their heads and shook them, as though they would have clenched every word that fell from him with a blow of the fist.

Daisy Medland sat just behind her father, exulting in his triumph, and, at every happy stroke, glancing at Norburn, and by sharing her joy with him doubling his. When the Premier had finished, and the last resolution had been carried, she ran to him, crying, "Splendid! I never heard you so good. Wasn't he splendid?" and looking so completely joyful that Medland was sure she must quite have forgotten Dick Derosne. She took his arm, and they made their way together to a carriage which was in waiting. An escort of police surrounded it, to save the Premier from his friends, and he, with Daisy, Norburn, and Mr. Floyd, the Treasurer, got in without disturbance. The coachman drove off rapidly down the main avenue, distancing the enthusiasts who would have had the horses out of the shafts. They passed a long row of carriages, belonging to people who had not feared to come and look on from a distance, and at last, knowing the procession would go back another way, Medland bade his driver stop under the trees, and lit a cigar.

"And I wonder if it will all make any difference!" said he, puffing delightedly. He had all an old political organiser's love for a big meeting, which does not exclude scepticism as to its value.

"Oh, you gave it 'em finely," said the Treasurer.

"I believe it'll frighten two or three anyhow," observed Norburn.

"I *know* we shall win to-morrow," cried Daisy, squeezing her father's arm.

"Ah! here's a special Sunday evening paper—how we

encourage wickedness!" said the Premier, seeing a news-vendor approaching. "Let's see what they say of us!"

"I've seen it all for myself," remarked Daisy, and she went on chattering to the other two, who were ready to talk over every incident of the meeting, as people who have been to meetings ever are. On they went, reminding one another of the bald man in the third row who cheered so lustily, of the fat woman who had somehow got into the front row and fanned herself all the time, of rude things shouted about Messrs. Puttock and Coxon, and so forth. The Premier, listening with one ear, opened his paper; but the first thing he saw was not about his procession. He started and looked closer, then gave a sudden, covert glance at his companions; they were busy in talk, and, with breathless haste, he devoured the meagre details of Benham's wretched death. The end reached, he let the paper fall on his knees, lay back, and took a long pull at his cigar. He was shocked—yes, he supposed he was shocked. He had known the man, and it was shocking to think of his throat being cut; yes, he had known him, and he didn't like to think of that. But—The Premier gave a long-drawn sigh of relief. That unknown murderer's hand had done great things for him. His daughter was safe now—anyhow, she was safe. She could never be subject to the degradation the dead man had once hinted at; and when he thought of what the man had threatened, pity for him died out of Medland's heart. More—although Kilshaw no doubt knew something—there was a chance that Benham had kept his own counsel, and that his employer would be helpless without his aid. Medland's sanguine mind caught eagerly at the chance, and in a moment turned it into a hope—almost a conviction. Then the whole thing would go down to the grave with the unlucky man, and not even its spectre survive to trouble him. For if no one had certain knowledge, if there were never more than gossip, growing, as time passed, fainter and fainter from having no food to feed on, would not

Anthony Hope

utter silence follow at last, so that the things that had been might be as if they had never been?

"Well, what do they say about us?" asked the Treasurer.

"Oh, nothing much," he answered, thrusting the paper behind him with a careless air. He did not want to discuss what the paper had told him.

"What's happened to-day," said Daisy, "ought to make all the difference, oughtn't it, father?"

"I hope it will," replied the Premier; but, for once in his life, he was not thinking most about political affairs.

CHAPTER XX

THE LAW *VERSUS* RULE 3

Among the many tired but satisfied lovers of liberty who sought their houses that night, while an enthusiastic remnant was still parading the streets, illuminations yet shining from windows, and weary police treading their unending beats, was the doorkeeper, who had borne a banner in Company A of Procession 1. His friend the watchmaker came with him, to have a bit of supper and exchange congratulations and fulminations. Hardly, however, had the doorkeeper pledged the cause in a first draught when his wife broke in on his oration by handing him a letter, which she said a boy in a blue jersey had left for him about ten o'clock in the morning, just after he had started to join his company. The envelope was cheap and coarse; there was no direction outside. The doorkeeper opened it. It was addressed to no named person and it bore no signature. It was very brief, being confined to these simple words—"You did not see me last night. Remember Rule 3."

The doorkeeper laid the letter down, with a hurried glance at his friend, whose face was buried in a mug. He knew the handwriting; he knew who it was that he had not seen; he remembered Rule 3, the rule that said—"The only and inevitable penalty of treachery is death." He turned white and took a hasty gulp at his liquor.

"Who brought this?" he asked.

"I told you," answered his wife; "a lad in a blue jersey; he looked as if he might be from the harbour." She put food before them, adding as she did so—"I suppose you've been too full of your politics to hear much about the murder?"

"The murder?" exclaimed the watchmaker. The doorkeeper crumpled up his letter and stuffed it into the pocket of his coat, while his wife read to them the story of the discovery. The watchmaker listened with interest.

"Benham!" he remarked. "I never heard the name, did you?"

"You know him, Ned," said the doorkeeper's wife; "him as Mr. Gaspard used to go about with."

By a sudden common impulse, the eyes of the two men met; the woman went off to brew them a pot of tea, and left them fearfully gazing at one another.

"What stuff!" said the watchmaker uneasily. "It was only his blow. What reason had he—?" He paused and added, "Seen him to-day, Ned?"

"No," answered Ned, fingering his note.

"Wasn't he in the procession?"

"I didn't see him."

"When did you see him last?"

The doorkeeper hesitated.

"Night of our last committee," he whispered finally.

"Oh, there's nothing in it," said the watchmaker reassuringly. He had not a letter in his pocket.

The doorkeeper opened his mouth to speak, but seeing his wife approaching, he shut it again and busied himself with his meal.

"What was the letter, Ned?"

"Oh, about the procession," he answered.

"Then you got it too late. Who was it from?"

"If you'd give us the tea," he broke out roughly, "and let the damned letter alone, it 'ud be a deal better."

"La, you needn't fly out at a woman so," said Mrs. Evans. "It ain't the way to treat his wife, is it, mister?"

"Mister" gallantly reproved his friend, but pleaded that they were both weary, and weary legs made short tempers. Giving them the tea, she left them to themselves; her work was not finished till three small children were safely in bed.

The sensation of having one's neck for the first time within measurable distance of a rope must needs be somewhat disquieting. The doorkeeper, in spite of his secret society doings, was a timid man, with a vastly respectful fear of the law. To talk about things, to vapour idly about them over the cups, is very different from being actually, even though remotely, mixed up in them. Ned Evans was a man of some education: he read the papers, accounts of crimes and reports of trials; he had heard of accessories after and before the fact. Was he not an accessory after the fact? He fancied they did not hang such; but if they caught him, and all that about Gaspard and the society came out, would they not call him an accessory before the fact? The noose seemed really rather near, and in his frightened fancy, as he lay sleepless beside his snoring wife, the rope dangled over his head. The poor wretch was between the devil and the deep sea—between stern law and cruel Rule 3. He dared not toss about, his wife would ask him what ailed him; he lay as still as he could, bitterly cursing his folly for mingling in such affairs, bitterly cursing the Frenchman who led him on into the trap and left him fast there. How could he save his neck? And he restlessly rent the band of his coarse night-shirt, that pressed on his throat with a horrible suggestion of what might be. Where was that Gaspard? Had he fled over the sea? Ah, if he could be sure of that, and sure that the dreaded man would not return! Or was he lurking in some secret hole, ready to steal out and avenge a violation of Rule 3? The doorkeeper had always feared the man; in the lurid light of this deed, Gaspard's image grew into a monster of horror, threatening sudden and swift revenge for disobedience or treachery. No; he must stand firm. But what of the police? Well, men sleep somehow, and at last he fell asleep, holding the band of the night-shirt away from his throat: if he fell asleep with that pressing on him, God knew what he might dream.

"It's very lucky," remarked the Superintendent of Police, who had a happy habit of looking at the bright side of things, to one of his subordinates, "that this Benham seems to have had no relations and precious few friends."

"No widows coming crying about," observed the subordinate, with an assenting nod.

"Nothing known of him except that he came to Kirton a few months back, did nothing, seemed to have plenty of money, took his liquor, played a hand at cards, hurt nobody, seemingly knew nobody."

"Why, I saw him with Mr. Puttock."

"Yes; but Mr. Puttock knows nothing of him, except that he said he came from Shepherdstown. That's why Puttock was civil to him. The place is in his constituency."

"Got any idea, sir?" the subordinate ventured to ask.

The Superintendent was about to answer in the negative, when a detective entered the room.

"Well, I've found one missing man for you," he said, in a satisfied tone.

"One missing man!" echoed his superior, scornfully. "In a place o' this size I'd always find you twenty."

The sergeant went on, unperturbed,

"François Gaspard, known as politician and agitator, didn't go home to his lodgings in Kettle Street last night, was to have acted as Marshal in Company B of Procession 3 to-day, didn't turn up, hasn't turned up to-night, don't owe any rent, hasn't taken any clothes."

"Oh!" said the Superintendent morosely. "Left an address?"

"Left no address, sir."

"How did he go, and where?"

"Not known, sir."

"Good Lord!" moaned the Superintendent, "and what's

your salary?"

The sergeant's good-humour was impregnable.

"Give me time," he said, and the sentence was almost drowned in a loud knock at the door. An instant later Kilshaw rushed in.

"What's this, Dawson?" he cried to the Superintendent; "what's this about the murder?"

"You haven't heard, sir?"

"I went out of town to avoid this infernal row to-day, and am only just back."

Dawson smiled discreetly. He could understand that the proceedings of the day would not attract Mr. Kilshaw.

"But is it true," Kilshaw went on eagerly, "that Mr. Benham has been murdered?"

"Well, it looks like it, sir," and Dawson gave a full account of the circumstances.

"And the motive?" asked Kilshaw.

"Robbery, I suppose. His pockets were empty, and according to our information he was generally flush of money; where he got it, I don't know."

"Ah!" said Kilshaw meditatively; "his pockets empty! And have you no clue?"

"Not what you'd call a clue. Did you know the gentleman, sir?"

Kilshaw replied by saying that Mr. Puttock had introduced Benham to him and the acquaintance had continued—it was a political acquaintance purely.

"You don't know anything about him before he came here?"

Kilshaw suddenly perceived that he was being questioned, whereas his object had been to question.

"You say," he observed, "that you haven't got what you'd call a clue. What do you mean?"

"You can tell Mr. Kilshaw, if you like," said the Superintendent to the sergeant, who repeated his information.

"Gaspard! why that's the fellow the Premier—" and Mr. Kilshaw stopped short. After a moment, he asked abruptly, "Were there any papers on the body?"

"None, sir."

"I suppose there's nothing really to connect this man Gaspard with it?"

"Oh, nothing at present, sir. Did you say you'd known the deceased before he—?"

"If I'm called at the inquest, I shall tell all I know," said Kilshaw, rising. "It's not much."

"Happen to know if he had any relations, sir?"

"H'm. He was a widower, I believe."

"Children?"

"Really," said Mr. Kilshaw, with a faint smile, "I don't know."

And he escaped from pertinacious Mr. Dawson with some alacrity. When he was outside, he stopped suddenly. "Shall I tell 'em to apply to Medland?" he asked himself, with a malicious chuckle. "No, I'll wait a bit yet," and he walked on, wondering whether by any chance Mr. Benham had been done to death to save the Premier. This fanciful idea he soon dismissed with a laugh; it never entered his head, prejudiced as he was, to think that Medland himself had any hand in the matter. After all, he was a man of common sense, and he quickly arrived at a conclusion which he expressed by exclaiming,

"The poor fool's been showing his money. Who's got my five hundred now, I wonder?"

His wonderings would have been satisfied, had Aladdin's carpet or other magical contrivance transported him to where the steamship *Pride of the South* was ploughing her way through the waves, bound from Kirton to San Francisco, with liberty to touch at several South American ports. A thick-set, short man, shipped at the last moment as cook's mate, in substitution for a truant, was lying on his back, smoking a cigarette, looking up at the bright stars, and ever and again gently pressing his hand on a little lump inside his shirt. He seemed at peace with all the world, though he was ready to be at war, if need be, and his knife, burnished and clean, lay handy to his fingers. He turned on his side and composed himself to sleep, his chest rising and falling with regular, uninterrupted breathing. Once he smiled: he was thinking of Ned Evans, the doorkeeper; then he gave himself a little shake, closed his eyes, and forgot all the troubles of this weary world. So sleep children, so—we are told—the just: so slept M. François Gaspard, on his way to seek fresh woods and pastures new.

CHAPTER XXI

ALL THERE WAS TO TELL

The custom in New Lindsey was that every Monday during the session of Parliament the Executive Council should meet at Government House, and, under the presidency of the Governor, formally ratify and adopt the arrangements as to the business of the coming week which its members had decided upon at their Cabinet meetings. It is to be hoped that, in these days, when we all take an interest in our Empire, everybody knows that the Executive Council is the outward, visible, and recognised form of that impalpable, unrecognised, all-powerful institution, the Cabinet, consisting in fact, though not in theory, of the same persons, save that the Governor is present when the meeting is of the Council, and absent when it is of the Cabinet—a difference of less moment than it sounds, seeing that, except in extreme cases, the Governor has little to do but listen to what is going to be done. However, forms doubtless have their value, and at any rate they must be observed, so on this Monday morning the Executive Council was to meet as usual, although nobody knew where the Cabinet would be that time twenty-four hours. Lady Eynesford, who wanted her husband to drive her out, thought the meeting under the circumstances mere nonsense—which it very likely was—and said so, which betrayed inexperience, and Alicia Derosne asked what time it

Anthony Hope

took place.

"Eleven sharp," said the Governor, and returned to the account of the murder.

Time after time in the last few days Alicia had told herself that she could bear it no longer. At one moment she believed nothing, the next, nothing was too terrible for her to believe; now she would fly to Australia, or home, or anywhere out of New Lindsey; now a straightforward challenge to Medland alone would serve her turn. Sometimes she felt as if she could put the whole thing on one side; five minutes later found her pinning her whole life on the issue of it. Under her guarded face and calm demeanour, the storm of divided and conflicting instincts and passions raged, and long solitary rambles became a necessary outlet for what she dared show to none. She shrank from seeing Medland, and yet longed to speak with him; she felt that to mention the topic to him was impossible, and yet, if they met, inevitable; that she would not have strength to face him, and yet could not let him go without clearing up the mystery. She told herself at one moment that she hardly knew him, at the next that between them nothing could be too secret for utterance.

What she hoped and feared befell her that morning. She went out for a walk in the Park, and before long she met the Premier, with his daughter and Norburn. The two last were laughing and talking—their quarrel was quite forgotten now—and Medland himself, she thought, looked as though his load of care were a little less heavy. The two men explained that they were on their way—a roundabout way, they confessed—to the Council, and had seized the chance of some fresh air, while Daisy was full of stories about yesterday's triumph, that left room only for a passing reference to yesterday's tragedy.

"I didn't like him at all," she said; "but still it's dreadful—a man one knew ever so slightly!"

Alicia agreed, and the next instant she found herself practically alone with Medland; for Daisy ran off to pick a wild-flower that caught her eye in the wood, and Norburn followed her. Not knowing whether to be glad or sorry, she made no effort to escape, and was silent while Medland began to speak of his prospects in that evening's division.

Suddenly she paused in her walk and lifted her eyes to his.

"You look happier," she said.

Medland's conscience smote him: he was looking happier because the man was dead.

"It's at the prospect of being a free man to-morrow," he answered, with a smile. "You know, Cincinnatus was very happy."

"But you're not like that."

"No, I suppose not. Say it's—"

"Never mind."

After a pause she made another attempt.

"Mr. Medland!"

"Yes?"

"You've been very good to me—yes, very good."

He turned to her with a gesture of disclaimer. She thought he

Anthony Hope

was going to speak, but he did not.

"Whatever happens, I shall always remember that with— with deep gratitude."

"What is going to happen?" he asked, with an uneasy smile.

"Oh, how can I?" she burst out. "How can I say it? How can I ask you?"

As she spoke she stopped, and he followed her example. They stood facing one another now, as he replied gravely,

"Whatever you ask—let it be what it will—I will answer, truthfully." A pause before the last word perhaps betrayed a momentary struggle.

"What right have I? Why should you?"

"The right my—my desire to have your regard gives you. How can I ask for that, unless I am ready to tell you all you can wish to know?"

"I have heard," she began falteringly, "I have been told by— by people who, I suppose, were right to tell me—"

In a moment he understood her. A slight twitch of his mouth betrayed his trouble, but he came to her rescue.

"I don't know how it reached you," he said. "Perhaps I think you might have been—you need not have known it. But there is only one thing you can have heard, that it would distress you to speak of."

She said nothing, but fixed her eyes on his.

"I am right?" he asked. "It is about—my wife?"

She bowed her head. He stood silent for a moment, and she cried,

"It was only gossip—a woman's gossip; I did wrong to listen to it."

"Gossip," he said, "is often true. This is true," and he set his lips.

The worst often finds or makes people calm. She had flushed at first, but the colour went again, and she said quietly,

"If you have time and don't mind, I should like to hear it all."

She had forgotten what this request must mean to him, or perhaps she thought the time for pretence had gone by. If so, he understood, for he answered,

"It's your right."

Her eyes sank to the ground, but she did not quarrel with his words. She stood motionless while he told his story. He spoke with wilful brevity and dryness.

"I was a young man when I met her. She was married, and I went to the house. Her husband—"

"Did he ill-treat her?"

"No. In his way, I suppose he was fond of her. But—she didn't like his way. She was very beautiful, and I fell in love with her, and she with me. And we ran away."

"Is—is that all? Is there no—?"

"No excuse? No, I suppose, none. And I lived with her till she died four years ago. And—Daisy is our daughter."

"And he—the husband?"

"He did not divorce her. I don't know why not, perhaps because she asked him to—anyhow he didn't. And he outlived her: so she died—as she had lived."

"And is he still alive?"

"No; he is dead now." He was about to go on, but checked himself. Why add that horror? How the man died was nothing between her and him.

"Have you no—nothing to say?" she burst out, almost angrily. "You just tell me that and stop!"

"What is there to say? I have told you all there is to tell. I loved her very much. I did what I could to make her happy, and I try to make up for it to Daisy. But there is nothing more to say."

She was angry that he would not defend himself. She was ready—ah, so ready!—to listen to his pleading. But he would not say a word for himself. Instead, he went on,

"She didn't want to come, but I made her. She repented, poor girl, all her life; she was never quite happy. It was all my doing. Still, I think she was happier with me, in spite of it."

A movement of impatience escaped from Alicia. Seeing it he added,

"I beg your pardon. I didn't want you to think hardly of her."

"I don't want to think of her at all. Was she—was she like Daisy?"

"Yes; but prettier."

"I don't know what you expect me to say," she exclaimed. "I know—I suppose some men don't think much of—of a thing like that. To me it is horrible. You simply followed your— Ah, I can't speak of it!" and she seemed to put him from her with a gesture of disgust.

He walked beside her in silence, his face set in the bitter smile it always wore when fate dealt hardly with him.

"I think I'll go straight home," she said, stopping suddenly. "You can join the others."

"Yes, that will be best. I'm not due at the Council just yet."

"I suppose I ought to thank you for telling me the truth. I—" Her false composure suddenly gave way. With a sob she stretched out her hands towards him, crying, "Why didn't you tell me sooner?" and before he could answer her she turned and walked swiftly away, leaving him standing still on the pathway.

She was hardly inside the gates of Government House when she saw Eleanor Scaife, who hurried to meet her.

"Only think, Alicia!" she cried. "Dick is on his way home, and with such good news. We've just had a cable from him."

"Coming back!"

"Yes. He's engaged! He met the Grangers on their tour round the world—you know them, the great cotton people?—at

Sydney, and he's engaged to the youngest girl, Violet—you remember her? It all happened in a fortnight. Mary and Lord Eynesford are delighted. It's just perfect. She's very pretty, and tremendously well off. I do declare, I never thought Dick would end so well! What a happy thought it was sending him away! Aren't you delighted?"

"It sounds very nice, doesn't it? I don't think I knew her more than just to speak to."

"Dick'll be here in four days. I've been looking for you to tell you for the last hour. Where have you been?"

"In the Park."

"Alone, as usual, you hermit?"

"Well, I met the Medlands and Mr. Norburn, and talked to them for a little while."

"Alicia! But it's no use talking to you. Come and find Mary."

"No, Eleanor, I'm tired, and—and hot. I'll go to my room."

"Oh, you must come and see her first."

"I can't."

"She'll be hurt, Alicia. She'll think you don't care. Come, dear."

"Tell her—tell her I'm coming directly. Eleanor, you must let me go," and breaking away she fled into the house.

Eleanor went alone to seek Lady Eynesford. Somehow Alicia's words had quenched her high spirits for the moment.

"Poor child! I do hope she hasn't been foolish," she mused. "Surely after what Mary told her—! Oh dear, I'm afraid it isn't all as happy as it is about Dick!"

And then she indulged in some very cynical meditations on the advantages of being a person of shallow emotions and changeful fancies, until she was roused by the sight of Medland and Norburn walking up to the house, to attend the Executive Council. From the window she closely watched the Premier as he approached; her mood wavered to and fro, but at last she summed up her impressions by remarking,

"Well, I suppose one might."

Anthony Hope

CHAPTER XXII

THE STORY OF A PHOTOGRAPH

Mr. Coxon may be forgiven for being, on this same important Monday, in a state of some nervous excitement. He had
a severe attack of what are vulgarly called "the fidgets," and
Sir John, who was spending the morning at the Club (for his
court was not sitting), glanced at him over his eye-glasses
with an irritated look. The ex-Attorney-General would not sit
still, but flitted continually from window to table, and back
from table to window, taking up and putting down journal
after journal. Much depended, in Mr. Coxon's view, on the
event of that day, for Sir John spoke openly of his
approaching retirement, and an appointment sometimes
thought worthy of a Premier's acceptance might be in
Coxon's grasp before many weeks were past, if only
Medland and his noxious idea of getting a first-class man out
from England could be swept together into limbo.

"What's the betting about to-night?" asked the Chief Justice,
as in one of his restless turns the brooding politician passed
near.

"We reckon to beat him by five," answered Coxon.

"Unless any of your men turn tail, that is? I hear Fenton's

very wobbly—says he daren't show his face in the North-east Ward if he throws Medland over."

"Oh, he's all right."

"Been promised something?"

"You might allow some of us to have consciences, Chief Justice," said Coxon, with an attempt at geniality.

"Oh, some of you, yes. But I'll pick my men, please," remarked Sir John, with a pleasant smile. "Perry's got a conscience, and Kilshaw—well, Kilshaw's got a gadfly that does instead, and of course, Coxon, I add you to the list."

"Much obliged for your testimonial," said Coxon sourly.

"I add any man I'm talking to, to the list," continued the Chief Justice. "I expect him to do the same by me. But, honestly, I add you even in your absence. You're not a man who puts party ties above everything."

Mr. Coxon darted a suspicious glance at the head of his profession, but the Chief Justice's air was blandly innocent.

"My party's my party," he remarked, "just so long as it carries out my principles. I don't say either party does it perfectly."

"I dare say not; but of course you're right to act with the one that does most for you."

Again the Chief Justice had hit on a somewhat ambiguous expression. Coxon detected a grin on the face of Captain Heseltine, who was sitting near, but he could not hold Sir John's grave face guilty of the Captain's grin.

"I see," remarked the Captain, perhaps in order to cover the retreat of his grin, "that they've discharged the woman who was arrested last night for the murder."

"Really no evidence against her," said the Chief Justice. "But, Heseltine, wasn't this man Benham the fellow Medland had a sort of shindy with at that flower-show?"

"Yes, he was. Kilshaw seemed to know all about him."

"He was talking to Miss Medland."

"And the Premier had her away from him in no time. Queer start, Sir John?"

"Oh, well, he seems to have been a loose fellow, and I suppose was murdered for the money he had on him. But I mustn't talk about it. I may have to try it."

"Gad! you'll be committing contempt of yourself," suggested the Captain.

"Like that snake that swallows itself, eh?"

"What snake?" asked the Captain, with interest.

"The snake in the story," answered the Chief Justice; and he added in an undertone—"Why can't that fellow sit still?"

Mr. Coxon had wandered to the window again, and was thrumming on the panes. He turned on hearing some one enter. It was Sir Robert Perry.

"Well," he began, "I bring news of the event of the day."

"About to-night?" asked Coxon eagerly.

"To-night! That's not the event of the day. Ministers are a deal commoner than murders. No, last night."

Coxon turned away disappointed.

"The murder!" exclaimed the Captain.

"Don't talk to me about it, Perry," the Chief Justice requested, opening a paper in front of his face. He did not, however, withdraw out of earshot.

"They've got a sort of a clue. A wretched hobbledehoy of a fellow, something in the bookseller's shop at the corner of Kettle Street, has come with a rigmarole about a society that he and a few more belonged to, including this François Gaspard, who is missing. He protests that the thing was legal, and all that—only a Radical inner ring—but he says that at the last meeting this fellow was dropping hints about putting somebody out of the way. Dyer—that's the lad's name—swears the rest of them disowned him and said they'd have nothing to do with it, and hoped he'd given up the idea."

"I suppose he's in a blue funk?" asked the Captain.

"He is no doubt alarmed," said Sir Robert. "He gave the police the names of the rest of their precious society, and, oddly enough, Ned Evans, of the House—you know him, Coxon?—was one."

"Heard such an awful lot of debates, poor chap," observed Captain Heseltine.

"Well, they went to Evans' and collared him. For a time he stuck out that he knew nothing about it, but they threatened him with heaven knows what, and at last he confessed to having seen this Gaspard in company with the murdered man in Digby Square a little before twelve on the night."

"By Jove! That's awkward!" said the Captain.

Coxon showed more interest now, and remarked,

"Why, Gaspard was one of Medland's organisers. I saw him with both Medland and Norburn on Saturday."

"I don't suppose they were planning to murder this Benham. Indeed, I don't see that the thing can have been political at all. What did it matter whether Benham lived or died?"

"I don't see that it did, except to Benham," assented the Captain. "But what's become of Gaspard?"

"Ah, that they don't know. He's supposed to have taken ship, and they've cabled to search all ships that left the port that morning."

"He'll find the man in blue—or the local equivalent—on the wharf," said the Captain. "Rather a jar that, Sir Robert, when you're in from a voyage. What are they doing now?"

"Well, the Superintendent said they were going to have a thorough search through the dead man's lodgings, to see if they could find out anything about him which would throw light on the motive. The police don't think much of the political theory of the crime."

"Dashed nonsense, *I* should think," said the Captain, and he sauntered off to play billiards.

"That young man," said the Chief Justice, "is really not a fool, though he does his best to look like one."

"That queer conduct seems to me rather common in young men at home. I noticed it when I was over."

"Is it meant to imply independent means?"

"I dare say that idea may be dormant under it somewhere. My wife says the girls like it."

"Then your wife, Perry, is a traitor to her sex to make such confessions. Besides, they didn't in my time."

"Come, you know, you're a forlorn bachelor. What can you know about it?"

"Bachelors, Perry, are the men who know. Which gathers most knowledge from a vivisection, the attentive student or the writhing frog?"

"The operator, most of all."

"Doubtless."

"And that's the woman. Therefore, Oakapple, you're wrong and my wife's right."

"The deuce!" said the Chief Justice. "I wonder how I ever got any briefs."

In the afternoon, when these idlers had one and all set out for the Legislative Assembly, some to work, others still to idle, Mr. Kilshaw felt interest enough in the fate of his late henchman to drop in at the police office on his way to the same destination. He was well known, and no one objected to his walking in and making for the door of the Superintendent's room. An officer to whom he spoke told him that Ned Evans was in custody, and that it was rumoured that some startling discoveries had been made at Benham's lodgings.

"Indeed, sir," said the man, "I believe the Superintendent wished to see you."

"Ah, I dare say," said Kilshaw. "Tell him I'm here."

When he was ushered into the inner room, the Superintendent confirmed the officer's surmise.

"I was going to send a message to ask you to step round, sir," he remarked.

"Here I am, but don't be long. I don't want to miss the Premier's speech."

"Mr. Medland speaking to-day?"

"Of course. It's a great day with us at the House."

"I think it looks like being a great day all round. Well, Mr. Kilshaw, you told me you knew the deceased."

"Yes, I knew Benham."

"Benyon," corrected the Superintendent.

"Yes, that was his real name," assented Kilshaw.

"At his lodgings there was found a packet. That's the wrapper," and he handed a piece of brown paper to Kilshaw.

"In case," Kilshaw read, "of my death or disappearance, please deliver this parcel to Mr. Kilshaw, Legislative Assembly, Kirton."

"I'm sorry to say, sir," said the Superintendent, "that the detective sergeant conducting the search took upon him to open this packet in the presence of one or two persons. It ought to have been opened by no one but—"

"Myself."

"Pardon me, but myself," said the Superintendent, with a slight smile. "Owing to the inexcusable blunder, I'm afraid something about what it contains may leak out prematurely. Those pests, the reporters, are everywhere; you can't keep 'em out."

"Well, what does it contain?" asked Kilshaw. He was annoyed at this unsought publicity, but he saw at once that he must show no sign of vexation.

"That, for one thing," and the Superintendent handed Kilshaw a photograph of two persons, a young woman and a young man. "Look at the back," he added.

Kilshaw looked, and read—"My wife and M."

"That's the deceased's handwriting?"

"Yes."

"And you know the persons?"

"I've no doubt about them. It's the Premier—and—and Mrs. Medland."

"Exactly. Now read this," and he gave him the copy of a certificate of marriage between George Benyon and Margaret Aspland.

"Quite so," nodded Kilshaw.

"And this."

Kilshaw took the slip of newspaper, old and yellow. It contained a few lines, briefly recording that Mrs. Benyon had left her home secretly by night, in her husband's absence, and could not be found.

Kilshaw nodded again.

"It doesn't surprise me," he said. "I knew all this. I was in Mr. Benyon's confidence."

"Perhaps you can tell us how he lived?" hazarded the Superintendent, with a shrewd look.

Mr. Kilshaw looked doubtful.

"The inquest is fixed for to-morrow. The more we know now, the less it will be necessary to protract it."

"I have been helping him lately," admitted Kilshaw; and he added, "Look here, Superintendent, I don't want that more talked about than necessary."

"You needn't say a word to me now unless you like, sir; but I only want to make things as comfortable as I can. You see, the coroner is bound to look into it a bit. Had you given him money lately?"

"Yes."

"Much?"

Kilshaw leant forward and answered, almost in a whisper,

"Five hundred on Friday night," and in spite of himself he avoided the Superintendent's shrewd eye. But that officer's business was not to pass moral judgments. Law is one thing, morality another.

"Then the thing's as plain as a pikestaff. This Gaspard got to know about the money, and murdered him to get it. We needn't look further for a motive."

"I suppose all this will have to come out? I wonder if Gaspard knew who Benham was?"

"It's not necessary to suppose that, unless we believe all Evans says. Certainly, if we trust Evans, Gaspard hinted designs on some one before he could have known Benyon had this money. Could he have known he was going to have it?"

"Benyon may have told him I had promised to help him."

"Well, sir, we must see about that. We shall want you at the inquest, sir."

"I suppose you will, confound you! And I should think you'd want a greater man than I am, too."

The Superintendent looked grave.

"I am going up to try and see the Premier at the House to-day," he said. "I think we shall have to trouble him. You see, he knew Gaspard as well as the deceased."

"I'll give you a lift. You can keep out of the way till he's at leisure."

At this moment one of the police entered, and handed the Superintendent a copy of the *Evening Mail*.

"It's as you feared, sir," he remarked as he went out.

The Superintendent opened the paper, looked at it for an instant, and then indicated a passage with his forefinger.

"It is rumoured," read Mr. Kilshaw, "that certain very startling facts have come to light regarding the identity of the deceased man Benham, and that the name of a very prominent politician, now holding an exalted office, is likely to be introduced into the case. As the matter will be public property to-morrow, we may be allowed to state that trustworthy reports point to the fact of the Premier being in a position to give some important information as to the past life of the deceased. It is said that a photograph of two persons, one of whom is Mr. Medland, has been discovered among the papers at Mr. Benham's (or we should say Benyon's) lodgings. Further developments of this strange affair will be awaited with interest."

"I wish," commented the Superintendent grimly, "that my men could keep a secret as well as their man can sniff one out."

But Mr. Kilshaw was too excited to listen.

"By Jove," he cried, "the news'll be at the House by now! Come along, man, come along!"

And, as they went, they read the rest; for the paper had it all—even a copy of that marriage certificate.

CHAPTER XXIII

AN ORATOR'S RIVAL

The House was crowded, and every gallery full. Lady Eynesford and Eleanor Scaife, attended by Captain Heseltine, occupied their appointed seats; the members of the Legislative Council overflowed from their proper pen and mingled with humbler folk in the public galleries; reporters wrote furiously, and an endless line of boys bearing their slips came and went. The great hour had arrived: the battle-field was reached at last. Sir Robert Perry sat and smiled; Puttock played with the hair chain that wandered across his broad waistcoat; Coxon restlessly bit his nails; Norburn's face was pale with excitement, and he twisted his hands in his lap; the determined partisans cheered or groaned; the waverers looked important and felt unhappy; all eyes were steadily fixed on the Premier, and all ears intent on his words.

For the moment he had forgotten everything but the fight he was fighting. No thought of the wretched Benham, who lay dead, no thought of his daughter, who watched him as he spoke, no thought of Alicia Derosne, who stayed away that she might not see him, crossed his brain now, or turned his ideas from the task before him. It was no ordinary speech, and no ordinary occasion. He spoke only to five men out of all his audience—the rest were his, or were beyond the power of his charm; on those five important-looking, unhappy-feeling men he bent every effort of his will, and played every device of his mind and his tongue. Now and then he distantly threatened them, oftener he made as though to convince their cool judgment; again he would invoke the sentiment of old alliance in them, or stir their pity for the men whose cause he pleaded. Once he flashed out in bitter mockery at Coxon, then jested in mild irony at Puttock and his "rich man's revolution." Returning to his text, he minutely dissected his own measure, insisting on its promise, extenuating its fancied danger, claiming for it the merits of a courageous and well-conceived scheme. Through all the changes that he rang, he was heard with close attention, broken only by demonstrations of approval or of dissent. At last one of his periods extorted a cheer from a waverer. It acted on him as a spur to fresh exertions. He raised his voice till it filled the chamber, and began his last and most elaborate appeal.

Suddenly a change came over his hearers. The breathless silence of engrossed attention gave place to a subdued stir; whispers were heard here and there. Men were handing a newspaper about, accompanying its transfer with meaning looks. He was not surprised, for members made no scruple of reading their papers or writing their letters in the House, but he was vexed to see that he had not gripped them closer. He went on, but that ever-circulating paper had half his attention now. He noticed Kilshaw come in with it and press it on Sir Robert's notice. Sir Robert at first refused, but when Kilshaw urged, he read and glanced up at him, so Medland thought, with a look of sadness. Coxon had got a paper now, and left biting his nails to pore over it; he passed it to Puttock, and the fat man bulged his cheeks in seeming wonder. Even his waverer, the one who had cheered, was deep in it. Only Norburn was unconscious of it. And, when they had read, they all looked at him again, not as they had looked before, but, it seemed to him, with a curious wonder, half mocking, half pitying, as one looks at a man who does not know the thing that touches him most nearly. He glanced up at the galleries: there too was the ubiquitous sheet; the Chief Justice and the President of the Legislative Council were cheek by jowl over it, and it fell lightly from Lady Eynesford's slim fingers, to be caught at eagerly by Eleanor Scaife.

"What is it?" he whispered impatiently to Norburn; but his absorbed disciple only bewilderedly murmured "What?" and the Premier could not pause to tell him.

Now followed what Sir Robert maintained was the greatest feat of oratory he had ever witnessed. Gathering his wandering wits together, Medland plunged again whole-heartedly into his speech, and slowly, gradually, almost, it seemed, step by step and man by man, he won back the thoughts of his audience. He wrestled with that strange paper rival and overthrew it. Man after man dropped it; its course was stayed; it fell underfoot or fluttered idly down the gangways. The nods ceased, the whispers were hushed, the stir fell and rose no more. Once again he had them, and, inspired by that knowledge, the surest spur of eloquence, there rang from his lips the last burning words, the picture of the vision that ruled his life, the hope for the days that he might not see.

"Believe!" he cried, in passionate entreaty, "believe, and your sons shall surely see!"

He sank in his seat, and the last echo of his resonant voice died away. First came silence, and then a thunder of applause. Men stood up and waved what they had in their hands, hats or handkerchiefs or papers; women sat with their eyes still on him, or, with a gasp, leant back and closed their lids. He sat with his head sunk on his breast, till the tumult died away. No one rose. The Speaker looked round once and again. Could it be that no one—? Slowly he began to rise. The movement caught Sir Robert's attention: he signed to Puttock, who sprang heavily to his feet. Puttock was no favourite as a speaker, and generally his rising was a signal for the House to thin. He began his speech with his stolid deliberation. Not a man stirred. They waited for something still.

"And now," whispered Medland to the Treasurer, who sat by him, "let's see what it was in that infernal paper."

The Treasurer handed him what he asked.

"You ought to see it," he whispered back.

Mr. Puttock's voice droned on, and his sheaf of notes rustled in his hand. No one looked at him or listened to him. Their eyes were still on Medland. The Premier read—it seemed so slowly—put the paper down, and gazed first up at the ceiling; then he glanced round, and found all the attentive eyes on him: he smiled—it was just a visible smile, no more—and his head fell again on his breast, while his hand idly twisted a button on his coat.

The show was over, or had never come, and the deferred rush to the doors began. They almost tumbled over one another now in their haste to reach where their tongues could play freely. Kilshaw and Perry, the Treasurer and the waverers, all slipped out, and Norburn, knowing nothing but simply wearied of Puttock, followed them. Scarce twenty were left in the House, and the galleries had poured half their contents into the great room which served for a lobby outside. There the talk ran swift and eager. The very name of

"Benyon" was enough for many, who remembered that it had always been said to be the maiden name of Medland's wife. Could any one doubt who the other person in that strangely revealed photograph was, or fail to guess the relation between the man they had been listening to and the man who was dead? A few had known Benyon, more Gaspard, all Medland—the three figures of this drama; many remembered the fourth, the central character, who had not tarried for the end of it: the man was rare who did not spend a thought on the bright girl, whose face was so familiar in these walls, and who must be dragged into it. Where was she? asked one. She was gone. Norburn, with rapid instinct, as soon as he had read, had run to her and forced her to go home. He was back from escorting her now, and walked up and down with hands behind him, speaking to no one among all the busily babbling throng.

The waverers stood in a little group by themselves, talking earnestly in undertones, while men wondered whether the paper would undo what the speech had done, and whether the Premier's words had won a victory, only for his deeds to leap to light and rob it from him again.

Inside, the debate lagged on, surely the dullest, emptiest, most neglected debate that had ever decided the fate of a Government. The men who had been set down to speak came in and spoke and went out again; a House was kept, but with little to spare. Sir Robert went in and took his place, opposite Medland, who never stirred through all the hours. Presently Sir Robert wrote a note, twisted it, and flung it to the Premier. "A splendid performance of yours, *mes compliments*," it said, and, when Medland looked across to acknowledge it, Sir Robert smiled kindly, and nodded his silver head, and the Premier answered him with a glad gleam in his deep-set eyes. These two men, who were always fighting, knew one another, and liked one another for what

Anthony Hope

they knew. And this little episode done, Sir Robert rose and pricked and pinked the Premier's points, making sharp fun of his heroics, and weightily criticising his proposals. Now the House did fill a little, for after all the debate was important, and the hour of the division drew near; and when the question was put and the bell rang, nearly half the House trooped out with virtuous air to join the other half, persistently gossiping in the lobby, and, with them, decide the fateful question.

One more strange thing was to happen at that sitting.

It was not strange that the Government were beaten by three votes, that only one of those wavering men voted with his old party at last, but it was strange that when this result was announced, and Medland's followers settled sturdily in their seats to endure the celebration of the triumph, the celebration did not come. There was hardly a cheer, and Medland himself, whom the result seemed hardly to have roused, woke with a start to the unwonted silence. It struck to his heart: it seemed like a tribute of respect to a dead enemy. But he rose and briefly said that on the next day an announcement of the Government's intentions would be made by himself—he paused here a moment—or one of his colleagues. He sat down again. The sitting was at an end, and the House adjourned. Members began to go out, but, as the Premier rose, they drew back and left a path for him down the middle of the House. As he went, one or two thrust out their hands to him, and one honest fellow shouted in his rough voice—he was a labouring-man member—"You're not done yet, Jimmy!"

The shout touched him, he lifted his head, looked round with a smile, and, just raising again the hat he had put on as he neared the door, took Norburn's arm and passed out of the House.

When Sir Robert followed, he found the Chief Justice waiting for him, and they walked off together. For a long while neither spoke, but at last Sir Robert said peevishly,

"I wish this confounded thing hadn't happened. It spoils our win."

The Chief Justice nodded, and whistled a bar or two of some sad ditty.

"I'm glad she's dead, poor soul, Perry," he said.

"There's the girl," said Sir Robert.

"Ay, there's the girl."

They did not speak again till they were just parting, when the Chief Justice broke out,

"Why the deuce couldn't the fellow take his beastly photograph with him?"

"It's very absurd," answered Sir Robert, "but I feel just the same about it."

"I'm hanged if you're not a gentleman, Perry," said the Chief Justice, and he hastened away, blowing his nose.

Anthony Hope

CHAPTER XXIV

THREE AGAINST THE WORLD

Though the House had risen early that evening, the Central Club sat very late. The smoking-room was crowded, and tongues wagged briskly. Every man had a hare to hunt; no one lacked irrefragable arguments to prove what must happen; no one knew exactly what was going to happen. The elder men gathered round Puttock and Jewell, and listened to a demonstration that the Premier's public life was at an end; the younger rallied Coxon, whose premature stateliness sometimes invited this treatment, dubbing him "Kingmaker Coxon," and hilariously repudiating the idea that he did not enjoy the title. Captain Heseltine dropped in about eleven; cross-questioning drew from him the news that communications had passed, informal communications, he insisted, from the Governor to Sir Robert, as well as to the Premier.

"In fact," he said, "poor old Flemyng's cutting up and down all over the place. Glad it's his night on duty."

Presently Mr. Flemyng himself appeared, clamorous for cigars and drink, but mighty discreet and vexatiously reticent. Yes, he had taken a letter to Medland; yes, and another to Perry; no, he had no idea what the missives were about. He believed Medland was to see the Governor to-morrow, but it was beyond him to conjecture the precise object of the interview. Was it resignation or dissolution? Really, he knew no more than that waiter—and so forth; very likely his ignorance was real, but he diffused an atmosphere of suppressed knowledge which whetted the curiosity of his audience to the sharpest edge.

A messenger entered and delivered a note to Puttock and another to Coxon. The two compared their notes for a moment, and went out together. The arguments rose furiously again, some maintaining that Medland must disappear altogether, others vehemently denying it, a third party preferring to await the disclosures at the inquest before committing themselves to an opinion. An hour passed; the noise in the streets began to abate, and the clock of the Roman Catholic cathedral hard by struck twelve. Captain Heseltine yawned, stretched, and rose to his feet.

"Come along, Flemyng," he said. "The show's over for to-night."

He seemed to express the general feeling, but men were reluctant to acknowledge so disappointing a conclusion, and the preparations for departure were slow and lingering. They had not fairly begun before Mr. Kilshaw's entrance abruptly checked them. Instantly he became the centre of a crowd.

"Now, Kilshaw," they cried, "you know all about it. Oh, come now! Of course you do! Secret? Nonsense! Out with it!" and one or two of his intimates added imploringly, "Don't be an ass, Kilshaw."

Kilshaw flung himself into a chair.

"They resign," he said.

"At once?"

"Yes. Perry's to be sent for. Medland, I'm told, insists on going. For my own part, I think he's right."

"Of course," said somebody sapiently, "he doesn't want to dissolve with this affair hanging over him."

"It comes to the same thing," observed Kilshaw. "Perry will dissolve; the Governor has promised to do it, if he likes."

"Perry dissolve!"

"Yes," nodded Kilshaw. "You see—" He paused and added, "Our present position isn't very independent."

Everybody understood what he hinted. Sir Robert did not care to depend on the will of Coxon and his seceders.

"And what about Coxon and Puttock?" was the next question.

"Haven't I been indiscreet enough?"

"Well, what are you going to do yourself?"

"My duty," answered Mr. Kilshaw, with a smile, and the throng, failing to extract any more from him, did at last set about the task of getting home to bed in good earnest.

They could rest sooner than the man who occupied so much of their interest. It had been a busy evening for the defeated Minister; he had colleagues to see, letters to write, messages to send, conferences to hold. No doubt there was much to do, and yet Norburn, who watched him closely, doubted whether he did not make work for himself, perhaps as a means of distraction, perhaps as a device for postponing an interview with his daughter. He had seen her for a minute when he came in, and told her he would tell her all there was to tell some time that night; but the moment for it was slow in coming. Norburn had been struck with Daisy's composure. She had seen the *Evening Mail*, and, without attempting to discuss the matter with him, she expressed her conviction that there could be nothing distressing behind the mysterious paragraph. Norburn did not know what to say to her. He felt that in a case of this sort a girl's mind was a closed book to him. He had himself, on the way back from the House, heard a brief account of the whole matter from the Premier's lips; it seemed to him, in the light of his ideas and theories, a matter of very little moment. He was of course aware how widely the judgment of many would differ from his, and when his mind was directed to the political aspect of the situation, he acknowledged the gravity of the disclosure. But honestly he could not pretend to think it a thing which should alter or lessen the esteem or love in which Medland's friends held him. And even if the original act were seriously worthy of blame, the lapse of years made present severity as unreasonable as it would be unkind. In vain Medland reminded him that, let the act be as old and long past as it would, the consequences remained.

"What!" Norburn cried, "would any one think the worse of Daisy? The more fools they!" and he laughed cheerfully, adding, "I only wish she'd let me show her I think none the worse of her. Why, it's preposterous, sir!"

"Preposterous or not," answered Medland, "half the people in the place will let her know the difference. I may agree with you—God knows how I should like to be able to!—but there's no blinking the fact. Well, I must tell her."

He recollected telling the same story to the other woman he

Anthony Hope

loved, and he shrank in sudden dread, lest his daughter should say what Alicia had said, "To me it is—horrible!" The words echoed in his brain. "Ah, I can't speak of it," she had cried, and the gesture of her hand as she repelled him lived before his eyes again. Surely Daisy would not do that to him!

"I should be like Lear—without a grievance," he said to himself, with a wry smile. "The very height of tragedy!"

It was near midnight before he put away his work. Norburn had left him alone two hours before, and he rose now, laid down his pipe, and went to look for his daughter in her little sitting-room. His heart was very heavy; he must make her understand now why a man who made love to her should be hastily sent away by his friends, what her father had condemned her to, what manner of man he was; he must seem to destroy or impair the perfect sweetness of memory wherein she held her mother.

He opened the door softly. She was sitting in a large armchair, over a little bit of bright fire; save for gleams suddenly coming and going, as a coal blazed and died down again, the room was in darkness. He walked up to her and knelt by the chair, his head almost on a level with hers.

"Well, Daisy, what are you doing?"

She put out a hand and laid it on his with a gentle pressure.

"I'm thinking," she said. "Do you want a light?"

"No, I like it dark best—best for what I have to say."

Suddenly she threw her arms round his neck, drawing him to her and kissing his face.

"I'd do the same if you'd killed him yourself," she whispered in the extravagance of her love, and kissed him again.

"But, Daisy, you don't know."

"Yes, I do. He told me. He's been here."

"Who?"

"Jack Norburn. He said you would hate telling me, so he did. You mustn't mind, dear, you mustn't mind. Oh, you didn't think it would make any difference to me, dear, did you? What do I care? Mrs. Puttock may care, and Lady Eynesford, and all the rest, but what do I care if I have you and him?"

"Me and him, Daisy?"

"Yes," she answered, smiling boldly. "He's asked me to marry him—just to show he didn't mind—and I think I will, father. We three against the world! What need we care? Father, we'll beat Sir Robert!" and she seized his two hands and laughed.

In vain Medland tried to tell her what he had come to say. Mighty as his relief and joy were, he still felt a burden lay on him. She would not hear.

"Don't you see I'm happy?" she cried. "It can't be your duty to make me unhappy. Jack doesn't mind, I don't mind!" Her voice sank a little and she added, "It can't hurt mother now. Oh, don't be unhappy about it, dear—don't, don't!"

They were standing now, and his arm was about her. Looking up at him, she went on,

"They shan't beat us! They shan't say they beat us. We

three, father!"

He stooped and kissed her. There is love that lies beyond the realm of giving or taking, of harm or good, of wrong, or even of forgiveness. With all his faults, this love he had won from his daughter, and it stood him in stead that night. He drew himself up to his height, and the air of despondency fell from him. The girl's brave love braced him to meet the world again.

"No, by Jove, we're not beat yet, Daisy!" he said, and she kissed him again and laughed softly as she made him sit, and herself sat upon his knee.

CHAPTER XXV

THE TRUTH TOO LATE

By four o'clock the next afternoon the Club had gathered ample materials for fresh gossip. The formalities attendant on the change of government, the composition of the new Cabinet, the prospects of the election—these alone would have supplied many hours, and besides them, indeed supplanting them temporarily by virtue of an intenser interest, there was the account of the inquest on Benyon's body. Medland had gone to it, almost direct from his final interview with the Governor, and Kilshaw had been there, fresh from a conference with Perry. The inquiry had ended, as was foreseen directly Ned Evans' evidence was forth-coming, in a verdict of murder against Gaspard; but the interest lay in the course of the investigation, not in its issue. Mr. Duncombe, a famous comedian, who was then on tour in New Lindsey and had been made an honorary member of the Club, smacked his lips over the dramatic moment when the ex-Premier, calmly and in a clear voice, had identified the person in the photograph, declared the deceased man to have been Benyon, and very briefly stated how he had been connected with him in old days.

"The lady," he said, "is Mrs. Benyon. The other figure is that of myself. I had not seen the deceased for many years."

"You were not on terms with him?" asked the coroner, who, in common with half the listeners, had known the lady as Mrs. Medland.

"No," said Mr. Medland; "I lost sight of him."

"You did not hear from—from any one about him?"

"No."

He gave the dates when he had last seen Benyon in old days. Asked whether he had communicated with him between that date and the dead man's reappearance, he answered,

"Once, about four years ago. I wrote to tell him of that lady's death," and he pointed again to the picture, and went on to tell the details of Benyon's subsequent application to him for a post under Government.

"You refused it?" he was asked.

"Yes, I refused it. I spoke to him once again, when we met on a social occasion. We had a sort of dispute then. I never saw him again to speak to."

"It was all done," said Mr. Duncombe, describing the scene, "in a repressed way that was very effective—to a house that knew the circumstances most effective. And the other fellow—Kilshaw—he gave some sport too. The coroner (they told me he was one of Medland's men, and I noticed he spared Medland all he could) was inclined to be a bit down on Kilshaw. Kilshaw was cool and handy in his answers, but, Lord love you! his game came out pretty plain. A monkey! You don't give a man a monkey unless there's value received! So people saw, and Mr. Kilshaw looked a bit uncomfortable when he caught Medland's eye. He looked at him like that," and Mr. Duncombe assumed the finest wronged-hero glance in his repertory.

"Oh, come, old chap, I bet he didn't," observed Captain Heseltine. "We've seen him, you know."

Duncombe laughed good-humouredly.

"At any rate he made Kilshaw look a little green, and some of the people behind called out 'Shame!' and got themselves sat upon. Then they had Medland up again and twisted him a bit about his acquaintance with Gaspard; but the coroner didn't seem to think there was anything in it, and they found murder against Gaspard, and rang down the curtain. And when we got outside there was a bit of a rumpus. They hooted Kilshaw and cheered Medland, and yelled like mad when a dashed pretty girl drove up in a pony-cart and carried him off. Altogether it wasn't half bad."

"Glad you enjoyed yourself," observed Captain Heseltine. "If it amuses strangers to see our leading celebrities mixed up in a murder and other distressing affairs, it's the least we can do to see that they get it."

The Captain's facetiousness fell on unappreciative ears. Most of Mr. Duncombe's audience were too alive to the serious side of the matter to enjoy it. To them it was another and a very striking scene in the fight which had long gone on between Medland and Kilshaw, and had taken a fresh and fiercer impetus from the well-remembered day when Medland had spoken his words about Kilshaw and his race-horses. Nobody doubted that Kilshaw had kept this man Benyon, or Benham, as a secret weapon, and that the murder had only made the disclosure come earlier. Kilshaw's reputation suffered somewhat in the minds of the scrupulous, but his partisans would hear of no condemnation. They said,

Anthony Hope

as he had said, that in dealing with a man like Medland it would have been folly not to use the weapons fate, or the foe himself by his own misdeeds, offered. As for the disapprobation of the Kirton mob, they held that in high scorn.

"They'd cheer burglary, if Medland did it," said one.

"Well, he wants to, pretty nearly," added a capitalist.

"But the country will take a very different view. Puttock'll rub it into all his people: *they*'ll not vote for him. What do you say, Coxon?"

"I think we shall beat him badly," said that gentleman, as he rose and went out.

Captain Heseltine soon followed, and was surprised to see Coxon's figure just ahead of him as he entered the gates of Government House.

"Hang the fellow! What does he want here?" asked the Captain.

Mr. Coxon asked for Lady Eynesford. When he entered, she rose with a newspaper in her hand.

"What a shocking, shameful thing this is!" she said. "What a blessing it is that the Government was beaten!"

Coxon acquiesced in both these opinions.

"I never thought well of him," continued the lady. "Now everybody sees him in his true colours. And it's you we have chiefly to thank for our deliverance."

Coxon murmured a modest depreciation of his services, and said,

"I hope Miss Derosne is well?"

Something in his tones brought to his hostess one of those swift fits of repentance that were apt to wait for her whenever she allowed herself to treat this visitor with friendliness. He was so very prompt in responding!

"She is not very well," she answered, rather coldly.

"I—I hope I shall have the pleasure of seeing her?"

Mr. Coxon's wishes were fulfilled to the moment. The door opened and Alicia came in. On seeing him she stopped.

"Come in, Alicia," said Lady Eynesford. "Here's Mr. Coxon come to be congratulated."

Coxon stood up with a propitiatory smile.

"How do you do, Mr. Coxon?" said Alicia, giving him a limp hand. "Shall I ring for tea, Mary?"

"They'll bring it. You haven't wished him joy."

"Oh, are you in the new Ministry?"

"I have that honour, Miss Derosne. I hope you are on our side?"

"I don't quite know which side you are on—now," observed Alicia, in slow but distinct tones.

Coxon grew red.

"I—I have joined Sir Robert Perry's Ministry," he answered.

"Of course he has, Alicia," interposed Lady Eynesford hastily.

Alicia seated herself on the sofa, remarking as she did so,

"Well, you do change a good deal, don't you?"

"Really, Miss Derosne," he stammered, "I don't understand you."

"Oh, I only mean that you were first with Sir Robert, then with Mr. Medland, and now with Sir Robert again! And presently with Mr. Medland again, I suppose?"

"She doesn't appreciate the political reasons," began Lady Eynesford, with troubled brow and smiling lips; but Coxon, frowning angrily, broke in,

"Not the last, I promise you, anyhow, Miss Derosne."

"What, you think he's finally beaten then?"

"That's not the question. Beaten or not, he is discredited, and no respectable man would act with him."

"We needn't discuss—" began Lady Eynesford again, but this time Alicia was the interrupter. She spoke in a cold, hard way, very unlike her own.

"If he won, you would all be at his feet."

Coxon was justified in being angry at her almost savage scorn of him; regardless of anything except his wrong, he struck back the sharpest blow he could.

"I know some people are very ready to be at his feet," he said, with a sneering smile.

His shaft hit the mark. Alicia flushed and sat speechless. A glance at Lady Eynesford's face told him the scene had lasted too long: he rose and took his leave, paying Alicia the homage of a bow, but not seeking her hand. She took no notice of his salute, and Lady Eynesford only gasped "Good-bye."

The two sat silent for some moments after he had gone; then Lady Eynesford remarked,

"Were you mad, Alicia? See what you laid yourself open to! Oh, of course a gentleman wouldn't have said it, but you yourself didn't treat him as if he was a gentleman. Really, I can make a great deal of allowance for him. Your manner was inexcusable."

Alicia did not attempt to defend herself.

"You are out of temper," continued her sister-in-law, "and you choose to hit the first person within reach; if you can do that you care nothing for my dignity or your own self-respect. You parade your—your interest in this man—"

"I shall never speak to him again."

"I'm glad to hear it, and, if you come into my drawing-room, I will thank you to behave yourself properly and be civil to my guests," and Lady Eynesford walked out of the room.

Alicia huddled herself in a heap on the sofa, turning her face to the wall. She felt Lady Eynesford's scornful rebuke like the stroke of a whip. She had descended to a vulgar wrangle, and had been worsted in it: the one thing of all which it

Anthony Hope

concerned her to hide had by her own act been opened to the jeer of a stranger; she had violated every rule of good breeding and self-respect. No words—not even Lady Eynesford's—were too strong to describe what she had done. Yet she could not help it; she could not hear a creature like that abuse or condemn a man like Medland—though all that he had said she had said, and more, to Medland himself. She was too miserable to think; she lay with closed eyes and parted lips, breathing quickly, and restlessly moving her limbs in that strange physical discomfort which great unhappiness brings with it.

A footstep roused her; she sat up, hurriedly smoothing her hair and clutching at a book that lay on the table by her. The intruder was her brother, and fortunately he was too intent on the tidings he brought to notice her confusion.

"Great news, Al!" he cried. "They've offered me Ireland. We shall start home in a month."

"Home in a month?" she echoed.

"Yes. Splendid, isn't it?"

"You're pleased, Willie?"

The Governor was very pleased. He liked the promotion, he liked going home; and finally, pleasant as his stay in New Lindsey had been on the whole, there were features in the present position which made him not sorry to depart.

"I shall just see the elections through, and Perry well started —at least, I suppose it'll be Perry—and then we'll be off. Shan't you be glad to see the old home again, Al?"

"It's so sudden," she said. "I shall be sorry to leave here."

"Oh, so shall I—very sorry to leave some of the people too. Still, it's a good thing. Where's Eleanor? I must tell her. I say, Dick gets here to-morrow."

"Oh, I'm so glad."

The Governor hurried out again, and Alicia returned to the sofa. The knot of her troubles had been rudely cut. Perhaps this summary ending was best. She herself would not, she knew, have had the strength to tear herself away from that place, but if fate tore her—perhaps well and good. Nothing but unhappiness waited there for her; it seemed to her that nothing but unhappiness waited anywhere now; but at least, over at home, she would not have to fear the discovery of her secret, the secret she herself kept so badly, nor to endure the torture of gossip, hints, and clumsy pity. No one, over at home, would think of Medland; they might just know his name, might perhaps have heard him rumoured for a dangerous man and a vexatious opponent of good Sir Robert. Certainly they would never think of him as the cause of bruising of heart to a young lady in fashionable society. So he would pass out of her life; she would leave him to his busy, strenuous, happy-unhappy life, so full of triumphs and defeats, of ups and downs, of the love of many and the hate of many. Perhaps she, like the rest, would read his name in the *Times* now and then, unless indeed he were utterly vanquished. No, he was not finally beaten. Of that she was sure. His name would be read often in cold print, but the glow of the life he lived would be henceforth unknown to her. She would go back to the old world and the old circle of it. What would happen after that she was too listless to think. It was summed up in negations; and these again melted into one great want, the absence of the man to whom her imagination and her heart blindly and obstinately clung.

Lady Eynesford had left her newspaper, and Alicia found her

hand upon it. Taking it up, she read Medland's evidence at the inquest. A sudden revulsion of feeling seized her. Was this the man she was dreaming about, a man who calmly, coolly, as though caring nothing, told that story in the face of all the world? Was she never to get rid of the spell he had cast on her before she knew what he really was? For a man like this she had sacrificed her self-respect, bandied insults with a vulgar upstart, and brought on her head a reproach more fitting for an ill-mannered child. She threw the paper from her and rose to her feet. She would think no more of him; he might be what he would; he was no fit subject for her thoughts, and he and the place where he lived and all this wretched country deserved nothing better than to be forgotten, resolutely, utterly, soon.

"I am very sorry, Mary," she was saying, ten minutes later; "I deserved all you said. I don't know what foolishness possessed me. See, I have written and apologised to Mr. Coxon."

And Lady Eynesford kissed her and thanked heaven that they would soon have done with Mr. Coxon and—all the rest.

CHAPTER XXVI

THE UNCLEAN THING

A few days later, Mr. Dick Derosne was walking in the Park at noon. He had been down to the Club and found no one there. Everybody except himself was at work: the politicians were scattered all over the colony, conducting their election campaign. Medland himself had gone to his constituency: his seat was very unsafe there, and he was determined to keep it if he could, although, as a precaution, he was also a candidate for the North-east ward of Kirton, where his success was beyond doubt. His friends and his foes had followed him out of town, and the few who were left were busy in the capital itself. Such men as these when at the Club would talk of nothing but the crisis, and, after he had heard all there was to hear about the Benyon affair, the crisis began to bore Dick. After all, it mattered very little to him; he would be out of it all in a month, and the Medlands were not, when he came to think of it, people of great importance. Why, the Grangers had never heard of them! Decidedly, he had had enough and to spare of the Medlands.

Nevertheless, he was to have a little more of them, for at this instant he saw Daisy Medland approaching him. Escape was impossible, and Dick had the grace to shrink from appearing to avoid her.

"The deuce!" he thought, "this is awkward. I hope she won't—" He raised his hat with elaborate politeness.

Daisy stopped and greeted him with much effusion and without any embarrassment. Dick thought that odd.

"I was afraid," she said, "we were not going to see you again before you disappeared finally with the Governor."

"Oh, I came back just to settle things up. I hope you are all right, Miss Medland?"

"Yes, thank you. Did you have a pleasant trip?"

"Yes, very," he answered, wondering if she knew of his engagement.

"We missed you very much," she went on.

"Awfully kind of you to say so."

"You started so suddenly."

"Oh, well—yes, I suppose I did. It just struck me I ought to see Australia."

"How funny!" she exclaimed, with a little laugh.

"Why funny?" asked Dick, rather stiffly.

"I mean that it should strike you just like that. However, it was very lucky, wasn't it?"

"You mean I—"

"Yes, I mean you—" said Daisy, who had no intention of

saving Dick from any floundering that might befall him. Mercy is all very well, but give us justice sometimes.

"You heard of my—my engagement?"

"I saw it in the papers. A Miss Granger, isn't it?"

"*A* Miss Granger!" thought Dick. Everybody knew the Grangers.

"I'm sure I congratulate you. You lost no time, Mr. Derosne."

Dick stammered that it was an old acquaintance renewed.

"Oh, then you've been in love with her a long while?" asked Daisy, with a curiosity apparently very innocent.

"Not exactly that."

"Then you did fall in love very quickly?"

"Well, I suppose I did," admitted Dick, as if he were rather ashamed of himself.

"Oh, I mustn't blame you," said Daisy, with a pensive sigh.

Dick, on the look-out for a hint of suppressed suffering, saw what he looked for. She was taking it very well, and it was his duty to say something nice. Moreover, Daisy Medland was looking extremely pretty, and that fact alone, in Dick's view, justified and indeed necessitated the saying of something nice. Violet Granger was leagues away, and a touch of romance could not disquiet or hurt her.

"Indeed I am anxious to hear that you don't," he said, accompanying his remark with a glance of pathetic anxiety.

"Why should I?" she asked.

This simple question placed Dick in a difficulty, and he was glad when she went on without waiting for an answer.

"Indeed I should have no right to. Love is sudden and—and beyond our control, isn't it?"

"And yet," said Dick, "a man is bound to consider so many things."

"I was thinking of a girl's love. She just gives it and thinks of nothing. Doesn't she?" and she looked at him with an appeal to his experience in her eyes.

"Does she?" said Dick, who began to feel uncomfortable.

"And when she has once given it, she never changes."

If this last remark were a generalisation, it was certainly an audacious one, but Dick was thinking only of a personal application. Daisy's words, as he understood their meaning, were working on the better nature which lay below his frivolity. He began to suffer genuine shame and remorse at the idea that he had caused suffering—lasting pain—to this poor unsophisticated child who had loved him so readily. Moved by this honourable, if tardy, compunction, he ejaculated,

"Oh, don't say that, Miss Medland. I never thought—I—I mean, surely you don't mean—?" And then he came to a dead stop for a moment; only to start abruptly again the next, with—"It would spoil my happiness, if I thought—you don't really mean it, do you? I don't know how I should ask you to forgive me, if you do."

Daisy's plot (which it is not sought to justify) had been crowned with success. A mischievous smile replaced her innocent expression.

"What do you mean, Mr. Derosne? Forgive you? I was speaking of my own feelings."

"Yes, so—so I understood, and I wanted to say that I hoped you wouldn't think I had been inconsid—"

"What does it matter to me, how long or how short your wooing is? They say lovers are self-centred, but really I think you're the worst I ever met. I must confess I wasn't thinking of you, Mr. Derosne."

"What?" exclaimed Dick.

"Is it possible you haven't heard of my engagement?" she asked in the sweetest tone.

"Your—"

"Yes—to Mr. Norburn," and she watched the effect with obvious pleasure.

Dick pulled himself together. She had made a fool of him; that was pretty clear now it was too late to help it.

"I hadn't heard. I congratulate you," he said, stiffly and awkwardly.

"Thanks. Of course that was what I meant when I said my feelings could never change. How odd you must have thought it of me, if you didn't know!"

"Well, I—I didn't quite understand."

"You seemed puzzled and I couldn't understand why. We were both thinking of ourselves too much, I suppose!"

"May I ask if you have been engaged long?"

"Oh, not actually engaged very long, but, like yours, it's been an old acquaintance, and—if you won't betray me—perhaps a little more for ever so long."

Dick was not quite sure whether he believed the lady or not. He ought to have wished to believe her; as a fact, he was extremely reluctant to do so, but Daisy's look was so candid and at the same time so naturally shy, in making her little avowal, that he was almost convinced that the semi-tragedy of their parting scene a few weeks before had been all acting on her side. Alicia could have undeceived him, but, for reasons tolerably obvious, Dick did not rehearse this interview to Alicia or to any one else.

"Ah! here comes Mr. Norburn!" cried Daisy, rosy with delight. "You must congratulate one another."

This very hollow ceremony was duly performed, and Dick left the lovers together. In fact he may be said to have made his exit in a somewhat shamefaced manner. Fortune put him at a disadvantage in that his partner was far away, while Daisy stood triumphant by the side of hers and watched him.

"Upon my honour," he exclaimed, hitting viciously at a flower, "I believe she was humbugging me all the time!" And from that day to this he thinks Miss Medland a flirt, and is very glad, for that among other weighty reasons, that he had nothing more to do with her.

Her behaviour towards Dick Derosne was fairly typical of Daisy Medland's attitude towards the world at large at this time. She made the mistake, natural enough, of being defiant, of emphasising outwardly an indifference that she did not feel, of anticipating slights and being ready to resent slurs which were never intended or inflicted. There are so many people in the world who want only an excuse for being kind, but yet do want that, and who are ready to give much, but must be asked. There were many among the upper circles of Kirton society who would have been ready enough to act a friendly part, to overlook much, to play protector to the girl, and do a favour to a man who had been and might again be powerful; but they too needed to be asked—not of course in words, but by a hint of gratitude waiting for them, a touch of deference, some kind of appeal from the loneliness and desolation of a doubtful position to the comfortable regions of unaspersed respectability. They could not help feeling that Daisy, though by no fault of hers, was yet one who should ask and accept as favours what among equals are no more than courtesies. The knowledge of this point of view drove Daisy into strong revolt against it: she was more, not less, offhand than of yore; more, not less, ready to ignore people with whom she was not in sympathy; more, not less, unscrupulous in outraging the small conventions of society. And, unfortunately, Norburn was a man to encourage instead of discouraging her in this course, for conventions and respectability had always been a red rag to him. In the result the isolation of the Medland household from most of the families of their own level in the town, and from all of a higher, if there were any such, grew from day to day, until it seemed that Daisy's "We three against the world!" was to come true so far as the world meant the social circle of their neighbours. Medland himself was too engrossed with larger matters to note the progress of this outlawry: when he did for a moment turn his thoughts from the campaign he was engrossed with, there was only one face in Kirton society whose countenance or aversion troubled him: and that one was sternly and irrevocably turned away.

Anthony Hope

Thus Daisy, though she might be cheered in the streets, and though she bore herself with exuberant gaiety out of doors, passed lonely evenings, especially when Norburn left her to help in the country elections. The Chief Justice had been to see her once, and Lady Perry had left a card, but she was almost always alone, and then the exuberant gaiety would evaporate. One evening about half-past nine, she was sitting alone, wishing her father or her lover would come back to her, when there was a knock at the door. Alicia Derosne came in, with a hasty, almost furtive, step.

"You are alone, aren't you? I saw Mr. Medland was away."

"Yes, I am alone," said Daisy, doubtful whether to put on her armour or not.

"Oh, Daisy, I've never been able to come and wish you joy yet. I wouldn't do it by letter. I'm so glad. You are happy, aren't you?" and she took Daisy's two hands and kissed her.

"Yes, I am very happy. It's sweet of you to come. How did you manage it?"

Neither cared to pretend that Lady Eynesford would approve of such a visit.

"Oh, I slipped out," said Alicia, nestling beside her friend. "Poor child! What things you have been through! Still—you have Mr. Norburn."

"Yes; with him and father I really don't mind." She paused, and then there slipped out, in lower tone, a tell-tale "Much."

Alicia answered it with a caress.

"How brave you are!" she said. "Does—does he mind?"

"Mr. Norburn?"

"I meant your father."

"He has no time to mind now. We are fighting," said Daisy.

"Ah, a man can fight, can't he?"

"Oh, but so can a girl. I'm fighting too."

"I've no one to fight for."

Daisy turned quickly towards her: there were tears in her eyes. Surely she was a sorry comforter: perhaps she had come as much seeking as to bring comfort.

"You don't look very happy," remarked Daisy.

"Don't talk about me, Daisy. It will never make the least difference between you and me. I wanted to tell you. You know we are going? You must write to me, dear, and some day you and Mr. Norburn must come to England and stay with me, when I have my own house. Promise now! I—I don't want to lose you quite."

"Of course I will write, but you won't care for our news when you are gone."

"Indeed I shall care to hear of you and Mr. Norburn, and—of your father too."

"Will you really? Oh, then I shall have lots to say. Father always gives one lots to say about him," said Daisy proudly.

"Tell him he mustn't despair."

"From you?"

"No, no. From you."

"Oh, of course I tell him that."

"I—I mustn't send him any message."

"You're not against him too, are you, Alicia?"

"I'm not much against him," whispered Alicia. "And, if any one says I am, Daisy, don't believe it of me. I must go, dear. I shall be missed. I shall come again."

"Do," said Daisy. "I'm just a little lonely now," and she nearly broke down, as Alicia took her in her arms.

Thus they stood when Medland, suddenly returned on an urgent matter, opened the door, and, standing, looked at them for a moment. Alicia seemed to feel his presence; with a start she looked up. He crossed the room, holding out his hand.

"It is like you," he said simply.

She shook her head.

"I—I did not know you were here."

"I am not supposed to be," he answered, kissing his daughter.

Alicia hastily said good-bye, Medland not trying to detain her. But he signed to Daisy to stay in the room and escorted Alicia down-stairs.

At the hall door he kept her, laying his hand on the door.

"Yes, that was very kind. Poor child! She wants friends."

"I can do very little—I—"

"Yes, I know. And you are going?"

"Yes, in three weeks."

He was silent for a moment: then he looked in her eyes.

"You know the worst now," he said in a low voice.

"Yes," she murmured, trying to escape his gaze.

"And you still say what you said before?"

"I—I say nothing. I must go."

"Very likely we shall never speak alone again as long as we live—perhaps never at all."

"Isn't it best?" she murmured.

"Best!" he echoed. "You are happy in it then?"

"I happy! Ah!"

He could not miss the meaning of her tone.

"Most people," he said, "would call me a criminal for what I am going to say—and you a fool if you listen. Alicia, will you face it all and come to me?" and he drew nearer to her. "I know what I ask—but I know too what I have to give."

"Let me go," she gasped, as though his hand were on her.

"Can you do it?" he asked. "I needn't tell you to think what it means."

"I don't mind that," she broke out suddenly. "Don't think it's that. I would face all that if—if I could—"

"Trust me?"

She bowed her head.

"You can never trust me again?"

"Why make me say it?"

"But it is so?"

Again she bowed her head.

"It is still—horrible?"

He drew back and opened the door, letting in the cool night air.

"Good-bye," he said. "It's your last word?"

She seemed to sway towards him and away again.

"I shan't ask again," he went on, still in that calm, low voice. "I shall accept what you say now. You think me—unclean?"

Her silence was answer as she stepped out into the path.

"For the last time!"

"I can't," she said, with a sob. "You—you know why."

"And yet, if you loved me!"

"Loved you!" she cried. "But no, no, no!" and she turned and disappeared in the gloom.

Anthony Hope

CHAPTER XXVII

THE DECISION OF THE ORACLE

"I see from Tomes," observed Eleanor Scaife to the Chief Justice, as he handed her a cup of tea, "that all the elections are on the same day in New Lindsey."

"They are," he answered. "A good thing, don't you think?"

"But if a man wants to vote in two places?"

"Then it's kind to prevent him, because if he does it he's sent to prison."

"Oh! And when do the results appear?"

"Here at Kirton? Oh, any time between nine and midnight, or an hour later. One or two are left over as a rule. They're published at the Town-hall, and it's generally rather a lively scene."

"And how is it going to go?"

The Chief Justice lowered his voice.

"Medland will be beaten. He can't believe it and his friends won't, but he'll be beaten badly all over the country, except here in Kirton. Kirton he'll carry pretty solid, but that won't be enough."

"How many seats are there here?"

"Oh, here and in this district, which is under Kirton influence, about two-and-twenty, and he ought to get eighteen or nineteen of them; but what's that out of eighty members?"

"And what's the reason? Merely his policy or—?"

"Well, his policy a good deal. All the manufacturers and capitalists are straining every nerve to give him such a thrashing as will keep him out for years, and they spare neither time nor money nor hard words. I don't blame 'em. And then, of course, the other thing counts. It hits him where he was strong—among the religious folk. Puttock's their special man, and Puttock never lets it alone."

"What, do they talk about it in public?"

"Well, I should rather think they did. Oh, we fight with the gloves off in New Lindsey."

"After all, if it's a matter that ought to count, it ought to be talked about," remarked Miss Scaife thoughtfully.

"I suppose so," answered Sir John doubtfully; "only it always sounds a little mean, you know."

Eleanor did not attempt to reconcile this seeming contradiction.

"So Sir Robert will be back? Well, Mary will be delighted."

"It doesn't so much matter to her, as you're going."

"No, but she will. For my own part, I like Sir Robert, but his Government rather lacks variety, doesn't it? It's not exactly thrilling."

"That's very high praise."

"I hardly meant it to be," laughed Eleanor. "However, as you say, it doesn't matter much now to us."

"No, nor to me."

"Then it's true you're resigning?"

"Yes, in a few weeks. I'm just holding on to—"

"See this crisis through, I suppose?"

"Oh dear, no. The crisis, as you call it, Miss Scaife, don't matter to me—nor I to it. I'm holding on to complete another year's service and get fifty pound more pension."

"You're very practical, Sir John."

"High praise again!"

"Perhaps hardly meant again!"

"I'm sure Lady Eynesford teaches her household the value of practicality."

"Well, Mary is practical; and I suppose Dick must be called so now—Miss Granger's an excellent match. Oh, I suppose we all pass muster pretty well, except Alicia."

"Miss Derosne is a visionary?"

"A little bit of one, I often tell her."

"It's an added grace in a pretty girl," said Sir John.

"I said *I* was practical," observed Miss Scaife.

"But you need no added graces," he returned, smiling.

"A palpable evasion!"

Some days had passed since Medland's interview with Alicia. He had left Kirton the morning after, and, as the day of the election drew nearer and nearer, news of him came from all parts of the colony. Wherever the opposition was strongest and hostility most bitter, he flung himself into the fray; at moments it seemed as though he would wrest victory from an adverse fate, but when he went away, the effect of his presence gradually evaporated, and his work was half undone before he had been gone a day. In the Governor's household the accounts of his doings were allowed to pass in silence; they had become a forbidden topic. Alicia might devour them in solitude, and the Governor himself watch them with an almost sympathetic interest; Lady Eynesford ignored them altogether, and seemed not to see Medland's colours and his watchwords that glared at her in the streets of Kirton. Sir Robert was quietly confident, and Kilshaw fiercely exultant; Medland's friends hoped against hope, and, secure of their position in the capital, flooded the country with eager missionaries. Passion ran high, and there had been one or two disturbing incidents. Sir Robert was refused a hearing in the Jubilee Hall; Kilshaw had been forced to escape violence by a hasty flight, when he tried to address a meeting in the North-East ward; and there had been something like a free fight between the factions in Kettle

Street. Captain Heseltine stated his opinion that if Sir Robert won, there would be "some fun" in Kirton, and was understood to mean that the Queen's Peace would be broken. Apparently the police authorities were of the same way of thinking, for at their request all preparations were made for calling out the Mounted Volunteers. Lord Eynesford declared that he would stand no nonsense, and a certain number of timid persons made arrangements to be out of Kirton on the all-important day.

At last it came, and wore itself away in a fever of excitement. While the poll was open there was no time to waste in quarrelling or parading, but in the evening, when the ballot-boxes were giving up their secret, the streets were crowded with dense throngs. The political leaders came dropping in from the country round. Medland was away and did not return, but Kilshaw was at the Club, and Puttock, all the local politicians, and most other men of note; for the Club was nearly opposite the Hall, where the crowd was thickest, and where the result would soon be proclaimed. Just below, one Todd, a well-known mob-orator, had mounted on a large packing-case and was exhorting the people to stand by Medland, happen what might; the police had tried to get near him and prevent him causing an obstruction, but his friends formed so dense a ring and offered such resistance that the attempt was prudently abandoned, and the sound of Mr. Todd's sweeping denunciations fell on the ears of the members as they talked within.

"I say, Kilshaw," called Captain Heseltine, who was by the window, "if you want to hear what you are, you'd better come here. Todd's letting you have it."

Kilshaw lounged to the window and put his head out, smiling scornfully.

"A lot of loafers and thieves," he remarked.

The crowd saw him. He was the especial object of their anger, ever since his share in Benyon's career had become public. He was greeted with an angry yell; the orator, seizing the occasion, shook a huge fist at him. Kilshaw laughed in reply, holding his cigar in his hand. There was an ugly rush at the Club door; an answering charge from the police; some oaths and some screams.

"You'd better vanish," suggested the Captain. "Your popularity is momentarily eclipsed."

"Damn the fellows," said Kilshaw. "They may storm the place if they like—I'll not move."

Matters were indeed becoming somewhat critical, when a loud shout was heard from in front of the Hall. The crowd forgot Kilshaw, forgot Mr. Todd, and rushed across the road. The first result was up!

For the next half-hour wild exultation reigned in the streets, and gloom predominated in the Club. The Kirton returns came out first, and, as the Chief Justice had prophesied, Medland swept the capital from end to end. A solid band of twenty members was elected in his interest, and he himself had an immense majority. The crowd was beside itself; all thought of defeat was at an end; they began to laugh, and smoke, and dive into the taverns in friendly groups to drink; they even flung jests up at Kilshaw, and only hooted good-humouredly when he cried,

"Wait a bit, my boys!"

Thus an hour passed without further news. Then the country results began to arrive. Among the first was that from

Medland's own constituency: he was beaten by above a hundred votes. Anticipated as this issue was, it was greeted with a loud groan, soon changed to an exultant cheer when it was declared that Coxon had lost his seat; no event, short of the defeat of Kilshaw himself, would have pleased the crowd so much; even in the Club men seemed very resigned; only Coxon's little band mourned the fall of their chief.

"A facer for him," remarked the Captain. Mr. Kilshaw smiled.

"Coxon generally falls on his feet," he remarked.

This victory was almost the last excuse the crowd found for cheering. The figures came in thick and fast now, and the tale they told was of Medland's utter defeat. By twelve o'clock the issue in seventy-five seats was declared; of the other five, four were safe for Sir Robert; and Medland had only twenty-nine supporters. Puttock and Sir Robert were returned, and Kilshaw had a triumphant majority. His was among the last announcements, and it was greeted with an angry roar of such volume that the Club window filled in a moment. The crowd, tired of their disappointing watch, turned away from the Jubilee Hall, and flocked together underneath the window.

"Why don't you return thanks?" asked Captain Heseltine.

Kilshaw was drinking a glass of brandy and soda-water. He jumped up, glass in hand, and, going to the window, bowed to the angry mob and drank a toast to his own success before their eyes. Mr. Todd's gross bulk pushed its way to the front.

"Come down here," he shouted, "and talk to us, if you dare!"

Kilshaw smilingly shook his head.

"Three cheers for Sir Robert!" he cried.

"How's your friend Benham?" shouted one.

"We'll serve you the same," yelled another; "come down;" and a third, whose partisanship outran his moral sense, proposed a cheer for Mr. François Gaspard.

"I think you'll have to sleep here," said the Captain.

"Not I," answered Kilshaw. "They daren't touch me."

"Hum!" said the Captain, doubtfully regarding the crowd. "I don't know that I'd care to insure you, if you go down now."

"We'll take you through," cried half-a-dozen young men, the sons of well-born or rich families, who were heart and soul with him, and asked for nothing better than a "row," with any one indeed, but above all with the mob which they scorned, and which had out-voted them in their own town.

The tramp of horses was heard outside. Two lines of mounted police were making their way slowly down the street. A moment later two voices sounded loud in alter-cation. The officer in command of the force was remons-trating with Big Todd; Big Todd was asserting that he had as much right as any one else to stand in the middle of Victoria Street and speak to his friends; the officer, strong in the letter of the law, maintained that no one, neither Big Todd nor another, had a right to adopt this course of action, or to do anything else than walk along the street whither his business might lead him.

"And they call this free speech!" cried Big Todd.

"Get on with you," said the officer.

"Now's your time," remarked the Captain. "Slip in between the two lines and you'll get through."

Kilshaw and his volunteer escort accepted the suggestion, and, linking arms, walked down-stairs. The Captain, after a brief inward struggle, followed them. Their appearance at the Club door was the signal for fresh hoots and groans.

"Now then, are you going?" said the officer to Big Todd.

The burly fellow cast a look round on his supporters.

"When I'm tired o' being here," he answered.

Kilshaw's band slipped in between the first and second rank. The officer touched his horse with the spur, and it sprang forward. Big Todd, with an oath, caught the bridle, and another man seized the rider by the leg. He struck out sharply, and the line of police moved forward.

"Stand up to 'em, boys," cried Big Todd, and he aimed a blow with his stick at his antagonist.

The young men round Kilshaw looked at one another and began to press forward. They wanted to join in.

A voice from behind them cried out warningly,

"None of that, gentlemen! You must leave it to us," and at the same instant the first rank seemed to leave them. The order to advance had been given, and the *mêlée* had begun. The rear rank advancing covered the members of the Club from attack.

"We seem to be spectators," observed Captain Heseltine, in a disappointed tone. He had earnestly hoped that some one would assault him.

Just ahead the fight was hot round Big Todd. The police were determined to arrest him, and had closed round where he stood. The big man was fighting like a lion, and some half-dozen were trying to protect him. On either side of this group the line of police passed on, driving the crowd before them. Their horses were trotting now, and the people ran before them or dodged into side streets and escaped. Big Todd and his little band were sore pressed. Todd was bleeding from the head and his right hand was numbed from a blow. He was down once, but up again in a second. As he rose, he caught sight of Kilshaw's scornful smile, and, swearing savagely, with a sudden rush he burst the ring round him and made for the arch-enemy. Kilshaw raised his arm to shield himself, Captain Heseltine stepped forward and deftly put out his foot. Big Todd, tripped in the manner of the old football, fell heavily to the ground, striking his bullet poll on the hard road.

Hector was slain. The Trojans scoured over the plain. Victoria Street was cleared, and Big Todd was borne on a stretcher to the police-station hard by.

"That fellow would have caught me a crack but for you, Heseltine," said Mr. Kilshaw.

A police-superintendent rode up.

"If you'd go home, gentlemen," he said, "our work would be easier. The trouble's not all over yet, I'm afraid. I'll send some of my men with you, Mr. Kilshaw, if you please, sir."

Kilshaw made a wry face.

"I wish I had my men," he said. "The Mounted Volunteers

would teach these fellows a lesson."

"Well, we may see that before we're many days older, sir," answered the officer. "Mr. Medland'll be here to-morrow, and heaven knows what they'll be up to then."

CHAPTER XXVIII

STEALING A MARCH

Alicia Derosne had a fantastic dream that night. She saw Medland again chasing a butterfly, as she had seen him on the day he came to Government House to receive his office. The butterfly floated always just over his head, and he always came near to catching it, yet never caught it. Then, by one of sleep's strange transformations, she seemed to be herself in spirit in the butterfly, and she knew that it flew so near because desire brought it, that it longed to be caught, and yet, at the last, by some sudden impulse, avoided his net. At last, as if wearied, he turned from her to another fluttering thing, and that he caught. And she heard a great murmur of voices applauding him, and he smiled and was content with his prize. Then she, the first butterfly, could not be happy unless she were caught also, envying the other, and she went and fluttered and spread her wings before his eyes, but he would not heed her, nor stretch the net over her, but smiled in triumph at the bright colours of his prize and the murmur of applause. And, with drooping wings, the first butterfly fell to the ground and died.

It needed no Joseph to interpret this dream. When he had called, she would not come. Now he would forget her and turn to the life of ambition and power that he loved. He would rule men, and trouble his head or his heart no more with the vagaries of girls and the strict scruples of their code. And she—what was there left for her? "The last time," he had said. There was nothing for her to do but what the neglected butterfly had done. In a few weeks more the sea would lie between them, and she would be no more to him, nor he to her, than a memory—a memory soon to fade in him, whose days and thoughts were so full; in her, it seemed, always to endure, ousting everything else, reigning in triumphant sorrow in an empty heart.

The news of the final result of the elections which Eleanor Scaife brought her in the morning while she was still in bed, presented to her mind another picture of the man, which appealed to her almost more strongly.

"It's a knock-down blow for Mr. Medland, isn't it?" asked Eleanor, sitting on the side of the bed. "As we're alone together, I may dare to say that I'm rather sorry. I didn't want him to win, but it's very hard on him to be crushed like this. How he must feel it!"

"He seems to have won in Kirton."

"Oh yes, just the town mob is with him. Fancy coming down to that! Of course he'll be quite powerless, compared to what he was. I wonder if he'll stay in politics. Captain Heseltine said some people thought that he'd throw the whole thing up and retire into private life."

"Yes, I'm sorry too," said Alicia, who lay all this while with her face away from Eleanor and towards the wall.

"And then his daughter's going to be married, and, of course, can never be such a companion to him as she has been; he'll be very much alone. Upon my word, Alicia, I'm getting quite sentimental about the man, and it's all his own fault, really. Why does he make it impossible for respectable people to follow him?" After a short pause, Miss Scaife suddenly laughed. "Do you know," she asked, "what that shameless Dick says? He says I ought to marry Mr. Medland, because we're both 'emancipated.' Really I'm not quite so 'emancipated' as Mr. Medland seems to be."

Alicia smiled faintly.

"What an idea!" she said, at last turning her face to her friend.

"He was only joking, of course. Assuming Mr. Medland asked me, and I'm sure nothing could be further from his thoughts, I'm afraid I should have to decline the honour. Wasn't it impertinent of Dick? It's lucky Mary didn't hear him. But, my dear, you must get up. All sorts of things are going on. It's most exciting."

"I thought all the excitement was over," said Alicia languidly.

"Oh, no. There was a riot in the streets last night, and they arrested some popular favourite and took him to prison. The mob's furious, and the police are afraid of a disturbance when he's brought before the magistrate this morning. Then Mr. Medland is to arrive at twelve o'clock, and they're afraid of another riot then. Sir Robert was here at half-past eight, and at his request the Governor authorised calling out the Mounted Volunteers to keep order. Lord Eynesford says he'll go with them. Do get up," and Eleanor went off, eager to hear the latest news. The present situation was justifying her tenacious opinion that new communities were interesting.

In spite of her many inquiries, her intelligence was not quite the latest. The police had stolen a march on the crowd, and Big Todd had been quietly brought before the seat of justice at nine o'clock, remanded for a week, and carried off to the prison, which was situated outside the town, about half-a-mile beyond Government House. The van containing the captive had rolled unsuspected through the streets, and it was not till the crowd had waited an hour outside the court that the secret leaked out. The outwitted men were in a fury. The mounted police lined the sides of the street, and their impassive demeanour seemed to rouse the mob to fresh anger. There had been a plan to rescue Big Todd, now it was too late, and men looked at one another in sullen wrath. The crowd drifted off towards the railway station, thinking to welcome Medland. The Mounted Volunteers were on guard there. They saw Kilshaw at the head of his company and hailed him with a groan. Behind the ranks, the Governor sat on his horse, flanked by his *aides-de-camp* and talking to Sir Robert Perry. No one was allowed within the station-yard, every one was compelled to move about, the preparations were complete, to riot would be to run against a stone wall.

Suddenly an idea, a suggestion, flew through the crowd. It was greeted with surly smiles and emphatic nods. To the surprise of the officers and of the Governor, the crowd began to melt away. Splitting up in twos and threes, it sauntered off, as if it had made up its mind to submit quietly to the inevitable. Soon only women and children were left, and the Governor began to feel that the array of force was almost ridiculously out of proportion to the need. The whole thing was, as Captain Heseltine regretfully observed, "fizzling out," and he proposed to go home to lunch.

Medland's train arrived half-an-hour later, and he came out of the station, looking round in surprise at the martial aspect of the scene. Then he smiled.

"We look rather asses," whispered Heseltine. "I wonder if they did it on purpose."

Medland came down the steps and found himself almost face to face with Kilshaw. The ex-Premier was smoking a cigar, and he took it out of his mouth, in order to smile more freely.

"If," he said to Kilshaw, "it's not dangerous to public order, I should like a cab."

Kilshaw heard a shamefaced, stifled giggle from his men behind him and turned very red. The next minute Sir Robert came up, holding out his hand.

"This is a great compliment to you," he said, smiling.

"Evidently beyond my deserts," answered Medland, getting into his cab. "To my house," he called to the man, and was driven rapidly away.

The Governor rode up to Sir Robert with a look of vexation on his face.

"The sooner we end this farce the better," he said. "I'm going home. I suppose you'll send the men to quarters."

"I really don't understand it," protested Sir Robert. "They looked like mischief."

"I suppose we frightened them. Oh, no doubt you were right," and the Governor turned his horse.

Suddenly the figure of a man on horseback, going at a gallop, was seen in the distance. The Governor drew rein and waited. The man came nearer, and, as soon as he was within earshot, he shouted.

"The prison! the prison! They've all gone to the prison."

"What?" cried the Governor.

"All the crowd," panted the messenger. "They mean to have Big Todd out. We've only got ten men there, and the people are threatening to burn the place down if he's not given up."

"By Jove, they've jockeyed us!" cried Captain Heseltine, and he turned to his chief for orders.

"We must be after them," exclaimed the Governor. "Let the orders be given. You, Heseltine, go and bring up the police. This looks like business."

The column was soon on the march, followed by a string of women and children, which was speedily outstripped when the word to trot was given. The outskirts of the town were reached; they met man after man who told them of a gathering crowd round the prison; they overtook more men, armed with cudgels, who slunk on one side and tried to hide their sticks. They reached the gates of Government House, and Lord Eynesford spied his wife and Alicia looking out of the windows of the lodge.

"Go and tell them what's up," he said to Flemyng. "Say there's no danger," and the column trotted on.

"This is what Mr. Medland has brought us to," observed Lady Eynesford, when Mr. Flemyng made his report. "I'm glad we've done with him, anyhow, aren't you, Eleanor?"

"Perhaps we haven't," suggested Eleanor. "I wonder if he's come back."

"No doubt he's encouraging this riot. I only hope he'll get the treatment he deserves."

Alicia stood by in silence. The little room felt close and hot. She was tired and worn out, for she had spent the morning writing a letter that seemed very hard to write.

"Mightn't we go into the garden?" she asked. "There's no danger to us, is there, Mr. Flemyng?"

"Oh dear, no, Miss Derosne. They're only thinking of Big Todd. I'll go on if you don't want me, Lady Eynesford."

He trotted off and overtook the rest just as they came in sight of the prison. The crowd was thick round it.

"By heaven, they've got the door open!" cried Heseltine.

They had. The heavy door hung on its hinges, and, as the Governor drew nearer, he saw the prisoner, Big Todd himself, in the centre of the crowd. There were near three thousand there, almost all men; most had sticks, here and there the sun caught the gleam of a knife or the glint from a revolver-barrel. A rude kind of rampart of the tables and chairs from the gaol formed a slight makeshift barricade, and behind it, the crowd, backed by the building, stood waiting for the attack.

The Governor halted.

"It really looks rather serious," he said.

Sir Robert Perry, whose fat cob was panting with unusual exertions, nodded assent.

"We don't want bloodshed, if we can help it," he observed.

Anthony Hope

"No, but we'll have that fellow," said the Governor curtly, "or I'll know the reason why."

His old instincts were astir in him. He had been a soldier in his time, and he almost regretted that his first duty was to reason with these men. Endeavouring to carry out this duty, he said to Heseltine,

"Go and say I'll give them three minutes to hand over Todd and disperse."

Heseltine rode forward till he came to the barricade and delivered his message, adding,

"Look sharp. There you are, Todd! Now come along, my man."

"Come and fetch me," grinned Big Todd.

"So we will," answered the Captain, smiling, "but you'd better come quietly."

"Look here, sir. Say no more about what happened last night and we'll give the Governor back his prison. We ain't hurt it, not to speak of."

Heseltine laughed.

"You're an insolent scoundrel," he said.

"You'd better get a bit further off before you talk like that, young man," growled a fierce-looking little fellow.

"Let the gentleman alone, Tim," said Big Todd. "He's a flag o' truce."

"Then you won't come?" asked the Captain.

"Declined with thanks, sir," bowed Big Todd.

Heseltine rode back and delivered the reply. An angry flush crossed Lord Eynesford's face.

"Very well," he said shortly, and turned to the Colonel. "Colonel," he said, "I want your men to scatter that crowd and bring Todd here. Don't fire without asking me again. Use the flat of the sword unless the crowd use knives or shoot; if they do, use the edge. I can't come with you, I wish I could."

"May I go, sir?" broke simultaneously from Dick and Heseltine.

"No," answered Lord Eynesford shortly.

"What a damned shame!" grumbled Dick.

The Colonel had spoken to the captains of his two companies, Kilshaw and another, and they in their turn had briefly communicated the Governor's orders to their men. Everything was ready, and the Colonel turned a last inquiring glance towards the Governor.

"Yes," said Lord Eynesford; but at the same moment a loud cheer rang out from the defenders of the gaol—

"Three cheers for Jimmy Medland!" they cried.

The Governor turned and saw the ex-Premier leaping from a cab and hurrying towards them.

"Stop!" cried Medland. "Stop!"

Anthony Hope

CHAPTER XXIX

A BEATEN MAN'S THOUGHTS

On reaching his home, Medland had found that Norburn had arrived before him, and was engaged in the task of consoling Daisy for the untoward issue of the fight. Daisy, on her part, was full of praise for the valour of Big Todd, and delighted to hear of the sort of fiasco that had waited on the military display at the station. Safe from the eyes of all save those who loved him, Medland did not maintain the indifferent air that he had displayed in public. In vain they reminded him of the swift reactions in political affairs, of the sturdy band that still owned his leadership, and of the devotion of all Kirton to him, or bade him think that he was himself almost a young man, and that this defeat was but a check and not an end to his career. For the moment the buoyancy was out of him; he did not care to discuss hopes or projects, and sat silent in his chair, while Norburn sketched new campaigns and energetic raids on Sir Robert's position. Daisy knew her father: these hours of despondency were the penalty he paid for the glowing confidence and rebounding hope that had made him the man and the power he was.

"Let him alone a little while," she whispered to her lover. "Something will rouse him soon, and he'll be himself again."

She put his letters by him, and the two left him to solitude in his study. He was vaguely surprised that no crowd had assembled to escort him to his house, and that the street was so quiet; he supposed that his adherents felt much as he did, too discouraged to make a parade, or try to hide their wounds under the pretence of a brave show; yet he was sensitive enough to every breath of popular sentiment to be hurt at the first sign of neglect. Perhaps they had had enough of him, perhaps they were looking for a new leader. No; that could hardly be, or they would not have elected all his friends. It was just that they felt as he did, beaten, soundly beaten, and had fled to their dens to lick their sores.

He listlessly stretched out his hand towards the letters and began to open them. Here were belated requests for help or advice, calculations of majorities and prophecies of victory, written at the last moment in unquenchable faith, to be read now with a weary smile of irony. Here too were honest, admiring condolences. "Better luck next time"—"Never despair," and so forth—side by side with anonymous and scurrilous gloatings over his fall. Once he laughed out loud: a zealous student compared him at length and in detail to Cleon, and ended with an ode of triumph which, he said, would appear in the press the next day or so. Medland pushed the heap away with an impatient sigh, but one note remained under his hand and he took it up, for it seemed different from the rest. He undid the envelope and glanced at the signature; then he sat up in sudden interest, for it was signed "Alicia Derosne."

"You will be surprised," she said, "that I should write; but I doubted if you understood the other night, and I can't be misunderstood by you. If you were what I once thought you, I would do all you ask, whatever it cost me, but I can't now. It's all different now. That thing makes it all different. You will think it a poor reason and a strange idea—I know you will; but your thinking it strange is just what makes it strongest to me. You may not understand—I'm afraid you won't—but you must believe that that is the only thing. Please don't try to see me, but send one line to say you believe me.—ALICIA DEROSNE. Good-bye."

At first he thought of what he read only as a fresh defeat, another drop of bitterness in a brimming cup, and he let the letter fall, despising himself for caring about such a matter. But he took it up again and re-read it, and the "Good-bye" at the end—the stifled cry of pain—touched him; she had finished the letter before she wrote that, for its ink was paler; the rest had dried, that had been hastily blotted; it was an after-impulse, a hint of the struggle with which she left her tenderness unexpressed. He pictured so well how she looked writing it, making her sacrifice at the altar of what she held holy in herself. Whether she were right or wrong seemed now to his softer mood to be of little moment. He could not think that she was right, and yet it suited her so well to be wrong on such a point that he could hardly wish her to have been what to his mind seemed right. With the strange feeling of the end of things, of finality, that his defeat and despondency had brought to him, her decision fitted well. She would not come to him, but the ideal of her rested beautiful in the delicate pride and fastidiousness of her scruples and her purity. The sort of life he must lead, no less than that he had led, must needs have soiled the image and stained its spotless white. He was conscious that his reception of what she said was half the outcome of the moment in which her decision reached him; but yet he could not look before him, and the idea of himself, restored to his former mind, scornfully mocking what now claimed reverence, angrily fighting against a merely fanciful hindrance, failed to dress itself like reality, though experience, half-smothered, protested that it would prove real. Now he was very sorry for her and for himself; but it was the sorrow of acquiescence, the pain of a vision that never could have had fulfilment not the fierce disappointment of well-grounded hope. Though she were passing out of his life, yet she would always be in it and of it, and their unhappiness seemed to him a tie as close as could have been knit between them by any union.

He was interrupted by the entrance of his daughter and Norburn. They were troubled, as a glance at their happy faces told him, by no sense of the end of things; they were at the beginning, and he was amused to find that, while they deplored his defeat sincerely and resented it hotly, it yet had a bright side to them. It set Jack Norburn at liberty; he had now no official ties and there would be a lull in politics. How should two young people use such an interval better than in getting married?

"How indeed?" said Mr. Medland, smiling.

"Then when we're comfortably married," said Daisy, "and you've had a little rest, we'll have at Sir Robert again, father! Oh, and I'm so glad those tiresome Eynesfords are going—except Alicia, I mean; I like her. I do hope the next people won't be quite so—" And Daisy's gesture indicated the inhuman exclusiveness and pride supposed to be harboured at Government House.

"Well, we go our way and they go theirs," said Norburn, with his good-humoured laugh. "We're happy in ours, I hope they're happy in theirs. Then, as soon as Daisy can be ready, sir?"

"Yes, as soon as Daisy can be ready," assented Medland.

When, after thanks and some more rose-coloured prophecies, they were gone together, he rose and, hands in pockets,

Anthony Hope

paced up and down the narrow room.

"Really, young Norburn has got the philosophy of it," he mused. "He takes my daughter, and his philosophy takes the only other woman I care about! But I believe, after all, that it's bad philosophy."

He stretched his arms in weariness.

"Ah, I feel burnt out!" he said, sinking back into his chair. "I must answer this," and he took up Alicia's note again, only to fold it up and put it in his pocket.

"I can't do it now. I must have some fresh air," he exclaimed petulantly. "This place suffocates me."

He opened the window and hailed a hack-victoria that was crawling by. Calling to Daisy to tell her he was going for a drive, he ran down-stairs and jumped in.

"Go to the Park," he said. "You needn't hurry."

The air revived his spirits. He leant back, sniffing its freshness, and finding the world very good. He met few people about and no one that he knew. The Park was empty, and the old horse jogged along peacefully. Insensibly he found himself thinking about what would happen when the new House met, and sparing a smile for Coxon's defeat, though he was afraid that gentleman would be only too well provided for. It struck him that a pitfall or two lay in Sir Robert's path, and he saw his way to giving Kilshaw a bad quarter of an hour over one of his election speeches. The only thing that he could not get away from was the thought of Alicia Derosne. He knew that there was to be nothing more between him and her, and that she was going away soon, never to return to, soon in all probability to forget,

New Lindsey; yet all his doings and activities in the future—and his brain began now to be swift to plan them again—presented themselves to him, not in the actual happening, but as they would look when read by her. This lover's madness irritated him so much that at last he took her letter from his pocket and tore it into little bits, scattering them on the breeze. He could answer it well enough from memory, and perhaps it would be easier to be his own man again when he had no tangible, material reminder of her with him. These things only made a man nurse and cosset fine-drawn feelings, spying curiously into a heart that might get well if it were covered up and left alone.

A cheery voice roused him, and his carriage stopped.

"Well, tearing up your bills, eh?" called the Chief Justice from the side-walk. "You must be glad to be out of it."

"Not I," answered Medland, smiling. "Among other things, I wanted to appoint your successor."

"Ah, dreadful, dreadful! Young Coxon, isn't it? I've been laid up with a cold, and seen and heard nothing, but I fancy that's right."

"I suppose he'll do pretty well, but he's not the right man to come after you. However, I am powerless now."

"Yes, order is safe again. By the way, I hear your friends made a little disturbance last night."

"Oh, yes; that headstrong fellow Todd. We can never hold him. It came to nothing, I suppose?"

"They arrested him, you know. But, Medland, I doubt—"

The driver turned round suddenly.

"Did you say Medland, sir?" he asked the Chief Justice. "Is this gentleman Mr. Medland?"

"What, didn't you know me?"

"No, sir; I'm only just out from England. But, if you're Mr. Medland, don't you know, sir—begging your pardon—what's happened about Todd?"

"No; what?"

"There's a fine row up at the prison, sir. Two or three thousand of 'em went up there this morning to take him out, and the Governor's up there with the Volunteers, and they say there's going to be a big fight and—"

"The fools!" exclaimed Medland. "I must go, Chief Justice."

"Why, what can you do?"

"Stop it, of course. Here, drive to the prison—drive like fury. Good-bye, Chief Justice. Come and see me soon. Get on, man, get on!"

The old horse was whipped up unmercifully, and the Chief Justice watched Medland disappear in a cloud of dust. He took off his hat to wipe his brow. Two little fragments of the white paper which Medland scattered had settled upon it.

"Poof!" The Chief Justice blew them off and they fluttered down on the grass. He stooped and picked up the larger bit. If he had looked at it, he would have read "Good-bye"; but he did not. The amber end of his cigarette-tube was loose: he unscrewed it, twisted the little bit of paper round the screw, and fitted the end on again.

"Capital!" said the Chief Justice. "It might have been made for it. Poor old Medland!"

CHAPTER XXX

THE END OF A TUMULT

"Stop!" he shouted; "stop!" and, taking advantage of the momentary pause, he made his way to the Governor.

"Let me speak to them, sir," he said; "I think I can bring them to reason."

But Lord Eynesford's spirit was roused.

"I must request you to leave the matter to me, Mr. Medland," he answered stiffly. "They have had their opportunity of submitting to the law peaceably, and they have chosen to disregard it."

"If you will give me five minutes, sir," said Medland very humbly. He loved the rough fellows who were acting so foolishly: perhaps something in his words had given them an excuse. He could not bear to think of them coming to harm, even through their own fault.

"I can't, sir," answered the Governor sharply. "I have the dignity of the Crown, which I represent, to think of. Pray stand aside, sir;" and he added to the Colonel—"Your orders are not altered."

Medland's quick eye measured the distance between him and the rioters. He was standing near the Governor, at the side of the troops, but a little in advance of their line. A run might bring him to them before the troops could reach them. If they did not resist there could be no bloodshed. There was yet a chance, and suddenly he dashed across in front of the line, crying, "Don't resist! don't resist!"

At the very moment of his start the Colonel had given the word to charge. No man saw clearly how it happened, but there was a forward dash, then an exclamation from one of the Volunteers, as he reined his horse back on its haunches, a wild cry from the barricade, and a loud shout, "Halt!" from Kilshaw. The line was stopped, and Kilshaw rode swiftly up to where the trooper had wrenched back his horse. Medland lay on the ground in front of the horse. The man had seen him too late to avoid him; he had been knocked down and trampled with the hoofs. His face was pale, and a slight twist of the features told of pain. He held his hand to his right side.

Kilshaw was off his horse in an instant.

"Back there, back!" he cried. "Don't crowd on him."

The Governor rode up; a group gathered round. There was no more thought of the charge. The rioters, after an instant, broke the barricade and came out, one by one, timidly making for the spot.

"Here," whispered Kilshaw to Dick Derosne, "you lift his head. He won't want to see me," and he drew back behind the wounded man.

The Governor dismounted and stood by his brother, but before Dick could lift Medland's head, a rough woman, in a coarse gown, pushed through, elbowing him and Lord

Anthony Hope

Eynesford aside.

"Let me, gentlemen," she said, her eyes full of tears, as she pillowed his head in her lap. "He's always been for us, Mr. Medland has," she explained. "Give me a clean hand-kerchief, one of you."

The Governor handed his, and she wiped the clammy moisture from the forehead and hands.

Medland opened his eyes.

"The horse kicked me in the side," he murmured faintly, "here, on the right—low down. I'm in pain."

Then he saw Dick Derosne.

"Mr. Derosne!" he called faintly, and Dick knelt down to listen. "Tell your sister I believe."

"What?" asked Dick in sheer surprise.

"You heard?" asked Medland petulantly.

"Yes—that you believe."

"Well, tell her," and he turned away his head.

There was a little bustle outside the group, and then Big Todd burst through.

"Is he killed?" he cried.

Medland saw him and stretched out his hand. Big Todd caught it, and the dying man pressed the fellow's knotted fist. Perhaps he saw in Todd the type of the "Great Beast," clumsy, often wrong-headed, but honest at heart, that he loved and worked for.

"What did you want to be such an infernal fool for, man?" he said, with a little smile. Then his eyes closed, and the woman wiped his forehead and kissed him.

The group round him drew back, leaving the woman and Todd near him. Presently some dozen of the rioters brought the top of a table from their barricade, and lifted him on to it. Then Big Todd spoke to the Governor.

"There'll be no more fighting," he said. "I'll give myself up, but I'd like to help the chaps to take him home first."

The Governor nodded, and they raised the table on their shoulders and set out for Kirton. Behind them came the woman and a few more of the same class; some children stole out from the back of the gaol and took their places. After them marched the rioters, and last of all the Governor, his party, and the troops. And in this order the procession passed along. And some time before it had gone far, Medland bled to death inwardly; his strength failed him and he gave a convulsive shiver, opened his eyes for the last time to the sky, and then lay still under the rough coat that Big Todd had thrown over him.

"Dick, Dick," whispered the Governor, when they came near Government House, "ride on and tell them."

Lady Eynesford, Eleanor Scaife, and Alicia were standing at the gate. They had hardly seen the procession turn a corner and come into sight before Dick galloped up.

"What is it, Dick?" cried Lady Eynesford. "Willie's not hurt?"

Anthony Hope

"No—it's—it's Mr. Medland."

Eleanor was standing by Alicia, and she felt a sudden clutch on her arm.

"What has happened?" she asked.

"I'm afraid he's very badly hurt," answered Dick, and drawing near his sister he whispered, "Al, he sent you a message. I don't know what it means, but—he believes."

One swift glance told him she heard, then her eyes fixed themselves on the advancing crowd, and the burden the men carried.

They halted a moment. The table was lowered; a man— apparently a doctor—had ridden up. He looked at the burden they bore, then he spread the rough coat again over the body and signed to them to go on. Dick stepped forward and asked a question. Returning, he said briefly,

"He's dead."

Alicia swayed heavily against Eleanor Scaife. Eleanor threw her arm round her waist, and answered the moan she heard with—"Hush, darling!" while Alicia, with parted lips and straining eyes, watched him carried by.

As they had escorted him home on the day when he first became their ruler, so they took him to his home now, the throng of mourners ever growing as the people poured out of the town to meet them, until they reached his house and halted before his door, waiting for some one who should dare to carry the news to the fair-haired girl who had met him in triumph when he came before.

In Kirton the name of "Jimmy Medland" is still remembered, and his grave does not lack continual flowers. In far-off England few remember him, and his name is seldom spoken, save when a very old white-haired man comes to stay with a lady in one of the Midland shires. Then, when they are alone, when her husband has gone hunting and the children are away, and there is no other ear to listen, Alicia will sometimes talk to Sir John of Mr. Medland, what he was and was not, what he did and dreamed, how he lived and died, and how the men of Kirton love his memory.

"It all seems like a dream now," she says, "but it's a dream I can never forget."

And Sir John presses her hand, for perhaps he guesses what she has not told him.

His daughter wrote on his tomb nothing except his name; but a wandering Englishman, who heard his story, and recollected the grave of another who died with his work undone, has rudely scratched at the base, near the ground, where the grass half hides it, an epitaph for him—*Plura moliebatur*. And he told Big Todd, whom he chanced to find smoking his evening pipe hard by, that it meant "He had more work in hand."

"Ay, trust old Jimmy!" said Big Todd, with a curious wave of his great hand towards the grave. Had such a thing been at all in his way, one might have thought it was a benediction.

THE END

Anthony Hope

ABOUT THE AUTHOR

Sir Anthony Hope Hawkins, better known as Anthony Hope, (February 9, 1863 – July 8, 1933) was a British novelist, born in London, and best remembered today for his short novel The Prisoner of Zenda (1894), set in the fictional kingdom of Ruritania, a prequel The Heart of Princess Osra (a collection of short stories set in 18C Ruritania) (1896) and a sequel Rupert of Hentzau (1898). His first novel was A Man of Mark (1890), and one of his most well-known works during his lifetime was The Dolly Dialogues (1894), published in the Westminster Gazette.

After being educated at Marlborough College and Balliol College (where he was President of the Oxford Union), he trained as a lawyer and barrister, being called to the Bar in 1877. He practised as a lawyer until 1894; he started writing full time after Zenda's success, completing many other novels and plays, including Sophy of Kravonia (1906), in a similar vein. He was knighted in recognition of his contribution to British propaganda efforts during World War I.

He published an autobiographical book, Memories and Notes, in 1927.

There is a blue plaque on his house in Bedford Square, London.

Other books by this author

A Man of Mark

Dolly Dialogues

Father Stafford

Frivolous Cupid

Rupert of Hentzau

Simon Dale

The Indiscretion of the Duchess

The Prisoner of Zenda

The Secret of the Tower

Anthony Hope

Choose from Thousands of 1stWorldLibrary Classics By

A. M. Barnard
Ada Leverson
Adolphus William Ward
Aesop
Agatha Christie
Alexander Aaronsohn
Alexander Kielland
Alexandre Dumas
Alfred Gatty
Alfred Ollivant
Alice Duer Miller
Alice Turner Curtis
Alice Dunbar
Allen Chapman
Alleyne Ireland
Ambrose Bierce
Amelia E. Barr
Amory H. Bradford
Andrew Lang
Andrew McFarland Davis
Andy Adams
Angela Brazil
Anna Alice Chapin
Anna Sewell
Annie Besant
Annie Hamilton Donnell
Annie Payson Call
Annie Roe Carr
Annonaymous
Anton Chekhov
Archibald Lee Fletcher
Arnold Bennett
Arthur C. Benson
Arthur Conan Doyle
Arthur M. Winfield
Arthur Ransome
Arthur Schnitzler
Arthur Train
Atticus
B.H. Baden-Powell
B. M. Bower
B. C. Chatterjee
Baroness Emmuska Orczy
Baroness Orczy
Basil King
Bayard Taylor
Ben Macomber
Bertha Muzzy Bower
Bjornstjerne Bjornson

Booth Tarkington
Boyd Cable
Bram Stoker
C. Collodi
C. E. Orr
C. M. Ingleby
Carolyn Wells
Catherine Parr Traill
Charles A. Eastman
Charles Amory Beach
Charles Dickens
Charles Dudley Warner
Charles Farrar Browne
Charles Ives
Charles Kingsley
Charles Klein
Charles Hanson Towne
Charles Lathrop Pack
Charles Romyn Dake
Charles Whibley
Charles Willing Beale
Charlotte M. Braeme
Charlotte M. Yonge
Charlotte Perkins Stetson
Clair W. Hayes
Clarence Day Jr.
Clarence E. Mulford
Clemence Housman
Confucius
Coningsby Dawson
Cornelis DeWitt Wilcox
Cyril Burleigh
D. H. Lawrence
Daniel Defoe
David Garnett
Dinah Craik
Don Carlos Janes
Donald Keyhoe
Dorothy Kilner
Dougan Clark
Douglas Fairbanks
E. Nesbit
E. P. Roe
E. Phillips Oppenheim
E. S. Brooks
Earl Barnes
Edgar Rice Burroughs
Edith Van Dyne
Edith Wharton

Edward Everett Hale
Edward J. O'Biren
Edward S. Ellis
Edwin L. Arnold
Eleanor Atkins
Eleanor Hallowell Abbott
Eliot Gregory
Elizabeth Gaskell
Elizabeth McCracken
Elizabeth Von Arnim
Ellem Key
Emerson Hough
Emilie F. Carlen
Emily Bronte
Emily Dickinson
Enid Bagnold
Enilor Macartney Lane
Erasmus W. Jones
Ernie Howard Pie
Ethel May Dell
Ethel Turner
Ethel Watts Mumford
Eugene Sue
Eugenie Foa
Eugene Wood
Eustace Hale Ball
Evelyn Everett-green
Everard Cotes
F. H. Cheley
F. J. Cross
F. Marion Crawford
Fannie E. Newberry
Federick Austin Ogg
Ferdinand Ossendowski
Fergus Hume
Florence A. Kilpatrick
Fremont B. Deering
Francis Bacon
Francis Darwin
Frances Hodgson Burnett
Frances Parkinson Keyes
Frank Gee Patchin
Frank Harris
Frank Jewett Mather
Frank L. Packard
Frank V. Webster
Frederic Stewart Isham
Frederick Trevor Hill
Frederick Winslow Taylor

Friedrich Kerst
Friedrich Nietzsche
Fyodor Dostoyevsky
G.A. Henty
G.K. Chesterton
Gabrielle E. Jackson
Garrett P. Serviss
Gaston Leroux
George A. Warren
George Ade
Geroge Bernard Shaw
George Cary Eggleston
George Durston
George Ebers
George Eliot
George Gissing
George MacDonald
George Meredith
George Orwell
George Sylvester Viereck
George Tucker
George W. Cable
George Wharton James
Gertrude Atherton
Gordon Casserly
Grace E. King
Grace Gallatin
Grace Greenwood
Grant Allen
Guillermo A. Sherwell
Gulielma Zollinger
Gustav Flaubert
H. A. Cody
H. B. Irving
H. C. Bailey
H. G. Wells
H. H. Munro
H. Irving Hancock
H. R. Naylor
H. Rider Haggard
H. W. C. Davis
Haldeman Julius
Hall Caine
Hamilton Wright Mabie
Hans Christian Andersen
Harold Avery
Harold McGrath
Harriet Beecher Stowe
Harry Castlemon
Harry Coghill
Harry Houidini

Hayden Carruth
Helent Hunt Jackson
Helen Nicolay
Hendrik Conscience
Hendy David Thoreau
Henri Barbusse
Henrik Ibsen
Henry Adams
Henry Ford
Henry Frost
Henry James
Henry Jones Ford
Henry Seton Merriman
Henry W Longfellow
Herbert A. Giles
Herbert Carter
Herbert N. Casson
Herman Hesse
Hildegard G. Frey
Homer
Honore De Balzac
Horace B. Day
Horace Walpole
Horatio Alger Jr.
Howard Pyle
Howard R. Garis
Hugh Lofting
Hugh Walpole
Humphry Ward
Ian Maclaren
Inez Haynes Gillmore
Irving Bacheller
Isabel Cecilia Williams
Isabel Hornibrook
Israel Abrahams
Ivan Turgenev
J. G.Austin
J. Henri Fabre
J. M. Barrie
J. M. Walsh
J. Macdonald Oxley
J. R. Miller
J. S. Fletcher
J. S. Knowles
J. Storer Clouston
J. W. Duffield
Jack London
Jacob Abbott
James Allen
James Andrews
James Baldwin

James Branch Cabell
James DeMille
James Joyce
James Lane Allen
James Lane Allen
James Oliver Curwood
James Oppenheim
James Otis
James R. Driscoll
Jane Abbott
Jane Austen
Jane L. Stewart
Janet Aldridge
Jens Peter Jacobsen
Jerome K. Jerome
Jessie Graham Flower
John Buchan
John Burroughs
John Cournos
John F. Kennedy
John Gay
John Glasworthy
John Habberton
John Joy Bell
John Kendrick Bangs
John Milton
John Philip Sousa
John Taintor Foote
Jonas Lauritz Idemil Lie
Jonathan Swift
Joseph A. Altsheler
Joseph Carey
Joseph Conrad
Joseph E. Badger Jr
Joseph Hergesheimer
Joseph Jacobs
Jules Vernes
Julian Hawthrone
Julie A Lippmann
Justin Huntly McCarthy
Kakuzo Okakura
Karle Wilson Baker
Kate Chopin
Kenneth Grahame
Kenneth McGaffey
Kate Langley Bosher
Kate Langley Bosher
Katherine Cecil Thurston
Katherine Stokes
L. A. Abbot
L. T. Meade

L. Frank Baum
Latta Griswold
Laura Dent Crane
Laura Lee Hope
Laurence Housman
Lawrence Beasley
Leo Tolstoy
Leonid Andreyev
Lewis Carroll
Lewis Sperry Chafer
Lilian Bell
Lloyd Osbourne
Louis Hughes
Louis Joseph Vance
Louis Tracy
Louisa May Alcott
Lucy Fitch Perkins
Lucy Maud Montgomery
Luther Benson
Lydia Miller Middleton
Lyndon Orr
M. Corvus
M. H. Adams
Margaret E. Sangster
Margret Howth
Margaret Vandercook
Margaret W. Hungerford
Margret Penrose
Maria Edgeworth
Maria Thompson Daviess
Mariano Azuela
Marion Polk Angellotti
Mark Overton
Mark Twain
Mary Austin
Mary Catherine Crowley
Mary Cole
Mary Hastings Bradley
Mary Roberts Rinehart
Mary Rowlandson
M. Wollstonecraft Shelley
Maud Lindsay
Max Beerbohm
Myra Kelly
Nathaniel Hawthrone
Nicolo Machiavelli
O. F. Walton
Oscar Wilde
Owen Johnson
P.G. Wodehouse
Paul and Mabel Thorne

Paul G. Tomlinson
Paul Severing
Percy Brebner
Percy Keese Fitzhugh
Peter B. Kyne
Plato
Quincy Allen
R. Derby Holmes
R. L. Stevenson
R. S. Ball
Rabindranath Tagore
Rahul Alvares
Ralph Bonehill
Ralph Henry Barbour
Ralph Victor
Ralph Waldo Emmerson
Rene Descartes
Ray Cummings
Rex Beach
Rex E. Beach
Richard Harding Davis
Richard Jefferies
Richard Le Gallienne
Robert Barr
Robert Frost
Robert Gordon Anderson
Robert L. Drake
Robert Lansing
Robert Lynd
Robert Michael Ballantyne
Robert W. Chambers
Rosa Nouchette Carey
Rudyard Kipling
Saint Augustine
Samuel B. Allison
Samuel Hopkins Adams
Sarah Bernhardt
Sarah C. Hallowell
Selma Lagerlof
Sherwood Anderson
Sigmund Freud
Standish O'Grady
Stanley Weyman
Stella Benson
Stella M. Francis
Stephen Crane
Stewart Edward White
Stijn Streuvels
Swami Abhedananda
Swami Parmananda
T. S. Ackland

T. S. Arthur
The Princess Der Ling
Thomas A. Janvier
Thomas A Kempis
Thomas Anderton
Thomas Bailey Aldrich
Thomas Bulfinch
Thomas De Quincey
Thomas Dixon
Thomas H. Huxley
Thomas Hardy
Thomas More
Thornton W. Burgess
U. S. Grant
Upton Sinclair
Valentine Williams
Various Authors
Vaughan Kester
Victor Appleton
Victor G. Durham
Victoria Cross
Virginia Woolf
Wadsworth Camp
Walter Camp
Walter Scott
Washington Irving
Wilbur Lawton
Wilkie Collins
Willa Cather
Willard F. Baker
William Dean Howells
William le Queux
W. Makepeace Thackeray
William W. Walter
William Shakespeare
Winston Churchill
Yei Theodora Ozaki
Yogi Ramacharaka
Young E. Allison
Zane Grey

www.ingramcontent.com/pod-product-compliance
Lightning Source LLC
Chambersburg PA
CBHW021329250626

47155CB00002B/658